The First
Spring

Morgan L. Booth

Copyright © 2013 Morgan L. Booth

Cover design by Morgan L. Booth

All rights reserved. No part of this publication can be reproduced or transmitted in any form or by any means, electronic or mechanical, without permission in writing from the author or publisher.

ISBN: 978-1-304-65463-2

For my family

because of their unending love and support

For my friends

thank you for your awesome ideas and excitement

And

For Oakview Elementary School

which gave me my start as a writer and as a published author. I am very glad and privileged to have participated in your Author Day assembly. Meeting all of your wonderful students and staff is an experience I will never forget. You guys are all very awesome. Keep on imagining!

Other books by Morgan L. Booth:

The Last Winter (Big Cat Seasons #1)

Fearless

Contents

Prologue - 1
1. *The Forest* - 5
2. *Fireflies* - 18
3. *Nightmare* - 34
4. *River Bird* - 48
5. *Touch* - 61
6. *Dreams* - 74
7. *The Past* - 88
8. *Man* - 105
9. *The Dark Place* - 120
10. *Safe* - 134
11. *The She-Cub* - 148
12. *Sandra's Circus* - - - - - - - - - - - - - - - - - - - 164
13. *Betrayal* - 178
14. *The White Giant* - - - - - - - - - - - - - - - - - - 198
15. *Bullhook* - 214
16. *Promise* - 230
17. *Chak* - 249
18. *Fate* - 266

19. *The Pseudopanthera* - - - - - - - - - - - - - - - - - -282
20. *Pit* -300
21. *Screams* - 317
22. *Trust* - 333
23. *Safe Haven* -352

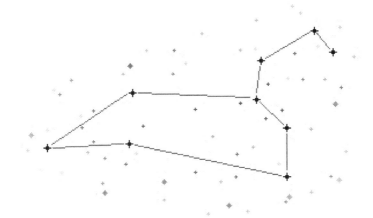

Prologue

"Help us! Please! Save us!"

"Escape! Escape!"

"Let us go! Free us!"

The screams were earsplitting. Loud cries of despair, agony and anger twisted in the air and resonated off the walls of the confinement. The horrible sounds hurt her ears, pierced her head like knives. She flattened her ears. She couldn't block them out, and they wouldn't stop screaming.

"Savior! Savior!"

"I don't want to die. Please, let us out!"

"Freedom! Set us free!"

She realized that the screams were directed at her. She opened her eyes. Darkness. Blindness. But she wasn't blind. It was this place, this world of screams, that was completely dark. No light, no hope in this place. Just darkness.

And screams.

She couldn't hear anything else. She squeezed her eyes shut. She wished they would stop, that the voices would silence for just once. She'd heard them all her life; the screams, the pain, the agony were all she knew. She wanted to scream back at them, to silence them herself, when suddenly she realized she was standing in something wet and warm. She looked down at the ground.

She was standing in blood.

With a frightened gasp, she leaped away, and that's when she saw the man. He was dead, lying face-up in the center of the red pool, which was fed by his torn, bleeding neck. His skull had been crushed, and his eyes bulged out of their sockets. His mouth was open in a silent, eternal scream. He had been killed.

She had killed him.

She could taste the blood on her lips. It was her jaws that had crushed his skull, her fangs that had ripped his throat, she who had spilled his blood. She crouched and stepped back, out of the pool of blood, backing away from her sin. Her ears flattened against her large head, and she cowered in the darkness.

"*Run away! Escape!*"

"*Don't leave us! Don't let us die!*"

"*They're coming! They're coming! Get out, now!*"

It was true. They were coming. She could head the footsteps, coming closer, accelerating with her heartbeat. They were attracted by the screams, the sound of the man's death and the roars of his killer. She bared her fangs. They would kill her. They would spill her blood in acts of vengeance, to make up for the man blood she'd spilled. She snarled in panic. She had to get out. She had to get away.

"RUN!"

She sprang away from the dead man. She ran, ran far from the blood, the death, the screams, and the dark. She did not look back. She kept running, running, running.

Chapter 1

The Forest

Beneath the steamy canopy of trees, all was dark. Very little light penetrated the dripping green leaves above, and thus created a sense of perpetual twilight for all who lived on the forest floor. The moisture in the air was as heavy as the largest tree in the forest, and hot, too – sweltering. The humidity was like a giant monster bearing down on the forest, and the moister on the sweating leaves was like his saliva, left over from the time when the monster dragged his tongue across the jungle – that monster being the gray clouds, and that tongue being the rain they produced.

It was through the darkness of the leaves that the jaguar ran, ran desperately for her life. They were following her. They were hunting her. They would kill her if they caught her. Her heart pounded in her chest.

Giant leaves and tangling vines rushed at her face, threatening to hinder her run, threatening to trap her and give her up to the hunters. The jungle was a haven, but it would kill any unwelcome guests. She did not know the jungle so well, nor did it know her. She feared that her choice of hiding places may have been the last foot dug in her grave. She had to get away. She had to hide. She had to live.

The she-cat swerved to avoid tree trunks as orchids and white trillium flowers brightened her way. She tried her best not to leave a trail, but the ground was muddy and she left a stream of prints in her wake, guiding the hunters to their prey. The jaguar was panicking, as she swerved right and left, leaping over the flora that grew on the ground, landing on the rot of plants long deceased. She panted loudly, saliva spiraling from her mouth, as she ran in the dark.

Her yellow eyes were well adapted to seeing in the low light. She had never known anything more than darkness. She had lived in it all her life. Her paws punched into the soft mud, kicked up the decomposing leaves as she leaped forward. Up ahead, behind a tree, there was light. Without slowing down, she dove into it.

The light was sunlight, shining onto the earth from high above, letting its warmth feed the smaller plants that rose up from the ground, racing to get to the top of the canopy, devouring as much sunlight as they could before it went away forever. This tiny clearing in the jungle was formed when a large tree fell to its death weeks before – its body still lay on the ground, its bark gray and dying, its giant carcass already decomposing, returning to the earth.

She entered the clearing for only a second, sliding to a stop in the mud when she saw the obstacle before her. The sunlight shined onto her pelt, illuminating the yellowish-orange fur decorated by her own unique pattern of black rosettes, shiny with sweat. Quickly, she turned her large head to look behind her, to see if they were still following her. A loud bang answered her question, and a bullet struck the dead tree just above her ears, shattering the bark into splinters. Instantly she turned and returned to the shadows.

The she-cat continued her full-out run, dodging a tangling web of vines before rounding quickly around the dead tree's roots, which fanned out in all directions. Once around the tree, she continued in a straight line, panting and wheezing hard. She was not used to running so long, running so hard and running so fast. Cats are not built with endurance, and the jaguar was no exception. The jaguar's main asset was her strength, the muscles in her legs and her powerful bite. But those were useless to her now. She had to keep up her pace. She could not turn around and fight. She would lose. She would die.

Saliva trailed from her jaws as she ran full-stride, her ears back and her tail whipping behind her. She could still barely hear them behind her – their loud shouts, their raucous laughter as they followed her trail, thinking of how easy she would be to kill. Thinking of how fun this hunt was turning out to be, how much of a challenge it was. Only Man would think of a challenging hunt as fun.

It was Man who was hunting her.

She cursed between pants as she fought to stay ahead of them. Her muscles screamed from the effort of having run so long and so hard. She had been running ever since she escaped, ever since she left the place of screams, the Dark Place – ever since she killed that man. That was why Man was hunting her now. They wanted her blood. They wanted revenge.

A long string of cat curses trailed from her mouth as plant after plant struck her in the face and chest. She needed to hide; she couldn't keep running like this. But as she ran on, she saw no place to conceal herself. Again, more curses sounded to the air as the she-cat roared in frustration. She wanted to fight, to turn and face the hunters, the men behind her, but she kept running, because she knew that the second she stopped, her fate would be sealed by bullet wound.

Capuchin and spider monkeys in the high canopy screamed at her as she ran beneath their troops, and she snarled at their high-pitched voices. Sloths lazily turned their heads to watch the jaguar run by before moving slowly to a new tree branch. Marsh deer grazing on small foliage and brush leaped away as the she-cat crashed through. The Amazon rainforest was ablaze with noise as animals fled from the running cat and the hunting men.

The jaguar leaped through the giant leaves of a ground plant and nearly ran headfirst into a kapok tree that grew on her path. She skidded on the plant rot, stopping inches away from it, and leaped back up on her feet. The dead tree she had gone around earlier had slowed the humans, and the she-cat was further ahead of them now. Yet she could still hear them, crashing through the brush, stomping the decay. She had to lose them. The she-cat thought ahead, and turned around.

She began to double back, running left for several yards before turning left again. Now she was running back the way she came. The ground she ran on now was not as wet, and so her trail was less noticeable. She ran and her muscles protested, until she saw a dark hole at the base of a tree ahead of her – a hollow. A hiding place. The hollow was obscured by a large plant, and so barely noticeable by lesser creatures. The she-cat herself wouldn't have seen it if not for her sharp eyes. She dove into the hollow, and froze.

Silence. The jaguar could not hear anything but her own heart pounding in her ears. The forest around her had gone silent;

the monkeys in the trees chattered almost inaudibly, while the birds had flown away as they heard the advent of the hunters. Even the insects were quiet for once – the forest had become eerie with anticipation. The she-cat fought to control her breathing, as she could hear it clearly even through the blood pounding in her ears. As she managed to silence herself, they came.

First, their voices. Strange, alien sounds, deliberate noises purposely made in their throats to produce words. Like high-pitched growls, monkey chirps with melody in the sound. Their laughter was like battle cries, snarls of challenge that the she-cat could not allow herself to answer. She listened, her eyes wide and dilated with fear, her heart beating faster and faster with each laugh.

Then, their footsteps, coming closer and closer and closer. Leaves crackled and crunched beneath their weight, and brush crashed as they forced their way through. The she-cat sank deeper into the hollow, trying to make herself small and unnoticeable, like the ants that marched on the leaves of the plant that shielded her.

Then, they came. A leg appeared before the jaguar's eyes, standing just a few feet away from the hollow. The leg was much different than most animal legs. Brownish in color, with wiry fur that did not cover the skin. To make up for their lack of fur, the humans used artificial skins to cover their real skin, but their legs below their knees were always bare. The she-cat watched that leg with fear in her eyes as its sibling came to join it. Both legs then stepped out of view, followed by another pair a little further away. This pair was much like the first. It also soon stepped away.

Then the third pair of legs came into view, and stayed in front of the hollow for a long time. The she-cat's heart raced as she saw the scar, the ugly, pink gash on the left leg, running from the knee to the ankle. She recognized that scar. She had seen it so many times before. She forced herself to keep from snarling.

"Where'd that darn cat run to?" one of the men said angrily after looking around the clearing. The she-cat heard him kick the brush.

"How the heck do I know?" another man answered. The first man let out a string of curse words. The fun and laughter was gone now.

"We lost her again!" the first man snarled. The she-cat flinched from the horrible roar.

"It can't have gone far," the man with the scar said plainly, shifting his weight from one leg to the other. "It's probably still heading east. Look for the tracks."

"There aren't any tracks!" the first man spat, kicking more brush. "I thought you were the tracker!"

"I was until the cat doubled back."

"We should have caught it by now!"

"We will catch it. That cat has never lived in the wild. It doesn't know how to survive out here. And we know the jungle better than it. We'll catch it, and if we don't, hunger and God will."

The first man snarled in anger and said nothing. The she-cat heard a grinding, clicking sound, and her heart froze – she knew that intimidating sound all too well. The sound of a rifle being cocked.

"Tell you what," the man with the scar purred. The she-cat now saw the gun as the man stuck the tip of the barrel into the ground and leaned against it like it was a walking stick. "When we find the thing, you'll get to shoot it. How 'bout that?"

A snarl and another string of curse words answered the proposal. Then, in a clearly frustrated voice: "Fine."

"*Bueno.* Here," the man with the scar picked up his rifle and tossed it to the angry man. "You can carry the gun."

More swears. Then the three men walked away.

It was a long time before the jaguar finally summoned enough courage to leave her hideout. The humans had long since gone away – it had been hours since she last moved. Her muscles ached horribly and she limped the first few steps as she forced herself to move out of the hollow. She poked her head through the leaves of the shielding plant and smelled the air. The human smell was still strong, but was slowly becoming stale. They were gone.

Sound had already returned to the jungle. The birds, having watched the men leave, began their incessant song once more, lending their beautiful, melodic voices to the forest. Howler monkeys groaned into the evening air, as they watched from the canopy the sun set over the horizon. The day insects had gone into hiding now, and the night insects were coming to take their place, to lend out their voices to replace the tired ones. Frogs began to chirp, and the first ocelot growled into the night as it began its nocturnal hunt.

The she-cat began to run again as the light faded. Her muscles protested, but she forced them to move, pouring her will into them to fight the soreness. She needed to put as much distance between her and the hunters as possible. She made herself run and run.

A small rivulet glinted with the fading light of the sun. The she-cat plunged into it, shattering its glassy surface. She waded the short distance to the other side, her paws occasional brushing the bottom of the shallow stream, as fish bumped up against her, wondering who she was to disturb their waters. The she-cat walked up to the other bank and shook her fur, spattering the dark foliage around her with muddy water. Then she started running again.

She ran until the forest became pitch black. As the moon rose into the sky, hidden by the canopy leaves, the she-cat still ran, and only when the vampire bats flew out of their hidden caves and swarmed in the night sky did she finally allow herself to slow to a trot.

As she wandered through the forest with no aim or direction, fighting sleep as it haunted her eyes, a bright green light suddenly flashed before her face. The she-cat jerked her head back in surprise, uttering a growl, as the little green light faded away to darkness. The she-cat relaxed and put her nose to the place where the light had flashed, but there was nothing there. Puzzled, the she-cat started walking on, until she saw the flash again, this time a little ways ahead of her, near the trunk of a tree.

A star? The she-cat didn't know what the thing was, as it blinked near the tree trunk, beckoning to her. The she-cat stepped forward to see the blinker, but before she could find it, the light had moved again. The jaguar began to chase it, ignoring the scream of pain her muscles made. She ran after the moving star for about a mile, until finally it stopped moving, and continued to blink in just one spot, a small leaf of a dying ground plant.

The she-cat, panting, now put her nose to blinking leaf, and discovered not a star, not just a light, but an insect. A glowing beetle that flashed its light in her face as she stared. Then the bug buzzed its wings and lifted off from the leaf, away from the breath of the she-cat. She watched it go, realizing now what the insect was.

A firefly.

She had never seen one before, only heard stories about these glowing insects that danced in the warm nights of the Amazon. She'd heard the stories of them, how they were the messengers of the god of the cats' religion, how they only danced in the forests protected by Panthera. How they were the eyes of the Lord of all Cats, how through their lights he saw the world and watched over the cats. How they guided and protected the night hunter as he prowled through his haven. The she-cat thought she'd never see one in her life. And here she was, watching one float away, blinking its neon, chemical light.

Suddenly the she-cat noticed that more glowing lights were blinking around her, more insects, more fireflies. Green stars were glowing all over the jungle, on every leaf, on every tree, in the high canopy and on the ground, choking the air. They blinked in unison, creating lightning in the forest. The she-cat sat down and marveled at it all. She watched the fireflies dance, and as she did, she remembered:

"When you see the fireflies dance in the forest, you will know that you are safe. For they are Panthera's messengers, the friendly forest guardians, who speak of safety in their light. And

only in a truly safe place, a haven, will the fireflies dance for you. Only when you are free."

The she-cat was free. And the fireflies fluttering all around her proved it.

Two weeks. Two weeks had gone by since she had escaped from the dark and licked the blood of a man off her paws. Two weeks she had been running from hunters. Two weeks she had been in the jungle, and never had she felt safer than she did now. The fireflies, those beautiful, glowing bugs, were dancing for her, and all would be fine now. She was safe. She was free.

For the first time in such a long time, the she-cat lay down in the open. She lowered her head to rest on her paws. Her eyes closed, and she fell into a deep and peaceful sleep.

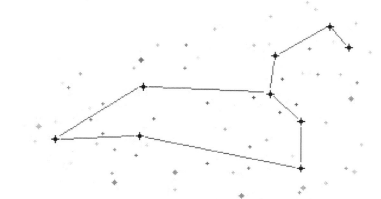

Chapter 2

Fireflies

It was summer.

A full year had passed since the she-cat had eluded the hunters and became free. Since then she had traveled still more miles to make sure she would never be followed again. After two months of nomadic wandering, she finally settled down and marked a territory of her own, within a lush, green area of the Amazon overflowing with food and water.

A large area of land, the territory was about twenty square miles across, and included a small stream that served as the western border of her territory. To the northeast was a large meadow of lush green grass, speckled with beautiful flowers blooming beneath a yellow sun. Near to the center of her territory and less than a mile from the meadow was the she-cat's den, a hollow in the side of a fallen kapok tree. And filling the rest of her territory was thick, impenetrable jungle crammed to the high canopy with life.

This territory was abundant with prey. Marsh deer and tapirs would travel miles just to roam this part of the rainforest. They would gather early in the mornings at the meadow to feast on the grass while the mist swirled around them, cooling them as they grazed. And the forest was never quiet of birdsong and bug chatter – that beautiful melody was always welcome and always heard. The song of the rainforest could be heard both day and night, and the music was only ever broken by the screech of the lone harpy eagle soaring above the canopy, searching for a capybara to snatch.

In the jungle, there is life in all layers of the canopy, and that abundance of life was best represented by this small piece of forest owned by the she-cat. Almost every animal the Amazon had to offer could be found among these leaves. Capybaras and anteaters dominated the ground floor, and the understory layer was home to insects and small snakes. The middle canopy was home to most birds, as they enjoy the fruit that grew at this layer. It was also the favorite place for the sloth to hang and rest all day in the low light. The high canopy belonged to the monkeys of the Amazon – the capuchin, the spider monkey, the howler monkey, the squirrel monkey – every monkey; every animal imaginable could be found in this territory.

That was why it was the perfect place to raise a bound-to-be curious cub.

In her time, the she-cat eventually mated with a male jaguar that had wandered through her territory. Now, with labor pains wracking her body, she lay in her kapok tree den, in a nest she had made days earlier out of dry leaves and fur. She lay down and waited for her cub to arrive.

Twilight was descending over the land. Her den lay within a clearing, and so a view of the sky was present. This skylight in the high canopy formed when the kapok tree fell to its death months earlier. Through this hole in the leaves, the she-cat watched the thin clouds above turn pink in the fading light. As the sun set, the moon rose, and soon the stars and fireflies came out to dance.

As the night sounds began to fill the forest, a brand new sound joined them on this one night. In her den, the she-cat licked her newborn cub as he squeaked and crawled blindly around the den, crying for milk. The she-cat gently nudged him toward her stomach, where he drank his new life. She growled with tenderness in her voice as she licked his body clean, revealing his perfect tawny fur, decorated by his own pattern of black rosettes.

As the helpless kitten whimpered and nursed, the she-cat looked outside at the forest night. The fireflies were flickering in the trees, lighting up the land in flashes of brilliant green. She agreed with the message that their lights were sending – yes, this place was safe. This place would always be safe, for Panthera protects it. Her cub shall never live in fear or worry of Man. He would never get to them here. Here, the jaguars were safe.

The she-cat suddenly thought of the perfect name for her cub. Leaning her head close to him, she whispered it to his deaf ears.

"Fecir." The jaguar word for safe haven, for messenger. For firefly.

It was nighttime. The full moon shone over the sleeping jungle, the leaves of the trees catching the silver light within their dewdrops and reflecting it. The stars, scattered about in the sky like the dewdrops on the leaves, blinked like the fireflies that danced in the humid meadow beneath the clear night.

Another creature danced with them tonight, danced and played for the first time beneath the watchful stars. A cloud of fireflies burst from the grasses and dispersed as the young, two-month-old jaguar cub laughed and readied himself to pounce again. He leaped into the air, his body surfacing above the sea of grass like a spouting whale, before diving back under a split second later. Another swarm of insects lifted into the air, and the cub reached up to catch them in his mouth.

The young cat's tawny coat glowed silver beneath the white light of the moon. His yellow eyes were bright with curiosity, for tonight was his first time venturing from the den. His triangular ears were alert and alive to the sound of frogs and insects. His spotted face, at the moment speckled with the glowing flecks of crushed firefly, turned toward the edge of the grass, and he called.

"Look, mother! Look at all the fireflies I'm catching!"

"I see," said a gentle voice. The she-cat sat at the edge of the meadow, watching her son play in the grass with the glowing insects. She smiled and almost hated to call back out to him. "Fecir," she said softly. "It's time to go home."

"Oh, mother!" Fecir whined, his shining eyes suddenly appearing among the moonlit grass. "Do I have to?"

"Yes, Fecir," the she-cat sighed. "Come on now."

Fecir moaned and reluctantly wade through the tall grass toward her. He meekly approached his mother, who immediately began to lick his face, cleaning him of the firefly chemical that spotted his cheeks. Fecir pulled away with a stubborn growl. "But mother, I want to stay. I want to stay and play with the fireflies," he pouted.

The she-cat continued to lick him. "There will be plenty more nights to play with the fireflies," she growled patiently, rasping her tongue over his eyes. "There's always tomorrow, and the next night, and the next...."

"Mother?" Fecir piped, pulling away again. "What are those tiny lights in the sky?"

The she-cat lifted her head. Above her the fireflies, the forest guardians, spiraled in strange patterns, blinking beneath a black sky. The she-cat chuckled. "Have the insects gone to your head? Those were the fireflies you were chasing."

"Not the bugs!" Fecir growled in frustration. "The ones that *don't* move! The ones that are *really* far away!"

The she-cat immediately realized what he meant, and looked up again, focusing her eyes on the silver specks of light behind the glowing insects, high up in the sky and as far away as the moon. She sat down. "Those ones?" she asked. "Those lights are the stars, Fecir."

"What are stars? Are they like fireflies?"

"No, they're not bugs. In fact, I'm not entirely sure what they are. They've been there forever, never moving and never fading, ever since the dawn of time. Each star is a part of a pattern that looks like an animal. We call these patterns the Star Lords."

"What are Star Lords?" Fecir cocked his head to the side.

The she-cat grinned. "They are our gods, Fecir, the ones that created this world and all the creatures that walk it. And each of those creatures has their own Lord that they follow, from the cold-blooded lizard to the brightly-colored toucan. There is a Star Lord for every creature on this Earth."

"Do we follow a Lord?"

"We do." The she-cat smiled. "We follow Panthera, the Lord of all cats."

"Which pattern is his?" Fecir asked, looking straight up and searching the sky.

The she-cat did the same, lifting her head and searching for the constellation she knew well. She saw it, a pattern of nine bright stars outlining the Star Lord's shape. She rumbled deeply.

"Over there, Fecir. Do you see him? He is sitting on the canopy, right at the top of those trees."

Fecir followed her gaze. His eyes brightened. "I see him!"

The she-cat smiled again. "That is Panthera, the great white jaguar. He is a large cat, with long fangs and powerful jaws; the strongest hunter in the night. He is always crouching down on his front paws, drinking from the black water that is the night sky, for he is a thirsty Lord. Tonight he licks the moisture off the leaves, see?"

Fecir looked in wonder at the pattern, imagining the image his mother described.

The she-cat continued, "They say that his rosettes are the color of cinnamon, and that his fur is as white as snow."

"What's snow?" Fecir suddenly asked, flicking his ear.

The she-cat's whiskers twitched. "What is snow?" she repeated. "Snow is like a frozen rain, like cold clumps of clouds that fall from the sky. It piles up in white mounds on the ground and covers everything in sight. It makes the land cold and blank."

"Is there ever any snow here?"

"No Fecir. It doesn't snow in the jungle. Here it is always warm, always green. But, there once was a time when it was never warm, never green. The whole Earth was covered in snow." She paused. "I haven't told you the story of the Endless Winter yet, have I?"

Fecir shook his head. "Tell me."

The she-cat sighed. "I'll tell you," she said, "but only if you promise to go to bed without a fuss. Deal?"

Bargaining, the she-cat had found as a new mother, worked well when trying to get a rowdy, stubborn cub to do what he was told. This tactic always worked, and it did not fail her now.

"Deal!"

"Alright then," the she-cat grunted, lying down on the ground and stretching her paws out in front of her. Fecir jumped up laid down beside her, resting his cheek on her shoulder. The she-cat sighed again before beginning her story, the story her own mother had told her years ago.

"Many, many years ago, everything in this world was white. All the land was covered in snow, and all the seas were frozen as ice. The trees were bare, shivering skeletons, devoid of leaves. There was no grass, no trees, no life anywhere. It was the Endless Winter, the cold that lasted for centuries."

Fecir ears were perked and alert.

"But then, that all changed. The Pantheraseer came, and she banished the cold, banished the Winter, and brought forth the spring."

"What's a Pantheraseer?"

"The Pantheraseer was the only cat who could see Panthera when he came down to Earth. In the time of the Winter, the cats had a legend that when Panthera came down from the sky and touched the snow, spring would spread forth from his touch. But only the Pantheraseer would see him. And she had a job to do. She had to convince all the big cats to believe in Panthera, and then, once everyone believed, she had to experience the greatest of losses before Panthera would bring spring."

"What was the greatest of losses?" Fecir asked.

"The loss of her own life," the she-cat whispered slowly.

There was silence for a long time between them. Fecir flattened his ears and pondered those words for a while, while the night music swirled around them, and vampire bats flitted overhead. The she-cat shook her head as a mosquito buzzed in her ear.

Eventually, the silence broke. Fecir lifted his head and looked into his mother's eyes. "So ... she died?" he asked in a small voice.

The she-cat sighed and rested her chin on her paws. "Yes, Fecir," she said gently. "She died. But her sacrifice was necessary for spring to come. Without her, the world would still be white, and we would not exist."

"Who was the Pantheraseer?"

The she-cat smiled in admiration as she thought of her. "A Siberian tigress."

"I thought you told me that the tigers were extinct?"

"Back then they weren't," the she-cat grunted. "And not all the tigers went extinct, dear cub. Many lived on the edge of extinction until the Pantheraseer was born, and some lived to see the spring and beyond. Those cats still exist today – the Bengal and the Sumatran. The Malayan, too. They survived the Winter. The Siberian, however, did not. The Pantheraseer was the last of them. Her kind died out with her."

"Would we have died out, too?"

"Yes. Without her, all the cats would've died. The lion, the leopard, the tiger, and us. The Pantheraseer was a hero."

"What was her name?"

The she-cat paused and pondered for a bit, trying to remember. "I don't know, Fecir. I don't think anyone knows anymore. She lived so long ago."

Fecir paused to think of a new question. He was stalling, trying to draw out this story for as long as possible, for he did not want to go to bed, even if he'd made a deal to do so. He quickly came up with something. "What did Panthera look like, when he came down to Earth?"

"His spirit, you mean? What did his spirit look like?" the she-cat yawned.

"What's a spirit?"

"A spirit is a creature that cannot die. It doesn't eat or breathe to stay alive. It cannot bleed, for it has no blood. It's a creature that moves in a whisper of wind in leaves, and can phase into a shadow. A creature unseen by normal eyes."

"So Panthera's spirit, then?" Fecir's eyes were bright.

"No one is really quite sure of what he looked like. Though most cats say that he came as a white tiger with blue eyes, the way the tigers saw him in the sky."

"Do all the cats see him differently?"

"Yes," the she-cat murmured softly. "They all have different views. The lions see him as a hunter with a flowing mane and blood-red claws. The leopards see him as a small, peaceful cat, with a long, bushy tail and glowing pink eyes. The tigers see him with bright blue eyes and coal-black stripes. None of the cats see him the same way, but one thing is common among all the sights, and that is that Panthera's fur is always pure white."

"Like snow?"

"Like snow," the she-cat confirmed, licking Fecir's nose tenderly.

Fecir cringed away and stood. "Do you think Panthera will ever come again?"

The she-cat frowned and looked away, thinking. "Some cats think he will," she said. "They say that he will come again, and when he does, another Pantheraseer will be born, and the legend will start anew. But I don't know why that would ever happen again. The Endless Winter was banished. I don't believe Panthera will come."

"Oh," Fecir mewed, somewhat disappointed. He flexed his claws and scratched at the ground with sudden boredom. The she-cat lifted her head and looked up at the sky, then stood up quickly, startling Fecir. He looked up at her as her large head eclipsed the full moon.

"Time for bed," she grunted.

"But mother–!"

"You made a deal with me," the she-cat reminded him. "Come along." She started walking toward the jungle.

With a pout, Fecir scampered to follow.

They were home in no time at all, for the journey was not so long. However, Fecir had miscalculated how sleepy he was, and soon complained that he was too tired to continue walking. Eventually his mother resigned to carrying him by the scruff of his neck the rest of the way home. By the time the two arrived at their hollow, Fecir had fallen asleep in his mother's jaws.

In their den, the she-cat gently laid Fecir in the soft earth at the back of the den. With a sigh, he curled up into a tight little ball, his paws twitching from his dreams. The she-cat then laid herself down to sleep beside him. However, before she could close her eyes, she felt Fecir stir, and with a sigh she prepared herself for another round of questioning.

But this time, Fecir asked only one question, and he whispered it so softly that the she-cat had to lean close and strain her ears to listen. Fecir's eyes fluttered and his voice was slurred with dreams.

"Do you think there will ever be another Endless Winter?"

The she-cat sighed and looked out at the fireflies dancing through the night. They spoke their message of safety, and the she-cat closed her eyes and rested her chin on her paws. "No, Fecir," the she-cat whispered. "No, there will never be another Endless Winter. Panthera forbids it."

As the storm raged overhead, all was chaos below. Men ran around and yelled at each other, trying desperately to be heard over the thunder. Animals screamed in terror and paced their cages, snarling at the men as they passed. A train whistle blew, loud and crisp through the air, sending the animals into more frightened screams. The rain poured through the air and the lightning flashed in the dark, briefly illuminating the men as they worked in the wet and tried to control their animals.

As all the animals around him screamed in fright, only one creature was calm amidst the chaos. He stood inside his wooden boxcar, rocking back and forth on his legs, which were chained to the floor. He rumbled softly in a low voice, until suddenly the door to the boxcar slid open and a man entered. The man carried a rod in his hand. The rod had a steel hook at the end, and the man used that hook to jab at the animal. The animal moaned and stepped away, but was held back by the chains on his legs.

The man quickly unlocked the chains and jabbed the animal again, yelling at him. The animal growled and again stepped away to avoid the pain, yet made no move to fight back.

"Get going! ¡*Vas!*" the man snarled, hooking the giant creature again with the rod. The animal stepped toward the open door to his boxcar. A ramp had been laid down so the animal could walk safely to the ground. The man walked behind the animal and hooked him again, forcing him to move forward. The animal groaned and stepped out into the rain.

For a moment the animal hesitated as he stood on the ramp. He surveyed the scene in front of him and moaned. The lightning flashed overhead, briefly illuminating his brilliant white skin.

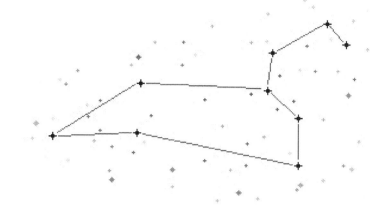

Chapter 3

Nightmare

It was dark.

That was all she could think about, the darkness. Though her eyes were open, no sight greeted them; just the blindness, the blackness. The deep void of shadows, open to her like a mouth, swallowing her, digesting her within the depths of its lightless stomach. The feeling was ... familiar.

The she-cat flattened her ears at the blindness, and reached out with her other senses to see the world. The earth beneath her paws was cold, hard, as if a mountain had mowed the jungle down and turned the dirt into smooth flat stone. Stone. The cold, smooth surface. The darkness, the sightlessness, why was it so familiar? Where was she?

She reached out further, calling to smell. There were many scents in the sightless world. There was a strong odor in the dark, the odor of fecal matter and urine. The smell was overpowering, yet one was stronger than it, overruled it. A sharp, metallic scent, cold and bitter to the nose, biting her sense of smell. This scent was also very familiar.

Light suddenly flickered on, flooded the giant room. The yellow glow, though somewhat dim, was shocking, nauseating, terrifying. But the she-cat did not fear the light. She feared what towered above her, on all sides of her, surrounding her, trapping her. Silver, cylindrical poles lined up to form walls. Smooth, metal bars. A cage.

Three walls of metal bars, one in front of her and one on each side. The fourth wall, the solid wall, the one she pressed against, was wooden. The once-smooth surface splintered with crisscrossing gashes, the marks made by the claws of a captive.

The she-cat pressed against the abused wall, pressed as hard as she could too it. Her ears were flat, her eyes were wide, her teeth were bared, snarling. The metal bars, the darkness. The smells, the flickering lights. She knew where she was. She remembered.

"No," she whimpered. "No, please. Not here. Not again."

The screams began. All around her, a thousand voices suddenly rose into the air. Her ears rang with their agony. The voices of animals, their pain twisting in the air, their fear sung for all to hear. Different animals, small and large, arguing, snorting in anger, bellowing. All captives, all prisoners, crying for freedom. The she-cat snarled at them. They were so loud, so scared. She hated them. She hated their screams. Jaguars, leopards, lions in the adjacent cages, all roaring, all screaming in anger, fear, desperation, hopelessness. Pacing, stalking in endless circles. They screamed in hopes of being heard.

"*Help me! Please!*"

"*Get me out of here! Don't let me die!*"

"*Panthera! Where is he? Save us!*"

The she-cat snarled, and her voice joined them as she roared. "No! No! No! Not again! No!" Tears dripped to the stained concrete floor. The she-cat was in the Dark Place again.

"*Sister!*" A voice was calling to her. "*Sister!*"

"Keko?" she yelped. She knew that voice. "Keko! Brother, where are you?"

"*Here!*" The she-cat saw him in the cage across from her, separated by an aisle of dust. A male jaguar, his coat golden in the yellow light, pacing in circles, his flanks rubbing against the imprisoning bars. His wide, amber eyes, the pattern of his rosettes – it was her brother. She remembered. "Keko!"

He reared, putting his paws on the bars. His teeth clashed against the metal. His claws scraped the silver as he slid down. A moan of despair. He looked into her eyes.

"*Swana!*" he coughed to the she-cat. "*Help me, Swana! Help me!*"

"What's wrong? What's happening?"

"*Help me, sister! I've been chosen!*"

Chosen. That word. That word stabbed through her like a burning knife. Her jaws opened in horror, eyes widened. She remembered that word. "No, Keko! Not you!"

"*They've chosen me!*" he cried mournfully. "*They're going to take me!*" His amber eyes shone in the yellow light, shone with fear. He moaned, hopeless pacing, back and forth, back and forth.

A screech of metal. A clang. Air flowed into the Dark Place. Clean air, brushing away the putrid fecal odor. A burning smell then came. Sharp as the metal. The animals shied away from the smell. The scent reached her nose, and she snarled. She knew that scent. She remembered.

It came, strolling between the stalls and cages. Rounded a corner and came into view. Man. He walked calmly, ignoring the animals, disregarding how they cowered. He came to the cat cages, and each cat hissed and growled at him before retreating away. The she-cat quickly saw why. The man had a rifle in his hand.

The she-cat wanted to reach between the bars, to hook him with her claws as he passed, but she feared that rifle. She knew of its power. The man stopped at Keko's cage, peered in. The she-cat saw the man's left leg, the ugly pink scar running from his knee to his ankle. She resisted the urge to hiss, as the man lifted his rifle.

Then she heard it. That sound. The sound that she would forever remember. A rifle being cocked. She watched her lift the hateful weapon to his eye. He stuck the muzzle through the bars, aimed it at the jaguar. The she-cat roared in fury, but she could do nothing. She closed her eyes.

"*Chosen!*" Keko wailed. "*Chosen!*"

The man pulled the trigger.

A pop was heard. The she-cat had expected a loud blast. But she only heard a pop. She opened her eyes as Keko roared furiously. He writhed on the concrete, hissing hysterically. He clawed at a red dart stuck in his thigh.

The man lowered his rifle and walked away, while Keko began to shudder. The liquid in the darts drained steadily into his blood, and Keko's movements became sluggish, tired. The animals murmured fearfully as his eyelids drooped, his roars morphed to moans, his breath slowed, relaxed. The drug was making him fall asleep.

"Keko, please! Open your eyes! Stand up, before he takes you away!" the she-cat screamed. Tears left streaks down her face as Keko's eyelids fluttered. His claws stretched out and he yawned indifferently. The she-cat threw herself at the bars. "Get up!"

But Keko's eyes were already closed. He was snoring peacefully. "Keko!" the she-cat shrieked desperately. "Get up!"

"*¡Cállate!*" An open palm banged her cage. The she-cat snarled at the annoyed man staring down at her. The rifle wasn't in his hands; instead, he held a coiled bit of orange nylon rope. The she-cat growled and stepped away, while the man turned to Keko's cage again. He watched the sleeping cat for a moment, then slowly unbolted the door. He opened the cage and stepped inside. He nudged Keko with his foot. Then he stooped down and tied the rope around Keko's hind legs. He dragged Keko out of the cage and onto the dirt.

The she-cat watched helplessly as her brother was dragged away. Her eyes followed as he rounded the corner and disappeared from view. Moments later there was a loud clang. The lights flickered off. Man and Keko disappeared.

Half an hour later, a sound vibrated through the wooden wall. A loud blast as a bullet was expelled from a gun barrel. Keko had died.

The she-cat woke up with a start. Her eyes were wide, her ears were back, and her fur was drenched with sweat. She panted hard in the darkness. For a moment she did not recognize where she was. It was only when she had calmed down that she saw that she was in her hollow, with Fecir sleeping peacefully beside her and the fireflies dancing in the trees outside. It had all been a dream.

No, the she-cat thought. *Not a dream. A memory.*

She had dreamed of her brother's death.

A scarlet macaw announced the arrival of the sun.

Bright orange light spilled over the land as the sun rose to sit on the tops of the kapok trees in the canopy. Rays of warmth threaded their way through the jungle, peeking behind thick tree trunks and illuminating giant leaves. The sunshine, as it brightened the forest, trapped itself in the dewdrops that sat glistening upon the green leaves, shimmering like diamonds as they reflected the dawn.

Morning mist encircled the trees at this time, a cloud wafting through the forest like a wraith, caressing the animals that walked in the fog. Silhouettes of marsh deer and peccaries drifted through a maze of wood, quietly making their way toward the meadow where they would eat the moist grass under the cover of the mist. Birds would fly carefully through the cloud, singing their morning song, waking the forest and shooing the night predators back into hiding. Monkeys in the canopy would wake and yawn before joining the birdsong with their own chorus of chatters, squeals, and howls.

It was the deafening music of the morning forest that made her ears twitch in the darkness of her hollow. The she-cat yawned, blinking her eyes that hadn't closed once since waking from her nightmare earlier that night. With a twitch of her whiskers, she quietly checked on Fecir, who was still asleep, curled up in a little ball in a corner of the hollow. The she-cat huffed quietly before leaving him to step out into the light.

With a yawn she entered the mist and shook her head to clear away her fatigue. She then began to groom herself, but as she did, memories of her brother's death came forward in her mind to haunt her. She growled as the visions played out in her head, and not even the music of the birds and monkeys could chase away the sound of those screams, his wails of despair, that rifle....

She shook her head again. She did not want to remember. For over a year she had suppressed those memories, in order to start a new life. But she couldn't keep them locked away anymore. She shook her head again, growling. She needed to find something to take her mind off the memories. She stood up and shook her fur; then, with a final yawn, the she-cat decided to go hunting. The thrill of the chase would surely take her mind off of her memories. She growled and trotted into the forest, heading towards the river.

In the cozy comfort of his hollow, Fecir heaved a heavy sigh as he rolled over in his sleep. His eyes were squinted shut, and his teeth bared slightly. His paws twitched, the claws sheathing and unsheathing as a strange dream troubled his resting mind.

His vision was gone. He saw nothing in this odd dream. There was no scent either. Fecir felt blinded. No sight, no smell. But sound. His ears were not blind. He could hear voices, calling, roaring into the darkness all around him. Voices he did not recognize. Voices he could barely understand.

"*Spring will come! Believe in him! Believe with all your life!*"

"Who is that?" Fecir said in his dream. "Who is talking to me?"

"*When the Pantheraseer is born and Panthera comes down to earth and touches the snow, spring will come as bright green as ever.*"

"Pantheraseer?" Fecir said, confused. "But … spring already came…. What's happening? What's going on?"

"*Panthera comes! Save us! Save us all!*"

"Save who!" Fecir cried out, but he still couldn't see anything. "What do you want from me? I don't understand! What is going on?"

"*Spring will come, Seragah. It will. I promise.*"

Fecir's mind froze. That name … he'd never heard it before, but somehow he knew it. Why? Why was it so familiar?

Seragah.

Suddenly Fecir's sight returned. The dark world diminished and his nostrils opened. He could see and smell again, but the sights and scents that met him were completely unfamiliar and alien.

The voices were gone. In their place was deafening silence. The world Fecir had entered was completely white. Gray trees with forking, naked branches surrounded him on all sides – a dying forest, bereft of green, of life. From the gray sky above fell giant white raindrops, drifting like leaves on a breeze. They collected on Fecir's pelt, and he shivered, suddenly cold. The rain was frozen. Snow.

Snow covered everything here in this frozen world. Beneath Fecir's paws was no mud, but the cold white. The earth was gone beneath it. Fecir's paws were numbing as he stood shivering in the cold. Clumps of the white powder sat on the branches of the trembling gray trees, and the skinny limbs somehow managed to hold the weight without snapping beneath the crushing cold.

Fecir's breath came in heavy pants, and moist steam rose from his mouth. His lungs felt bigger somehow, he noticed. He inhaled deeply, filling his lungs to capacity, then let it all out in a huff. He was amazed. He must've grown bigger within the last few minutes of standing in the cold.

Suddenly Fecir heard a voice. He twitched his ears, turned his head toward the sound. His eyes searched, and there, on a bare branch high off the ground to his left, he saw a white bird.

Fecir stared at this strange bird. It looked nothing like the colored toucans or the harpy eagles he so clearly knew, but its face did seem to closely resemble that of a spectacled owl. The bird's brilliant white feathers blended perfectly with its surroundings, and its eyes were large and took up most of the space on the owl's face. Those eyes were bright yellow, and they stared with pupils forever fixed on one spot.

On him. Fecir suddenly realized that the owl was staring directly back at him. When their eyes met, Fecir felt a strange sensation course through him. He couldn't identify the feeling. It was as if he'd seen those eyes somewhere before. Fecir blinked in confusion, when the owl puffed out its furry chest, took a breath, and exhaled, making that sound Fecir had heard earlier: "Who!"

"Who?" Fecir asked, then yelped in surprise. His voice was not his. It was too deep, too adult to be his own. He growled and felt the deep rumble in his chest. Fecir had no idea what was happening.

The owl suddenly screeched and opened its wings, swooping into the air. Startled, Fecir watched it leave, and then he suddenly noticed the pain in his belly.

The pain was like a fire, as if he had swallowed a burning log, and the flames were licking the inside of his stomach, scalding it, melting it. He moaned in agony. The fire in his gut was consuming him, and he wanted to collapse, to cry out from the pain. He had never felt this kind of pain before ever in his life. It was the pain of starvation.

A wafting smell suddenly flowed beneath his nostrils, and he breathed. The scent was faint, yet it immediately caught his full attention. Saliva began to pool in his mouth and leak from his lips onto the snow. Before he knew it, Fecir was trotting toward the source of the smell. It was the smell of meat.

Fecir noticed, as he crunched through the snow, that his paws were heavier than they normally were, bigger and wider. He stopped and glanced down at his legs for the first time, and gasped when he saw that the paws were not his. The paws that he stood on were white like the snow, larger and furrier than his own tawny cub feet, and the legs they were attached to were orange and ringed by black stripes. Fecir turned his head to look back at his body. It was orange as well, and his spots, his unique pattern of rosettes was gone, and in its place were ribbons of black winding all the way down his body and ending at the tip of his whipping tail.

Fecir had become a tiger.

The meat scent still had its grip on his nose, pulling him by the nostrils to its source. Fecir could not resist – not caring that he had become a tiger, he ran toward the meat. He craved it. He needed it. His belly seemed to burn even hotter as the smell became stronger, its source closer.

Fecir weaved his way through the skeleton forest until suddenly he came to a clearing. There, in the middle of the clearing, was some sort of den made out of short black trees. Inside the den was red meat. Without thinking, Fecir darted into the den. As his jaws clamped down on the frozen meat, a clang was heard behind him, and with a roar he turned around. More trees had appeared out of nowhere, forming a cage around Fecir. He was trapped.

With a roar Fecir attacked the bars of the cage, banging his large head repeatedly against the metal, until blood coated his eyes and his vision went dark.

In his sleep, Fecir writhed but did not wake. He turned over and over, in the coolness of his hollow, while the music of the Amazon lulled him into deeper sleep, deeper dreams, deeper nightmares.

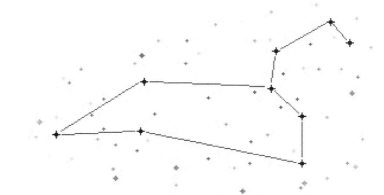

Chapter 4

River Bird

The stream bubbled a beautiful song beneath a shade of leaves.

The river was calm, it's surface like glass, reflecting the light that broke through the canopy above. Though not many feet from one bank to the other, it was deep in the middle, and thus almost all kinds of fish swam up this way, from the tiny cichlid to the enormous arapaima. Piranhas and electric eels were also common, but seldom did they come near the shore, and so weren't much of a threat. Otters would sometimes run along the bank, chattering and barking as they played and chased one another amongst their family groups, and a few turtles would come in the day to swim lazy circles within this tranquil part of the river, resting up for when they would brave the rapids the next day in order to reach their spawning grounds. The only creature absent from the river was the Amazon River dolphin, a creature that only came during the rainy season, when the stream flooded its banks and became deep enough to swim through.

On both sides of the stream was a bank of soft sand and mud, which the water lapped at it as it lazed its way downstream. Fringing the sandy banks was brush and thick foliage, in which the she-cat was hiding, waiting for her prey.

She lay down among the thick leaves and fronds, peeking through the brush every once and a while to look at the river. She had been waiting an hour already, but she was ever patient. She stayed absolutely still, becoming one with the jungle around her, listening, watching, waiting.

Eventually her patience was rewarded. In from a hole in the canopy above flew an egret, its white feathers glistening in the midmorning sun. It flew in a slow circle before landing gracefully in a shallow part of the bank, near where the she-cat was hiding. The she-cat shook when she smelled it, and began to drool. This was the prey she'd been waiting for.

But she could not leap out yet. She must wait. Wait for when her prey least expected an attack. The she-cat forced herself to stop shaking, watched the bird silently, as it lifted one of its long, slender legs out of the water. It stepped elegantly through the stream, finding a nice spot to stand. Then it was still, its head and beak staring into the water, listening, watching, waiting for its prey to swim by.

The she-cat watched in silence, drool dripping onto her paws. Her hungry belly thought of food, but her mind kept wandering elsewhere, as she watched her prey's movement. Her tired, drowsy mind couldn't focus on the bird. All she could think about was her brother.

"Help me, Swana, help me! I've been chosen!" She could still hear his voice clearly.

She snapped her mind away, focusing on the egret. She couldn't think about that right now. She was hunting.

She watched the egret intensely, never letting eyes wander from it. She focused on how it moved, how its head bobbed up and down when it walked. She watched it as it walked deeper into the water and stopped, standing still, watching the water. Waiting for a fish to swim between its legs. Listening, watching, waiting.

The she-cat's mind wandered again. She saw the man with the scar, saw him dragging her brother away. She wished she could chase after them, but the bars held her back. She wished she could've saved him.

She remembered the gunshot, that horrible, painful sound that ended her brother's life.

The she-cat snarled at the memory, then immediately regretted the noise. The egret barked in alarm and looked toward her. The jaguar lifted her head out of the ferns, and the bird squawked, seeing now who his hunter was. He turned quickly and opened his wings.

With a snarl and a loud curse, the she-cat sprang out of her hiding place, racing toward the bird. The egret began to beat the air with its white wings, barking in its croaky voice, trying to get airborne. It managed to lift about ten feet into the air when the she-cat ran up to him. Crouching low to the ground, she bunched up the muscles in her powerful hind legs, then released the tension in a fantastic leap. She soared up into the air beside the egret, and, opening her jaws wide as she neared him, she clamped her teeth around the bird's neck.

With a honk, the egret shuddered in the air, flapping its wings violently and battering the she-cat as they fell back to earth. The two animals landed with a loud splash in the center of the stream, and the water surged and swelled for a few moments as they disappeared beneath the glassy surface. A few moments later, a spotted head broke the surface, and the jaguar paddled back to shore, the dead egret in her jaws.

The she-cat dragged her kill onto the muddy bank and dropped it in the shade. Then she stood there panting for a few moments, as the kill rush left her exhausted on the beach. She stared at the egret while she calmed down, stared at its broken neck and its soggy feathers torn from the battle. As she stared, all she could think about was her brother.

Her brother had been killed by Man. He had been taken from her, taken from the Dark Place and brought outside, to the land of light, only to be killed. Such a cruel way to die. To see the light for the first time, even if only through drugged eyes, and then be snatched away from it by the dark clutches of death. Her brother had gone through that. He had died that way. He had been chosen.

He had called her "Swana."

Swana. The she-cat could hardly remember her own name anymore. Not since her brother's death had she heard the word, and in the years that followed she had steadily forgotten until she became nameless, a discarded nomad in the land of the Amazon. Now, as she stared down at the egret, more memories came flooding back to her, and she closed her eyes, as if to keep the visions from pouring out of them.

The she-cat remembered her mother. She remembered her first few weeks of life, when all she knew was her mother's warm breath, the soft sound of her gentle voice, and the taste of her milk. She remembered the feel of her brother kicking blindly at her as they fought for a place to nurse at their mother's side. And she remembered her name. The name her mother had whispered to her as she cleaned her with her tongue. Swana. The jaguar word for egret, for river bird.

She remembered why her mother had named her after the egret. She remembered her mother saying that when she was born, her legs were kicking furiously, in short bursts of force, as if she was leaping in her dreams. Her legs had come already equipped with thick, wiry muscles, which were constantly in motion during her first weeks. The mother cat had known at that moment that her daughter would be a jumper – that she would leap high into the air, like a river bird in flight.

The she-cat almost smiled at this memory. After her birth, Keko had come next, and their mother had named him after the other wonder of the Amazon: the pink river dolphin. She remembered how her mother had said their names over and over to their closed ears, until her soft voice had penetrated their deafness and the words became imbedded in their minds, became part of who they were.

The she-cat had been born in a wooden box, with straw bedding and only one opening to the outside. The box was cramped, and outside of it was a cage. Swana and Keko were born at the Dark Place, within this birthing box. There were several other boxes in other cages around them, where other she-animals bred by Man nested and gave birth. They called this place the "birthing center". It was the Dark Place of cubs.

The floors were made of cold concrete stained by defecation and blood from previous births. Swana remembered being warm in the box when she nursed from her mother. She remembered feeling safe and secure. As she grew older, her mother would tell her stories about the wild world, for it was from the wild that their mother came. Back then, Swana's favorite stories were about the fireflies, Panthera's messengers that danced in the forest night.

"When I was young, I roamed through the jungle, free to hunt and survive on my own," she remembered her mother saying. "My mother taught me how to survive the way the true jaguar should: by hunting her meat and marking her territory; by fighting off intruders and believing in Panthera. And by listening to the fireflies."

"What are fireflies?" Swana asked, cocking her head to the side.

"They are little insects that glow like stars. They dance in the sky with the moon and brighten the darkness of the fading day. They are the embodiment of safety, my mother told me. The eyes of Panthera himself. He sees through their light and watches over us all," she paused, "Remember these words well, my cubs. When you see the fireflies dance in the forest, you will know that you are safe. For they are Panthera's messengers, the friendly forest guardians, who speak of safety in their light. And only in a truly safe place, a haven, will the fireflies dance for you. Only when you are free."

Swana smiled at this memory. This story had stayed with her forever, even as the memory of her mother faded away. She was very fond of these memories, for her mother had been wise. She missed her dearly.

"The fireflies don't dance here, do they?" Keko growled almost scornfully.

"No, they don't," the mother cat snarled, baring her fangs slightly in the darkness of the box. "And they never will. For here we will never be safe. Here we will never be free."

"I wish I could see a firefly," Swana sighed, padding over to her mother's paws. "They sound pretty. Dancing with the moon."

"They are very pretty, my dear," the mother growled softly, nuzzling her daughter. "They are the most beautiful sight in the Amazon."

Swana growled and lay down across her mother's outstretched forelegs, burying her face into the fur of her great chest. "Do you think I will see one when I'm older? Do you think I can be a true jaguar, like you?" Swana asked, looking up at her from the tops of her eyes.

The mother cat stared into her daughter's eyes. "I hope so, Swana," she whispered softly. "I really hope so."

Suddenly the she-cat frowned. This memory ... she knew the part that came next. She growled, for she remembered: those were the last words her mother ever said to her.

The next few moments happened in a blur. Swana remembered a high-pitched snarl, and seconds later she was exposed to light. The birthing box was lifted away, and Swana was blinded by bright, burning fluorescents. Her undeveloped eyes smarted as she reeled from the shock of such an intense glow.

Her sensitive eyes could barely adjust before she heard the loud pop. Her mother roared in anger as a dart went into her thigh. She leaped away from her cubs and snarled, but then her legs gave out and she slumped to the floor with a moan.

Swana could not comprehend what was going on. In a daze, she noticed two shadows moving closer to her, behind the metal bars, silhouetted by white light. Swana was too small, too sick to move away.

The mother cat saw the shadows and moaned in anger. Though she had been drugged and was losing consciousness, she could still see the shadows clearer than her cubs. She knew what they were. Her eyes burned with hate for them. Man.

Swana squalled dizzily as a hand wrapped around her middle. Dazed and confused, she mewed as she was lifted off the ground and brought between the bars of the cage. She found herself cradled in the vice-like arms of a she-human, her brother next to her. Their mother roared in fury, but she could do nothing. Her body was numb, her limbs paralyzed. She could only moan in despair as she surrendered to sleep.

Swana's eyes finally cleared as she watched her mother lose consciousness on the concrete, imprisoned behind the bars. The other shadow – the male human – was there, stooped beside her, pulling the dart from her skin. Swana saw the scar on the man's leg, the gash that she would remember forever. She whimpered as the she-human walked away. That was the last time Swana saw her mother.

The next time Swana opened her eyes, she found herself in a glass box, barely big enough to turn around in. There were other boxes with other animals in them around her, most of them infants. There were birds and monkeys, too – small creatures, all crying, all screeching, all loud.

Humans often came to look at them. They peered at the animals, tapped on the glass, touched them, held them – some even took animals home. There was never a moment of privacy. The humans were always looking at her with greedy eyes. Swana learned to hate them.

Swana spent a few weeks in that place, until she outgrew the box. That place, filled with animal screams, the cries of children missing their mothers, was only a prequel of what was to come. That box prepared her for the cruelty ahead, when Swana and Keko were transferred to the Dark Place, the place she remembered best. The place where animals were chosen for death.

Swana gasped, opening her eyes wide. She was daydreaming again, and the memories had come back to haunt her. She was still standing by the river, with the egret in front of her, its body growing cold. The she-cat trembled as she stood there in the shade, panting as if she hadn't breathed once while asleep. The past still haunted her. The pain that she had buried for years had shattered all the barriers she had made in her mind, and the crash of memories had left her broken and breathless. She breathed heavily as she stared down at the river bird before her, its body stiffening in the brightening light.

    The she-cat growled and shook her head, sitting down to stare at the kill she had made. She had no idea how long she'd been dreaming. It must've been at least twenty minutes. Already the egret was being picked at by ants. Little insect armies crawled through the white feathers like living dirt crumbs. The she-cat shook her head again in disgust.

    "I need to stop doing this," she said to herself. "Stop getting distracted at the wrong times." She stood up on shaky legs and gently wrapped her jaws around the bird's neck. She lifted it up and worried it, loosening the ants from the flesh and scattering feathers to the mud. Then the she-cat settled down on the sand to eat her kill.

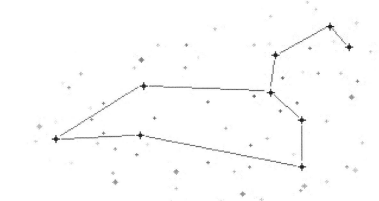

Chapter 5

Touch

In the shady hollow in the middle of the clearing, Fecir's eyes finally opened to greet the day.

At first he shut his eyes stubbornly, wanting to sleep again. He had been dreaming a strange dream earlier, but after a while that vision had faded into a hunting dream, one that Fecir would have liked to have finished. But the loud groan of a howler monkey had stirred him from his slumber, and he growled irritably as the primate moaned again somewhere in the canopy above. Fecir flattened his ears and rolled over, wanting to sleep in the shade forever, until he heard a different noise, one that made his ears perk up and his eyes open again.

The sound was unlike anything Fecir had ever heard; so different was it from the call of a monkey or bird that it silenced the forest for a moment or two, as the strange cry echoed throughout the whole jungle. Fecir rolled back over and lifted his head, listening intently for the sound again, as his triangular ears rotated like radar dishes, trying to locate the source of the noise. But the sound didn't come back, as the forest was once again swamped by bug chatter and bird calls.

Then, very suddenly, the sound came again, and the forest went dead as it echoed. It was like a loud scream, a trumpeting voice that pierced the air before dying down almost immediately as it began. This scream was soon followed by a low groan, almost a purring growl, and then silence.

Fecir's ears twitched. Curiosity surged through his veins and made every hair on his body stand on end. He had to investigate. Sniffing the air a couple times, he soon realized that his mother was not around. She wouldn't be back for a while. Fecir smiled mischievously and stepped out into the sunlight.

The humidity swamped him as soon as he was out of the shade, and he cringed in the blinding sunlight. Then, as his eyes adjusted to the light, the sound came again louder than ever. Whatever animal was making that sound, it was very close by. Fecir's sharp ears soon pinpointed its location, and, after checking to see if the coast was clear, he bounded off into the leaves, heading towards the meadow.

As he entered the jungle, Fecir's curiosity began to soar higher and higher. He had walked through the jungle before, but never had he done so alone. Now, as he moved through the leaves without a guardian, he felt completely alive and adventurous, as the wonders of the wild world came out of hiding to greet the curious cub.

He saw more birds and animals than he ever could imagine. A moriche oriole, a scarlet macaw, even a blue-crown motmot. He discovered sloths sleeping in the canopy and monkeys chattering above him. Even a marsh deer and her fawn – a rare sight in the forest, for marsh deer are as elusive as the jaguars that eat them. As Fecir marveled at all the wonders around, the noise came to him again, and he remembered his purpose in the jungle. He was getting closer to the sound. The loud, trumpeting bellow echoed throughout the forest, scaring birds into the sky and waking sloths from their slumber. Many animals scattered at the sound. Only Fecir moved toward the noise.

Fecir did not know why he didn't run away. The sound didn't seem to frighten him like it did the other animals. He felt drawn to the sound, as if there was a rope tied around his neck, pulling him towards the source of the noise. The voice, in some way, was calling to him, and he couldn't resist it. Fate made him pick up his paws and bound forward to meet the sound.

About halfway between the den and the meadow, Fecir finally halted his run. He could see light ahead of him, peeking out between the fronds of a giant fern, indicating that there was a clearing in front of him. From behind those leaves, the noise came, a mournful bellow of pain and fear, ending on a high note that made the trees tremble. Fecir crouched low in the shadows, suddenly cautious. The creature was there.

He could hear the animal breathing, deeply inhaling the moist air before blowing it forcefully back out. A low growl rumbled through the earth, vibrating beneath Fecir's paws. The creature was big. Fecir's fur stood on end, but he still was not afraid, even as the terrible scream came again through the trees. Deep in his mind, he once more felt that he was being called, and he couldn't help but feel that he needed to answer that call. This feeling was stronger than any emotion, hesitation or fear. Fecir stepped forward into the sunlight.

Slowly, Fecir nosed his head between the fern leaves. He blinked a few times, looking around the clearing, as the glare of the sun blinded him. He soon became aware of a giant shape silhouetted against the trees. As his eyes adjusted, he gasped at the sight.

An enormous creature stood in the middle of the clearing, its left side facing the tiny cub. Its body was round and supported by four long legs and flat paws. Its skin was like leather and its tail was like a short vine, with a few long strands of gray hair growing from the tip. Its neck was short, if it was there at all, for it was hidden by two giant, wing-like ears. Its head was at least half the size of its body, and protruding from the lower part of the animal's face were two curved tusks. But perhaps the most interesting and unusual part of this animal was its nose, which was so long it dragged on the ground and moved with a mind of its own, like a giant snake.

And on top of it all, the creature's skin was pure white.

As Fecir marveled at this strange creature, the white animal suddenly lifted its nose up and let loose that anguished scream that Fecir had heard earlier. The sound seemed to come from that long nose, and when the noise ended the animal dropped its nose and let it hang low to the ground. The animal moaned low in its throat – a strange, almost purring sound, as it shifted its weight and rocked back and forth on its strange legs.

Fecir's nose quivered as he smelled the animal. He realized that the creature had two scents. One smell was uniquely exotic, like strange grasses and wild plains, while the other was more sinister, like the harsh sharpness of metal and the stench of blood. Fecir realized that the more pleasant smell came from the white skin of the animal, while the metallic smell came from a red headdress, decorated with golden tassels hanging from the sewn edges of the fabric, attached to the beast's head via a harness. As Fecir watched, the animal touched the fabric with his nose repeatedly, flapping his head irritably. Fecir wondered where the headdress had come from and why it was strapped to the creature's face. He continued to stare curiously as the animal raised his head and bellowed.

The creature strained forward, and Fecir suddenly realized that the giant couldn't move. Its left hind foot was caught, tangled in a rope that had also tangled itself around a large tree at the edge of the clearing. The giant bellowed angrily, for he was unable to free his leg even with his skillful trunk. It was then that the creature noticed the little jaguar cub watching him, and looked straight at Fecir.

Fecir froze as their eyes met. The white giant's earth-brown eyes looked deep into the cub's yellow ones, and almost seemed to be searching for something, as his large pupils quivered ever so slightly. Neither of the two animals dared to breathe. Fecir was frozen, unable to even blink. The white giant continued to stare until suddenly, he tossed his head up. He had recognized something in Fecir's eyes. That very feeling of recognition seemed to calm the giant entirely.

Fecir finally gasped for breath. He felt as if he'd come out of a trance. He shook his head and looked at the giant, who had returned to rocking back and forth on his legs. He couldn't understand why he wasn't able to look away. As the white giant's eyes had searched his own and seen something in them, Fecir, too, had seen something in the white giant's eyes, something he still couldn't understand. He had seen those eyes before somewhere. That same feeling of recognition he'd felt in his dream the night before he felt now. He had recognized the giant's eyes, just like he'd recognized the owl's eyes.

The white giant moaned again, bobbing his head up and down and waving his nose in the air. As he did this, he watched Fecir out of one eye. Fecir realized that the giant was trying to get his attention. Throwing caution to the wind, he stepped out into the sunlight, toward the strange, unearthly animal.

The giant stopped moving when Fecir came near. Now the giant turned his head toward him and raised his trunk to his forehead. Fecir saw the twin tusks and his fur bristled, yet did not step back. Somehow, he knew that the creature would not hurt him.

Fecir boldly stepped forward again as the creature shifted his weight and let out a purring grumble from deep in his throat. Fecir found this noise to be almost soothing, and he was not afraid. Fecir was almost close enough for the white giant to reach out and touch him with his trunk when the creature suddenly strained forward and gave a violent tug against the rope. The tangled cord tightened around his ankle and the giant bellowed in frustration. Fecir took a step back and snarled.

"Stop struggling!" he growled to the beast. "You're making it worse."

To his surprise, the giant immediately went still, as if he had understood Fecir's words. He calmed down and watched Fecir out of the corner of its eyes. The young cub huffed.

"That's better," he said. "See? If you struggle, it just gets more tangled. Stop moving so much and it won't be so tight."

The creature nodded its head gravely and flapped its ears, rocking back and forth.

Fecir suddenly felt weird. He was talking to a giant white behemoth whom he knew absolutely nothing about. And what's more, the animal could understand him. Fecir's fur bristled all over. What was he doing? He thought about leaving, but then his eyes once again saw the tangled rope. He knew that the animal could not escape alone. He needed help. And Fecir was the only one around. He couldn't just abandon the creature. He stepped forward, and the white giant watched him.

"Hey," he said. "I'm going to help you out, alright? You need help, and I'm here. I'm going to cut the rope. But I'll only do it if I know that you won't hurt me once you're free." He eyed the giant's tusks. "So I'll make a deal with you, strange animal. If you promise not to hurt me, I'll bite through the rope. Deal?" He felt funny using his mother's bargaining tactic.

The giant, with its remarkable ability to understand Fecir's language, nodded its head in agreement. Without another word, Fecir leaped toward the giant's leg. He sunk his teeth into the thick, tough rope and gnawed. He became completely absorbed in his task, and thus he did not see the white giant turn his head toward him. He did not see the strange glint in the giant's eye. He did not notice the white giant reach his trunk out to him.

Fecir felt a light tap on his shoulder, and suddenly the world around him flashed brilliant white. His vision turned dark and his spine tightened and tensed, arching his back and curling his neck. He let go of the rope as his muscles contracted and seized. His eyes rolled to the back of his head, and time itself seemed to freeze around him, as strange images suddenly entered his mind.

The first image was of a darkened sky. No moon shone through the dark, and so the only light came from the stars littered across the night. A band of glowing dust streaked across the heavens, creating a dividing line between the completely dark and the growing light of dawn. Most of the stars were fading, but Fecir's mind was drawn to a small group of nine stars, glowing brighter than all the rest. These stars were organized to form the shape of a large animal. Fecir recognized Panthera, the white jaguar god, as he crouched to drink from the black water sky.

This image flashed away almost as instantly as it came. The next vision began immediately after, and Fecir found himself looking down on rolling seas of parched, yellow grass. The sunlight shining down was relentlessly hot, and Fecir could almost feel its heat, as animals suddenly entered his mind's eye. These creatures that lumbered through the tall grass very closely resembled the white giant. Their noses were long and their ears were large, but their skin was gray and not white. They did not wear headdresses as the white giant did, and they traveled in large groups, with members of all different ages. They trumpeted and bellowed to each other as they moved through the dry land, munching on the dying grass and trying to absorb what little nutrition could be found within the stalks. The animals kept moving, in hopes of finding food.

That image flashed away, and the next image came for only a split second. But it shocked Fecir completely. The animals that he had just seen moving together as a herd, now all lay dead among the shriveled grass, their bodies decaying beneath an angry sun, their exposed bones bleached white in the heat. A cold wind suddenly blew, sweeping away the grave image, and replacing it with a new one.

Now Fecir looked upon a wall of ice, as it encroached on the land of the gray giants. This massive glacier moved slowly, at the speed of a lava flow, yet no creature could move out of its path, for the wall encircled the globe. Eventually the glacier spread over the whole earth, encasing the planet in ice and snow that would not melt for thousands of years.

The Endless Winter, Fecir thought as the vision faded away, replaced by the images of animals living amongst the frigid snows. These animals Fecir could vaguely recognize, yet he had no name for them. A black-and-white parrot that flew underwater and laid her egg on the feet of her partner; a giant marsh deer with proud, broad antlers and a dangling beard; a strange mammal with almost catlike features, that sang a mournful song to a lonesome moon.

And one more creature, Fecir saw, as she ran through the powdery snow. A beautiful orange cat whose coat was adorned by ribbons of black. She halted her run and lifted her head, roaring with a voice like thunder. Fecir recognized this creature. A Siberian tigress.

A blast suddenly echoed through the air, and the tigress's roar was cut off. She fell to the snow and disappeared in a flash of white. Now Fecir was blind. His vision had gone dark, until suddenly two eyes opened in the darkness. The eyes were large and glowed yellow like the sun, with pupils forever fixated on one spot. Those glowing eyes illuminated the face upon which they sat – the face of the white owl. The owl opened its beak, but the image vanished before it had a chance to make a sound.

Now Fecir saw the tigress again, only this time she was no longer living. She lay on her side in a field of snow that stretched out to every horizon. Yellow flowers were growing out of her orange pelt, growing from her body. This image shocked Fecir, and the vision quickly disappeared, leaving him blind once more.

Darkness extended to oblivion all around him. Suddenly there was a metallic clang, and the darkness diminished, revealing the bars of a metal cage.

The visions suddenly released Fecir, and he came to, opening his eyes wide and gasping violently for breath. He nearly collapsed as his spine and muscles let go of all their tension. He coughed and choked down air, as if he hadn't breathed in years. As he struggled to comprehend what had just happened to him, he heard a low rumble and felt something brush his fur. Instantly he leaped away, as the startled white giant retracted its nose and curled it under its jaw.

Fecir hissed and glared at the white giant. It had done something to him, done something with that nose of his. The visions must've been triggered by his touch. Fecir became furious. The white giant had broken the deal.

Without saying a word, Fecir turned and ran off into the trees. The white giant roared after him, calling desperately for him to come back. Fecir kept running. He ran until the white giant's calls were lost to the rainforest music, and by then Fecir had returned to the den. He ran inside the hollow and curled up in a protective little ball. Shaking and shivering, yet feeling safe in his hollow, he eventually calmed down enough to sleep once more.

Chapter 6

Dreams

Dark clouds were gathering in the sky.

In the Amazon, thunderstorms and rain showers were a fact of life, happening almost all year round. Because of the jungle's position on the Earth's equator, and its tropical climate, storms were seen almost every day. Rarely were there breaks in the ceaseless bombardment of rain, and these storms could pop up without warning, as one was doing now.

Swana was nearly halfway to her den when she heard the first light patter of rain on the canopy leaves above, and the murmur of distant thunder reached her ears. Birds flitted all around her, looking for a place to stay dry, while bugs scurried back into their burrows. A troop of capuchins in the trees above jumped hurriedly from branch to branch, chattering nervously.

Swana looked up at the leaves. Through small breaks she could see the filtered gray light, the overcast clouds that were just a precursor of what was to come. She sensed deep in her gut that the storm coming was a bad one, and she too began to search for shelter, moving quickly beneath the troops of monkeys and hunkered-down birds. She knew in her mind that she needed to get back to Fecir soon, before the storm hit. Her pace quickened into a steady trot.

All afternoon, her mind had been swirling with thoughts of her past, but after eating the egret and resting for a bit by the river, she had come to terms with her thoughts, and had once again forced them down into the deepest recesses of her mind. She now thought of one thing only: her tiny cub, left alone in the den as the storm moved steadily closer.

The rain became more forceful. Soon the she-cat's fur was drenched, and as a cold wind blew, rustling the damp leaves, she shivered and shook her fur, spattering the foliage around her with wet. Her paws sunk into the muddy earth, and when she lifted them away, the ground sucked at them, as if trying to keep her from leaving. And the storm was coming ever closer. The murmur of thunder had grown into a low rumble. The she-cat began to run, fighting through the mud, trying to make it back to the den before the brunt of the storm hit.

Eventually she made it back to the clearing. The rain was coming down full force now, and the she-cat shook herself vigorously before crouching into her den. Once inside, she was safe and dry, and Swana immediately saw the tiny cub curled up in the corner of the hollow, just where she'd left him. His scruffy side was rising up and down gently with his breathing, and, with a gentle smile, the she-cat crept over to him. Lying down on her side, she curled up around her cub, sighed and closed her eyes. As the storm moved in, mother and child slept in each other's comforting warmth.

Fecir opened his eyes in a peculiar place.

He was in the meadow. But it was a different meadow than he remembered. Everything around him was dark. There was no jungle surrounding this meadow, just shadows, black nothingness that extended on forever. But that wasn't what caught Fecir's attention. The meadow that he had played in just days before was green. This meadow was white.

The grass was silvery color, reflective and shining like stainless steel. The stalks waved and danced, moved by some intangible breeze, one that carried no scent. The flowers in this meadow were a brilliant titanium white hue, the petals so ashen that they glowed with their own light. Fecir stood up and looked around at this white meadow, until he suddenly noticed that there were stars above him, twinkling in the night.

Fecir opened his jaws in awe. He had never seen so many stars. There were thousands of them, more stars than there were leaves in the jungle. So many that they formed a band of stardust that divided the sky in half. Fecir's eyes widened as he tried to see it all, and his open mouth curled into a smile.

Immediately he began to pick out the constellations that he knew. Cancer the crab, Corvus the crow, Hydra the serpent, the Gemini twins, and Panthera, the Lord of all cats. His eyes sparkled with admiration when he spotted the constellation. He imagined, looking upon those nine stars, that the great white jaguar was there in the sky, looking down on him. But as he stared at the constellation, his eyes widened in amazement. The cat suddenly appeared, crouching down on his front paws, his rear end standing in the air, his tongue lapping methodically at the darkness. His white coat glistened like the flowers in the meadow, and his rosettes, the color of warm cinnamon, rippled over his muscular body. Fecir's breath caught in his throat. Panthera was here.

The white jaguar's tongue abruptly stopped lapping, and he opened his eyes. The color was startling. They were the brightest green, like the color of new fern leaves, the stalks of newborn grass. They glowed intensely and looked directly down at the tiny jaguar cub in the white meadow.

Fecir froze. It was almost as if he were caught in a trance. He could not look away from those eyes. His ears flattened and his body went rigid, yet the white jaguar's eyes were not angry. Rather, they were calm, knowing, and oddly familiar. Fecir felt that same strange feeling that he perceived when he looked into the white giant's and the white owl's eyes. Somehow, he had seen those eyes before.

A thought passed through Fecir's mind. Why were these animals so familiar? Where had he seen them before? How were they all connected? Fecir couldn't stop staring at those green eyes.

The jaguar cub and the Star Lord held their gaze for a long time. Then, without warning, the white jaguar let out a roar that shook the white meadow. His deep, guttural voice rang out like thunder in the forest, shaking the stars and blowing away the flowers. Fecir covered his head with his paws. He squeezed his eyes shut, as the sky and the white meadow collapsed into empty, silent darkness.

Fecir awakened with a sharp gasp, as a clap of thunder vibrated through the hollow and shook the ground beneath his paws. Outside, lightning flashed violently, illuminating the forest with erratic bursts of light. The clouds rolled overhead, the thunder roaring furiously, a symbol clash following the steady drum beat of the pounding rain. Fecir shivered in the hollow, looking out at the den entrance. Another flash made him blink, but the following boom of thunder made him jump. The world went dark again, and Fecir trembled with his ears flat against his head, his eyes wide with fear.

"Mother," he whimpered. "Where are you, mother?"

"Here," came a calm voice above him. "I'm right here."

Fecir's eyes began to adjust, and he looked up to see the she-cat sitting upright above him. Growling tenderly, she lowered her nose to him and licked his face. Mewling, Fecir crawled beneath her stomach curled up into a tight little ball. Another rumble of thunder rolled overhead, and Fecir yelped, burying his face into his mother's warm fur.

The she-cat sighed. Fecir had always been terrified of thunder. Whenever a storm rolled through, Fecir would try to hide from the noise. He shivered uncontrollably beneath her, every hair on his back and shoulders standing straight up. She growled softly, in a soothing tone, trying to calm him as the lightning flashed outside.

"There, there," she said gently. "The thunder can't hurt you. You don't have to be afraid."

Fecir buried his face deeper into her fur.

The storm raged overhead, but eventually moved away to the east. The thunder began to fade, and the lightning struck less and less frequently. The rain softened to a light patter, and the fireflies came out to resume their nightly dance. Now Fecir finally relaxed. He stopped shivering and came out of hiding. He remained beneath his mother's body, but poked his head between her paws, looking out at the soaked Amazon jungle beyond the hollow. Both cats were silent for a long time.

"Mother?" Fecir suddenly asked. "Why do we dream?"

"Why do we dream?" the she-cat repeated. "I have no idea. I guess to keep our minds busy while we sleep."

"Do dreams ever mean anything?"

"Not that I know of," the she-cat growled.

"What are dreams, anyways?"

The she-cat growled almost irritably, searching for an answer. This topic was not something she was comfortable to discuss. "Dreams are just memories, Fecir," she said with a sigh. "Just random thoughts and memories all jumbled together to create an irrational plot. They don't mean anything. They just entertain our minds while we sleep. Just a replay of things you've seen before. Just ... memories." Swana's eyes darkened as she thought of her nightmares from earlier that day. A low, inaudible growl vibrated in her throat as she thought again of the Dark Place and its horrors.

Fecir did not see his mother's mood change. His mind was preoccupied with confusion. He flattened his ears and looked down at the ground. *Dreams are memories? How can that be?* he thought. *I've never seen the white meadow. I've never met a white cat. And I've certainly never been a tiger before! How can my dreams be my memories if those memories are not my own?* Fecir was silent for a while as he contemplated this in his mind. Then, suddenly, he thought of something else.

"Mother, what do you dream about?" he asked, looking up at her with a smile.

The question brought the she-cat out of her trance, and she looked down at Fecir questioningly. She turned away. "I'd rather not share," she said quietly.

Fecir frowned. He looked down at the ground, embarrassed. After a moment of hesitation, he asked in a small voice, "Are they bad dreams?"

The she-cat sighed. "Yes."

"Talking about them will make you feel better," Fecir said hopefully.

"No," Swana snapped. Then, in a softer voice, she said, "I don't want to talk about my dreams, Fecir. I just don't." *Spare you the horror that I go through every night,* she added silently.

Swana had never told Fecir about her past. She had never spoken a word about Man or the Dark Place. She had done this to protect him, so that he may grow up without fear of Man, without knowledge of him. She had sworn to never tell him anything, for his own good.

"Oh," Fecir said, a little disappointed. Both were silent again as they listened to the rain falling steadily and the frogs chirping in melody. Soon the she-cat yawned and laid down on her side, and Fecir curled up next to her. As he laid his head down to sleep, his eyes suddenly opened wide and ears perked up.

"Mother?"

"Hrrrmmm?" the she-cat groaned irritably. She had already closed her eyes.

"Have you ever seen a white animal? I don't mean like an animal that is supposed to be white, but an animal that should be a different color? Like a white tapir or a white snake?"

The she-cat grunted and moved her head. "Go to sleep, Fecir," she growled.

"Ok, ok," Fecir said, closing his eyes again. "Goodnight, mother."

"Goodnight, Fecir," Swana sighed. Not a moment later, she heard little snores next to her, and she knew that Fecir was fast asleep.

But somehow, Swana couldn't fall asleep. She opened her eyes, suddenly restless. Fecir's last question had completely unnerved her. A white animal? Where did Fecir get that idea?

She brushed the thought aside. He was a cub with a huge imagination. She had been like that herself once. He probably just made it up. Swana closed her eyes again. But just as she was drifting off into sleep, she remembered something: a part of the legend about the Pantheraseer. A part that said Panthera could come as any animal, so long as his skin was white.

Swana drifted off to sleep before she could remember anything else. Soon she was snoring as dreams filled her head. The she-cat and her cub slept within their dry, safe hollow, as the fireflies, the forest guardians, danced the night away in the dark forest outside.

Just a mile away, at the edge of the meadow, a tapir and her child wandered through the damp, rain-soaked brush, foraging for food. The tiny calf, sporting her white stripes proudly, stayed close to her mother's side as they moved through the dark. The adult waddled along, her long, dangling nose snuffling the ground, smelling out berries and fruit that the wind might've knocked out of the trees. But suddenly, she stopped, and her body went rigid. Her ears rotated forward, and she listened, her eyes growing wide. With an excited squeal, she quickly ushered her calf into the shadows, just as a monster came crashing through the brush.

This monster was unlike anything the jungle had ever seen. Its eyes cast beams of bright light, light brighter than the moon and stars. Its body was shiny, wet with rain, with smooth, solid skin. It breathed a horrible, gaseous breath that choked the clean, misty air, and its voice rumbled and gurgled like a dying howler monkey. Its circular paws moved by rotating, and for a fleeting moment the tapir mother thought that the monster would plow right into her, as she stared wide-eyed into its eyes. But then, abruptly, the monster halted atop the flattened foliage. Its voice stopped, and its gaseous breath ceased, yet its eyes remained open and glowed fiercely. The tapirs sank deeper into the forest, yet watched wearily this strange, intruding creature.

The creature gave birth. Two animals came out of its stomach, animals unlike any creature ever seen. These aliens walked upright on two legs as they moved around the shiny creature. They went to the monster's rear and removed from it a strange object. The aliens carried it into the light of their mother's eyes, and the beam reflected on the object's shiny, patterned surface. It was made of the same material as the monster's skin.

The aliens spoke to one another, in loud, raucous voices. The tapir could hear them, but could not understand them. They talked as they worked with the strange shiny object, unfolding it under the guiding light of the monster's eyes.

"How can you be sure that there are actually jaguars around here?" one of the aliens asked. He squatted down next the other alien, who was sitting on the wet ground and tampering with the shiny object.

"Oh, they're out here. Believe me," the other alien growled, "I know they're here."

"But how? How can you be sure?"

"I feel it in my gut. They're here. And there is evidence, too. Remember those bones and feathers by the stream? Jaguar killed a bird there. Fresh, too. They're here. They might even be watching us." The alien chuckled as he unfolding the shiny object into a bigger one.

The other alien looked about nervously. "Won't they attack us?"

"Naw, they won't. Don't you worry, boy. Help me set this thing up."

The younger alien stood up and started walking toward the edge of the forest. In the shadows, the frightened tapirs cringed away, their eyes wide with fear. The younger alien then called to the older one, "Hey, did you hear about the circus elephant that escaped last week?"

"Yeah, I heard," the older one grunted, standing up suddenly. He stooped over the shiny object and picked it up. "They probably caught it by now. Poor thing would stick out like a sore thumb around here."

"Yeah," the younger said. "This seems like a good spot."

"Alright. Let's set her up and get out of here," the older growled. He set the shiny object down where the younger alien had directed him, and tampered with it some more. Finally he stood up. "We're done here."

"*Bueno*," the younger said. "Let's go home."

The two aliens climbed back into the monster's stomach, and the angry creature roared back to life. The tapir could hold her fear no longer. With a sharp cry, she leaped away, leading her calf into the deeper jungle.

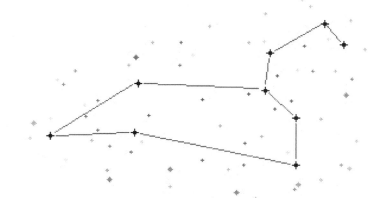

Chapter 7

The Past

A lone harpy eagle circling overhead announced the arrival of the morning, as warm yellow light spilled onto the canopy and peeked through the forest layers, dappled the leaves with dawn. The eagle's feathers, bristling in the high altitude air, captured the warmth in their tips, as the proud bird bathed in the golden light. With another loud screech, he wheeled away, as the forest, hearing his call, began to wake beneath him.

  In the hollow, Fecir's eyes cracked open. He twitched his whiskers, then his ears, and lifted a paw to rub his cheek. With a groan and another flick of his ears, he lifted his head and yawned, opening his maw wide enough to reveal his tiny teeth. He stood up and stretched his front legs, arching his back and yawning again.

Then he shook his pelt and looked over at his mother on the other side of the den.

She was sleeping. She lay on her side with her cheek resting on her forearm. Loud snores emanated from her mouth and nose. Her paws twitched slightly, the claws grasping at some invisible object. Her eyes drooped half open, and her pupils, rolled up into the back of her skull, jerked rapidly beneath her eyelids. Her whiskers twitched and trembled, as if she were snarling in her sleep. Fecir watched her curiously.

Is she dreaming? Fecir wondered, leaning in to sniff her jerking lips. *What is she dreaming about?* Tentatively, he reached out a tiny paw and touched her nose. His mother did not respond. Her face went on shuddering, and if anything her snores grew louder.

Fecir snorted. *Whatever she's dreaming about*, he thought, *it must be interesting.* He thought back to their conversation last night. Was she dreaming about a memory right now? Could it be a hunting memory? A cub-hood memory? *Either way,* Fecir concluded, *she won't be waking up anytime soon.*

His eyes suddenly lit up, and his lips curled into an impish grin. *Which means I have plenty of time to go looking for the white giant!* Fecir licked his lips at the thought.

Creeping around his mother, Fecir made his way to the circle of light that was the opening to the hollow. With one last glance back, he cautiously stepped outside. His body disappeared into the light.

Once outside, he yelped with glee of having eluded his mother. With an excited leap, he quickly bounded off into the jungle, heading towards the meadow. He didn't notice how strangely quiet the forest seemed, as he boisterously crashed through the brush, laughing as he went. The only creature that saw him leave was the harpy eagle, circling above the hollow, feeling the warmth of the sun on his feathers.

In the hollow, Swana continued on sleeping, twitching as dreams danced in her head. She whimpered suddenly, as if she had been injured, then snarled viciously, but did not open her eyes. For in her dreams her eyes were open, yet she could see nothing. The Dark Place was haunting her sleep again.

She couldn't remember much. This nightmare came to her broken in pieces. The light was dim and flickering. Her vision was blurred. The screams were warped, distorted. She couldn't understand them. She couldn't think straight. A broken image came before her. A fuzzy red dot on her thigh. Her vision cleared for a moment, and she saw what it was: a dart. Without thinking, she clawed it out of her skin. Liquid spurted from the tip. Her vision went dark.

When her eyes opened, a new image was in front of her. The top corner of her cage. A piece of metal connecting the door to the other wall, holding it in place. Something was wrong with it. She frowned, but couldn't comprehend it. The bolt wasn't in the right place. The door was unbolted.

She went under again. She felt like she was drowning, like she was swimming through thick mud. She couldn't see, couldn't hear, could barely move. Her limbs were numb, dragging behind her like weights. When the mud next cleared, she was in front of the cage door, and the door was wide open. The animals were screaming at her, clawing at her. She slumped to the ground. Her face hit the concrete. She dove back into the mud.

The mud gave way to clear water. She opened her eyes. Her vision wasn't blurry. Her limbs weren't as numb. She could hear better, move better. She stood up and staggered, off-balance. Her head hurt, her stomach heaved. She felt dizzy. A smell hit her nose. A burning, metallic scent. She snarled.

She looked up and saw him. The man. He was younger than the others, skinnier, shorter. A boy. He held a nylon rope. No rifle. He was harmless to her, weak and helpless. A bird with a broken wing. Food. Prey.

She wasn't thinking. Her head hurt. Her vision went red. The boy screamed, dropped the rope, turned to run. Swana was on top of him the next moment. Her claws went into his back. With a roar, she brought him down. He kicked, tried to fight, screamed for help. But Swana was the hunter, and he was the prey. Her teeth went into his throat.

It all happened too fast. Swana's vision went dark. She was aware of nothing. When next she opened her eyes, she wasn't sure of what had happened. Her head hurt, her ears rang. Her vision was completely clear. She was no longer drowning. She could feel her limbs. She was standing in something wet and warm. She looked down. Blood.

She saw the boy, leaped away from him. Her breath came in ragged gasps. What had she done? What had happened? She had killed him. She flattened her ears. She'd killed a man.

"They're coming! They're coming! Get out, now!"

With a roar, she leaped away. She ran through the rows of cages, the animals screaming at her as she went, clawing at her, but Swana dodged their claws. She rounded the corner and disappeared from the Dark Place forever.

When Swana woke up, she could still hear the screams. They still rang in her ears, as she sat up with a gasp. She lay for a long time, panting, unable to speak. Finally, after a few moments, she regained her breath. But the screams still echoed around her. Most of the voices had faded. All but one continued to cry for help.

Suddenly Swana realized that the scream was not a remnant of her nightmare. It was real, calling from the forest. At that exact same moment, Swana noticed that Fecir was nowhere to be seen. Instantly she was on her feet. "Fecir?!"

Fecir frolicked through the forest, laughing gleefully as he burst through the brush. He splashed through mud puddles and leaped over rivers of ants. He couldn't hear the white giant's calls, but he remembered where he was. He ran toward that clearing in the woods.

He eventually slowed to a trot as he neared the place where he last saw the giant. The ferns surrounding the clearing loomed up over him, the sunlight peeking through their leaves and dappling Fecir with warmth. He stopped just before entering. The giant's scent had been washed away by the rain. He could no longer smell its presence. Still, he hesitated. If the giant was there, it might do something strange to him again, scare him like last time. He waited cautiously for a moment, but eventually summoned his courage. Boldly, he stepped into the light.

The clearing was empty. The white giant was nowhere to be seen. There was an impression in the ground from where it had once stood and a few water-filled footprints, but the creature itself had vanished without leaving a scent. Fecir began to investigate, sniffing the footprints and puddles. He noticed the rope still tied to the tree and trotted forth to sniff it. The rope had apparently ripped in half, its end frayed and the length pulled taut around the tree. The giant had snapped the rope and escaped.

For a moment, Fecir felt a little disappointed. He had hoped the creature would still be there, and that perhaps if his mother could see it, she might be able to tell him about white animals. But that feeling soon vanished. He was deeply glad that the creature had escaped. Perhaps it was still around, maybe grazing at the meadow, if the thing even ate grass. Fecir's excitement renewed, he bounded out of the clearing and into the jungle, moving towards the meadow.

A little ways into darkness, Fecir's nose discovered an interesting scent. At first he thought it was the white giant, and his heart skipped with joy. The smell had that same metallic twinge to it that the giant's headdress had. decided to follow it, as it led him to the meadow

Near the edge of the meadow, Fecir found tapir scat, but he dismissed it. He was on the trail of something much more intriguing. Light began to filter in through the trees as he approached the end of the jungle, where brush and canopy met grass and open sky. Rounding a tree, he soon saw openness ahead of him. And there, on the edge of grass, the source of the strange smell – a metal object.

The object was rectangular in shape, with a transparent body that seemed to be made out of thin silver vines strung together in a mesh. There was only one opening to the outside, and the interior was hollow, almost like a den. Fecir stayed in the shadows for a while, staring at the metal den cautiously. He wondered where it could've come from. Could the white giant have left it there? He warily stepped toward the object to find out.

He circled the metal den, sniffing the air. The den had a wide variety of smells, most of them dwarfed by the bombarding metallic scent. Fecir could recognize none of them. He couldn't smell the white giant on it, either. Whatever the thing was, it wasn't from the jungle. It was completely alien.

Fecir moved closer and closer to the den, wondering what could live in it. His cub curiosity, the inquisitiveness hardwired into the brains of all growing children, was getting the best of him, as he sniffed the entrance. He stepped inside it, moving cautiously. As he moved deeper into the den, he saw a panel that was raised above the ground. Fecir sniffed it briefly, then stepped on it.

The panel went flat against the ground. At the same moment, Fecir heard a loud clang behind him. Whirling around with a snarl, he saw that the opening had been closed up by a wall of silver vines. The den had swallowed Fecir. He was trapped.

With a cry, he lunged himself at the wall, clawing at it, screaming as loud as he could. Birds resting among the grass in the meadow were startled into the air by the noise. Monkey troops lifted their heads and hooted at the sound. A mile away, a frantic mother heard the screams and came running.

Swana could hear the crying from anywhere in the world. The voice belonged to her baby, and her maternal instincts instantly kicked in. She charged through the brush, following the screams. All she could think of was that Fecir could be in trouble. With a terrified roar, she crashed through ferns and swerved around trees, running full stride. All the time, she shouted back to the voice, "Fecir! I'm coming! Hang on!"

Splashing through giant puddles and leaping over leaf rot, Swana's mind was filled with all sorts of thoughts. Is he hurt? Was he attacked? Is there another jaguar around? Did a marsh deer kick him? Did a snake bite him? Her eyes were white with fear.

Moments later, a smell hit her nose, and she almost skidded to a full stop. That smell. That sharp, metallic scent. She knew that smell. She knew it all too well. Her mind nearly froze with disbelief. Not a moment later, her eyes darkened with rage, and she quickened her pace. *If you dare hurt my cub,* she threatened in her mind. *If you dare to lay a hand on him, I'll kill you, just like I killed the other one. I won't let you hurt my child!*

With a terrible roar, she burst through the brush and into sunlight.

Fecir clawed and bit at the vines hysterically, trying to break them, but the thin wires were stronger than they appeared. He cried and wailed, ramming the walls with his shoulders and head, but they wouldn't budge. He howled for his mother, and relief surged through him when he heard her voice in the forest.

"Fecir!"

"Mother!" he shouted back.

"I'm coming, Fecir!"

Suddenly she came crashing through the ferns. Sunlight splashed onto her pelt as she ran immediately up to him and sniffed at him through the wires. Fecir mewed and pawed at her, and Swana growled in relief when she saw that he was unharmed.

"Mother, I can't get out," Fecir whimpered. He rose up on his hind legs and tried to touch his nose to his mother's. "I'm stuck."

"I'll get you out," Swana said gruffly, sniffing at the contraption. She recognized the thing immediately. It was a metal trap designed to catch live prey. She had seen them before while running from the Dark Place. She sniffed at the wires, snarling in anger when she smelled their scent. She couldn't believe that they had followed her this far. She let loose a roar of rage that made Fecir flatten his ears and shudder.

"Mother?" he asked timidly.

"Quiet, Fecir," she snapped as she circled the trap, looking for a way to open it as a torrent of thoughts swirled in her head. How did they manage to find her? How did they track her in the rain? Why, after a year, did they come back?

Swana put her front paws on the trap and began to rock it back and forth. Growling, she leaned her whole weight on it, trying to crush it, but the wires held. She batted at it, clawed it, sat on it, even knocked it completely sideways, but still couldn't get the thing to open. Eventually Fecir spoke again.

"Mother?"

"What?" Swana panted, the fury still fresh in her eyes.

"What is this thing?"

Swana took a deep breath. "It's a hunting trap. It's used to catch live animals."

"Why? What animal catches other animals alive?" Fecir asked.

Swana growled. "Only Man makes these traps," she said with a curl of her lip. "Only Man catches live animals from the forest."

Fecir was silent for a moment. "Man?"

Swana paused. She didn't want to tell him about Man. She had wanted to protect him. But she didn't have a choice now. She shook her head and growled, pacing around the trap angrily.

"Man is the world's most dangerous predator, Fecir. He is the cruelest, most merciless hunter out there. He hunts for the pleasure of hunting. He kills for the pleasure of killing. He is the world's most powerful creature, an animal that all others must fear."

"What does Man look like?" he asked, as his mother stalked dizzy circles around him.

"Man is like a hairless monkey. He walks upright on two legs without a tail to balance him. He has no fur and so covers himself with the skins of other creatures. His face is flat and his eyesight is poor. He can't smell or hear the things we can. His teeth draw no blood and he lacks claws."

"But that doesn't sound dangerous at all!"

"I know. He doesn't seem dangerous. But he is," Swana said slowly. "What makes Man dangerous is his mind. He can imagine things, do things with his mind that we would never understand. He can use his mind to build things, things like weapons. Long black rods called rifles that kill with a sound like thunder. He doesn't need teeth or claws. He has weapons that can kill an animal in the blink of an eye."

Fecir heard this and flattened his ears. An otherwise harmless animal can make something so powerful? What were these creatures? "Mother, how do you know so much about Man?"

Swana froze. Her muscles stiffened and she closed her eyes. Images of the Dark Place poured into her thoughts and she shuddered as she heard the screams all around her. She snarled and opened her eyes again. "I won't let them hurt you, Fecir. I promise. I'm going to get you out of that thing. I won't let Man hurt you."

Over the next several hours, Swana made many more attempts to break her cub free. By noon, the only progress she had made was a small dent in the trap's ceiling. The afternoon passed, and soon darkness began to fall as the sun disappeared behind the western horizon. As the crickets and frogs commenced their nightly musical, an exhausted Swana came over to lay down beside the cage. Fecir curled up next to her, getting as close at the cage would allow him. They sat in silence for a long time.

"Fecir," Swana eventually said, in a sad voice, "I'm sorry. I can't break the trap. I'm so sorry." Her body shook, silently sobbing.

Fecir was quiet for a moment. "What will happen now?" he whispered softly.

Swana sniffed and shook her head. "Man will come," she said at last. "He will come for us."

"What will he do?"

"I don't know. Most likely he will kill us." She paused. "That, or he'll take us to the Dark Place."

"What's the Dark Place?"

"The Dark Place," Swana growled suddenly, in a voice full of hatred. "It's a place ruled by Man. It is what they call a canned hunting farm, where Man keeps and raises animals to die at the hands of amateur hunters, all for our heads or our pelts to be taken as trophies." She curled her lip in disgust.

Fecir flattened his ears, but then he looked up at his mother curiously. He hesitated before asking, "Have you ever been there before?"

Swana sighed and closed her eyes, before turning her head to look at Fecir, looked into his innocent eyes. It was too late to keep secrets from him now. Man was already upon them. He had to know.

"Yes, Fecir," she sighed, turning away again. "Yes, I've been there before. I've been to the Dark Place." She paused. "Remember last night, when you asked me about my dreams? Well, I'm ready to tell you about them now."

Fecir listened quietly.

"My dreams are of a past I would rather forget," Swana began in a shaky voice. "I wasn't born in the jungle. I was born in the Dark Place. I came into life in a tiny wooden box within a metal cage, with a brother beside me. When I was just a few weeks old, Man took my mother away from me, and I never saw her again. My brother and I were separated and put in the Dark Place.

"When I was just over a year old, Man took my brother away from me, too. He was 'chosen' to die. They drugged him and dragged him out of the Dark Place, and a little while later, they killed him with rifles. That memory still haunts my dreams every night."

Fecir watched his mother in awe. He had never known, would've never known, that his mother carried so much pain on her shoulders. She had always been strong around him, stubbornly impervious to emotion. Seeing her like this, seeing her vulnerable, made Fecir feel afraid.

"That place was horrible, Fecir," Swana continued, closing her eyes. "I lived in the dark for two years. I never saw sunlight. I never knew grass or trees. All I knew were screams. The other animals screamed all the time. Screamed to be let free, to be liberated. Some wailed to be killed so they wouldn't have to live there anymore. We waited in the dark for the day when we, too, would be chosen for death, for that was the one sure thing in our future." She paused and shook her head, trying to swallow the lump in her throat.

Fecir broke his silence. "How did you survive?"

Swana closed her eyes, remembering. "I escaped," she said. "One night I was chosen and drugged. But the Man who drugged me left the cage door unbolted. I was able to open the door and run away, and...." She paused again, before snarling, "And in the process of escaping, I killed that Man."

Fecir's eyes grew wide.

"For several weeks after my escape, I was hunted," Swana continued. "I managed to elude the hunters, and for months afterward I traveled as far as I could away from the Dark Place. I ran to a place where no one would find me. And I found this place, and I knew I would be safe here." Swana sighed. "Or I *thought* I would be safe, at least."

Fecir suddenly became terrified of what was to come. He edged closer to his mother and pressed against her, wishing that he could crawl underneath her like he did during a storm. He shivered and asked in a small voice, "Are we going to the Dark Place?"

Swana hesitated. "I won't let them take you away, Fecir," she snarled. "I won't let you go there. I will fight them. I will fight them to the death, if I have to. I won't let them hurt you." She licked Fecir through the bars.

Fecir eventually fell asleep within the cage, pressed close to Swana's side. Swana growled softly as she looked out upon the shadowy forest, her watchful eyes guarding her child from the darkness. As she scanned the brush, she whispered in a silent, determined voice, "I'll never go back there. I'll never go back."

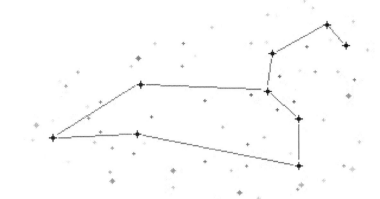

Chapter 8

Man

It was barely dawn when Fecir awoke to his mother standing in front of the cage, her body rigid and her hackles raised. Her ears were down and her yellow fangs were completely bared. Her claws dug into the soft earth and her pelt shuddered over rippling, angry muscles. From her throat came a deep, threatening growl, and in her eyes burned red with rage.

    Fecir also stood up and went rigid. His tail began to quiver and his back arched upwards. He skittered back, pressing close to the farthest wall of the cage. His mother barred his view of the meadow, but he need not use his eyes. A choking, gaseous odor was in the air, a putrid scent that made his throat burn and his eyes water. He coughed and gagged in disgust.

"Get low, Fecir," Swana suddenly spoke. Her back was to him and she barely moved.

"Mother, what is that smell?"

"Man is here. Get down and stay silent." Her voice was strangely gentle. It seemed to calm him down enough to obey. He lay himself flat on the ground.

A loud, roaring voice entered into the meadow. The voice chugged as it coughed up gas and exhaust, polluting the clean air. Innocent foliage and brush crashed loudly as a creature trampled over them. Swana growled when the chugging voice suddenly fell silent. The air became still and tense around them.

"Mother, what was that sound?" Fecir whispered hesitantly.

"Hush!" Swana hissed.

The forest was motionless. Not even the wind dared to make noise. Suddenly, a new sound came from the meadow. Strange voices, high-pitched like monkeys, yet their chatter was bizarre, alien. Swana growled deep in her throat as the voices reached her ears. She knew those sounds.

"Man," she said in a low voice. Fecir shivered.

Now they heard the footsteps wading through the tangling grass. Swana crouched low to the ground as they came closer and closer. There were four of them, judging by the number of footfalls. Their voices were becoming louder as they moved through the meadow.

"Do you think we caught anything last night, *¿tío?*" a young voice asked.

"You're too eager, *chico*, it's only been one night," an older voice answered. Swana listened intently, though she couldn't understand their words.

"But, you said that this was jaguar country. You said this place was crawling with them. That's why I wanted to come back and check today."

"*Necesitas paciencia, chico.* You need patience. Wait two days and you might have something. Wait a week and you'll definitely have something. Wait one night and all you'll have is *nada*," the older voice chuckled loudly.

Swana snarled, unable to control her hatred. Her voice sounded out through the silent forest.

The footsteps ceased at the sound of her anger. The voices fell silent, listening. The younger voice chuckled.

"Told you. I told you there were jags."

"I think we may have caught something, boys."

"Let's go! I want to see him!"

"*¡Oye, chico!* Wait!"

One of the creatures broke away from the group and started running toward the jaguars. Swana's tail swished furiously and she growled deeply. Her claws came out as she crouched lower, ready.

The footsteps became louder and louder, until finally, the creature came into view.

Fecir stared in wonder at the human being before them. It was young man, a teenager, with skinny arms and hairy legs and no visible weapons. Its skin was dark and covered by clothing, and its hair was short and wiry. And it walked upright on two legs.

Fecir only saw him for a split second before Swana leaped into the air.

By the time the boy saw Swana, it was already too late. She flew toward him, landing all of her weight on top of his body and digging her claws into him. The boy screamed in surprise and pain as he fell to the ground with the cat on top of him. Swana snarled in his face and sank her claws deeper.

Fecir watched, his eyes wide with fear, as Swana's vision went red and her mind went blank. She clawed at the boy, shredding his shirt and leaving long streaks of blood on his chest. The boy cried for help. He kicked and fought, his weak limbs helpless to stop the attack. Swana barely heard him over her own snarls. In her mind, she was back in the Dark Place, and the boy she killed was beneath her now. She roared in blind fury and opened her jaws wide.

"My cub," she snarled, her breath hot on the boy's face. "I won't let you hurt him. I'll die protecting him, and I'll take you down with me!"

Swana knew that she was going to die. She had known that as soon as she found Fecir in the trap. She knew that Man was going to come for her. There was no escape this time. Swana had already surrendered to her fate. She was going to die protecting her cub, and she promised to not die without taking Man with her. It was her last act of defiance. The boy's head went into her mouth. Her teeth grazed his scalp.

Before she could close her jaws, a gunshot rang through the air.

Swana fell over with a snarl. A gaping wound opened up in her shoulder. Blood leaked into her fur. Swana didn't even feel the pain. She was too furious to stop her attack. In moments, she was on her feet again, snarling. Another man stood at the edge of the meadow. In his hands he held a hunting rifle. Smoke trailed from the barrel as he pointed it at Swana again, focusing the crosshairs on her forehead.

With a roar, Swana leaped before he could pull the trigger. With a cry, the man fell beneath her paws. The rifle clattered away as Swana sank her claws into his flesh and ripped.

Fecir cried and paced in his cage. The smell of smoke and gunpowder was in his nose, and his eyes watered with the metallic scent of Man. He yelped at his mother as she tore and bit into the man furiously. The man kicked and shouted as Swana roared in his face. Her claws slashed through his left arm, leaving a long, bleeding gash. She kept the man pinned as he struggled and fought. She opened her jaws and sank her teeth into his collarbone. The man screamed.

A shot rang through the air. Swana tore her fangs away and looked up. Two more men were at the edge of the grass, and one of them had his rifle raised. With rabid anger, Swana leaped toward them, fierce eyes gleaming. The man with the rifle fired.

Three loud blasts rang out, and Fecir flinched at each one. Swana's roar was cut off. She fell mid-charge and hit the mud hard, sliding on her side. When she came to a complete stop, she was still. There were two bleeding holes in her shoulder and abdomen, and one right between her eyes. The she-cat was dead.

Fecir screeched when she hit the ground. He pawed at the wires, trying to reach her, as her wide open, unseeing eyes stared perpetually at him. He cried, but his voice would not wake her. She had died before she even hit the ground, from the bullet in her skull. Swana was gone.

"Mother!" Fecir wailed. "Mother!"

The man who had fired the shots, the oldest man with a furry chin, slowly lowered his weapon, while the other man with a clean-shaven face rushed toward the boy on the ground. The other injured man sat up and tied the remnants of his shirt around his bleeding arm. He wasn't injured as badly as the boy, who needed help to stand up as he bled from multiple cuts in his chest.

Fecir ignored them, still pawing at the wires, trying to get close to his mother. He refused to believe that she was gone. "Wake up!" he cried. "Get up, mother, please! Wake up!"

The injured man managed to stand up and limp away, while the clean-shaven man had to help the teenager walk. The three moved away, back into the sea of grass, while the bearded man surveyed the scene. He went over to the dead she-cat and knelt down beside her, feeling her fur.

Fecir snarled, outraged. "Don't touch her!" he shrieked. "Get your paws off her!" His vision was blurred by tears.

The bearded man looked up in surprise. For the first time, he noticed the cub in the trap. He stood up and walked over to him. Fecir hissed as his shadow fell over him. Bearded Man inspected him for a moment before shouting towards the meadow.

"*¡Oye!* Ricardo! Come see!"

After a few moments the shaved man came trotting back.

"What, Ángel? What do you want?"

"*Mira.*" Ángel pointed at the cage. "It's a cub."

Ricardo peered into the cage. He huffed. "How old?"

"Two months, I think. Just a little kitty." Ángel grinned.

Fecir snarled at them fiercely and tried to roar like an adult, but all that came out was a frightened squeak.

"Oh, a tough guy! Feisty!" Ricardo laughed. "Let's take him out, see how tough he is."

Ángel chuckled and tilted the wire cage. He reached his hand in and pulled Fecir out by the scruff of his neck. Fecir growled and tucked his neck as the man held him at arm's length.

"Who's a big, nasty kitty!" Ángel teased. Fecir snarled and swiped at him, but his claws did no damage. Fecir was helpless in the man's grip.

"Mother!" he cried, looking for her. "Mother, help me!"

The men just laughed at his cries. Ricardo walked over to Swana and grabbed her by the head. He dragged her bloody body close and then lifted her head to Fecir's. He touched her nose to Fecir's, and a drop of blood dripped onto Fecir's chin. He cringed away.

"Is that your mommy?" Ricardo teased, moving Swana's jaw to make her look like she was talking. Fecir whimpered as tears of hatred blurred his vision.

The men laughed and returned him to the cage. Ángel then lifted the cage and carried it away from the trees. Fecir cried as he was carried away from Swana and into the grass.

A red truck sat in the middle of the grass. Sitting on the tailgate was the injured man, who was busy plastering gauze on his wounds. The boy was sitting in the cab, barely conscious, his whole torso bandaged. Ángel sat the cage down on the tailgate while the injured man regarded it curiously.

"A cub?"

"*Sí*. The adult was its mother."

"So that's why." The man grinned. Wincing, he hoisted himself off the tailgate and made his way to the cab. "Hey, can you drop us off at the hospital on the way back?"

"Sure. But tell them you were attacked by a dog or something. Don't need to explain why we're hunting jags." Ángel pushed the wire cage onto the truck bed and tied it down with a rope. Fecir spat at him and hissed, and in response the man banged an open palm on the top of the cage. The sound made Fecir cringe. Ángel grinned in satisfaction before grabbing a tarp and walking away.

After a few moments both Ángel and Ricardo returned, carrying the blue tarp between them like a sling. In that tarp sling lay the still body of Swana. Together the two men hoisted her onto the truck bed and then folded the tarp over her, to cover her body, before tying her down. Her nose and forehead, however, lay uncovered, and her angry glazed eyes stared directly up at Fecir. He moved away and cowered, whimpering.

The truck suddenly rumbled to life, startling Fecir. The engine roared and chugged as it coughed up exhaust. Fecir's eyes burned as he inhaled the horrible scent. The wheels began to turn as the truck rolled away, roaring over the rough, uneven terrain. The trees began to whiz by as Fecir was jostled and thrown about in his cage.

Swana's head lolled about as the truck bumped and jerked over foliage and plants. Her dead eyes continued to stare forever outwards. Looking into those angry yellow orbs made Fecir feel helpless and afraid. He knew where he was going. He was going to the place of his mother's dreams. He was going to the Dark Place.

Fecir eventually passed out from the rocking, swerving, jerking movements of the truck navigating through the forest. The whirling of the trees and the insane motion was too much for him to bear. And the morning sun climbed higher into the sky.

Fecir did not know how long he was unconscious. When he awoke, it was because the blazing sun was beating down on him. He was dizzy and lethargic under that burning gaze, but he soon realized that they were no longer in the jungle. The truck was now moving across smoother ground, and it was rolling in a straight line. Fecir stood up and looked around. He could see the jungle in the distance behind them, a line of thick green that suddenly dropped off to cleared, deforested land, bleached yellow under the burning sun, the grasses shriveled and dead.

Fecir looked on in awe until suddenly the truck made a sharp turn onto a dirt road. A cloud of dust swelled up behind them, and Fecir's vision became choked. The truck then reduced in speed, and a sign suddenly appeared in the dust and whizzed by. Fecir could not read the words printed on the wood. The sign read, in large, bold letters: "RANCHO MATEO: *Caza Cautivo y Mascotas Exóticos.*"

Beneath those words was written in much smaller letters: "MATHEW'S RANCH: Captive Hunting and Exotic Pets."

The truck continued to reduce speed. Fecir saw more trucks come into view, as well as other vehicles. All of them seemed to be asleep, lined up in rows on a large, flat patch of dirt. The truck suddenly turned and strolled onto the dirt patch. It then found its own place to sleep, and it shuddered as its engine was shut off. Its roaring voice ceased and went silent. Fecir lifted his head and looked around.

The place they had come to was large and bustling with activity. Humans walked everywhere through the dust – some stood by their trucks, others talked in groups, many explored. Most of them carried rifles.

Mathew's Ranch stood on a cleared bit of land surrounded on all sides by thick jungle, which hid the illegal farm from the random passerby. The land was mostly loose brown dirt that turned into a thick cloud when walked upon. Sparse bits of parched yellow grass grew up here and there, around the buildings and between the parking spaces in the parking lot. The dust cloud that hung over this dry place was choking.

Seven buildings lay beyond the parking lot. One of which stood right next to the lot, and was labeled by a large sign reading

"TIENDA DE REGALOS – Gift Shop." Many people milled about this house-like building, with its dusty bleached walls, its rotting wood porch, and its chipping paint. An awning over the porch offered the only outdoor shade available on the whole property.

A supply building on the opposite side the parking lot stood in the shadow of a giant, towering wooden barn, its walls unpainted and its metal roof shining. As Fecir looked upon the giant building, he saw a human approach the metal door. When that heavy door opened, a great ruckus leaked out of the building – a menagerie of shrill animal cries and a mixture of sharp, pungent and putrid odors flowed out into the air until that door was once again closed, sealing the noise and smells inside. Fecir's ears flattened in fear of the building.

Attached to that building stood a tool shed, with the door hanging off of one hinge and unable to close. Inside that small shed was an assortment of items on racks – shovels, rakes, buckets, hammers, and an impressive collection of both tranquilizer and automatic hunting rifles.

Behind the giant building and tool shed were two more medium sized buildings, both hidden from Fecir's view and gated off from the public to explore. The larger of these two buildings was called the birthing center, the place where Swana was born. The other building, about the half the size of the birthing center, was the workshop, where trophy animals were taken after the hunt to be skinned or made into taxidermy.

The final building was another house-like building, although it was in much better shape than the gift shop. This building stood next to the birthing center and helped obscure it from view. This white-and-yellow painted building was labeled "CENTRO DE ADOPCIÓN – Adoption Center."

Fecir snarled as hands suddenly appeared above him, untying his cage from the bed of the truck. Without thinking, he lashed at the hands with his claws, pushing them through the wire mesh. He managed to nick the palm of one of the hands, and they both snapped away. Ángel uttered a loud curse before he banged his other hand against the top of the cage. Fecir shrank away at the noise.

"*Maldito gato,*" Ángel hissed. He finished untying the rope and jerked the cage into the air. He then stomped angrily towards the large building, swinging the cage at his side. Fecir cried in fear. He looked back at the truck behind them as they walked into the shadow of the massive building. He saw Ricardo drag Swana off the truck bed and plop her onto the dusty ground.

"Mother!" Fecir cried.

A gunshot rang out through the air, followed by the whooping of men over in the distance. Fecir, distracted from his mother, flinched and looked in that direction. A large corral stood a little ways away from the main area of the ranch. A group of men gathered around the wooden fence, cheering and hollering loudly. Another gunshot rang out from the corral, and Fecir flattened his ears as a guttural scream knifed into the air, followed by a sharp, defeated whimper. The smell of blood and death reached his nose. The men in the crowd whooped and rejoiced.

Fecir's eyes went wide and he crouched into a little ball, as Ángel opened the heavy metal door to the main building, and they both entered into darkness.

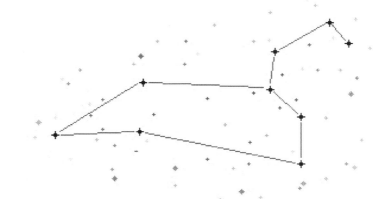

Chapter 9

The Dark Place

A dim light flickered on overhead.

It took a few moments for Fecir's eyes to adjust to the weak yellow light. It took him even longer to adjust to the sounds and smells of the building. The screams of animals filled the room, echoing off the walls. The humid interior was scorching, and Fecir could barely breathe. Not only was the air hot, it was putrid and disgusting, completely opposite to the clean, moist air of the jungle. It reeked of urine and feces, blood and disease, rot and decay. This must be the Dark Place, Fecir realized. The place of screams.

Fecir mewed in fear as Ángel walked through the rows of animal cages. The animals were organized by size and species. Near to the door of the massive building were two large pens made of rope and wooden poles. In one of these pens stood a large, gray animal with a massive horn on the tip of its nose: a rhinoceros. In the adjacent pen were six wildebeest, packed and huddled together like sheep.

Then there were four stalls, each stall about half the size of the large pens. Two of the stalls were crammed with prong horned antelope, packed so tightly together that they barely had room to breathe. The other two stalls contained different ungulates, ones that Fecir did not get a chance to see because Ángel suddenly turned down a corridor and walked between rows of new animals, each one as miserable as the first few.

These stalls were smaller and contained smaller animals. While the ungulate stalls were wooden, these ones were a mix of wooden walls and metal bars, and contained mostly familiar creatures. One stall contained marsh deer, and another had a very filthy, anemic anteater. The animals' eyes were dull with pain as they suffered in mournful silence.

Ángel turned again down a dead-end hallway. The dirt floor here was spattered with filth and dried blood. On either side of the walkway were rows of metal kennels, each one containing a big cat.

Fecir looked in awe. He had never seen so many cats in one place before, and never had he seen so many angry eyes. The cats paced in endless circles, moaning, snarling, roaring, screaming.

One of them, a small leopard, lunged at them as they passed by. Most of the others, many of which were native jaguars, just observed with sickly eyes as they walked past.

Ángel stopped at an empty cage. The concrete had been sprayed somewhat clean and a food dish in the corner contained kibble that seethed with roaches. The jaguar in the cage next door eyed the kibble with hungry eyes. When the door to the empty cage clanged open, he snarled and quickly retreated angrily away.

Ángel held the kennel door open with his foot while he opened the wire trap and thrust his hand inside. He lifted Fecir out by the scruff of his neck and then plopped him onto the concrete floor. Fecir immediately scurried to the far wall, the wall was marred by splintering gashes and scars. Fecir shivered as the kennel door banged shut and Ángel walked away. A few minutes later the lights went out, and there was a loud clang as the metal door closed. The animals were returned to darkness.

Immediately the noise became louder, the animals more rabid. They stalked their cages with claws outstretched, kicked and bit the walls and bars, chewed their own flesh until they bled. The large ungulates swayed their heads back and forth stereotypically, while the anteater began to rip out its own fur and claws. And the cats roared. They roared in anger, fear, and misery. Fecir shivered in terror as they paced around him, their eyes glowing with mad light.

"Hey, cub!"

Fecir jumped up, startled. The jaguar that had been eyeing the kibble earlier was staring right at him with ravenous eyes.

"Cub!" he snarled, yellow teeth glistening. "Give me your food."

"My f-f-food?" Fecir stammered.

"Food!" the jaguar demanded. "Give it to me, now!" He suddenly rammed the bars with his head and roared. Fecir moved away to other side and pressed against the bars.

A sharp nip on his rear made him jump. He leaped away from the bars and saw that the leopard in the other cage had bit him. The cat roared in fury and tried to claw at him through the bars, slobbering and foaming at the mouth.

"Food!" the jaguar in the other cage bellowed, ramming the bars again/ Fecir moved back to the scarred wooden wall and huddled against it, his heart racing. He had never felt more terrified in his life. He wished for his mother, but then he remembered: she was gone.

"Savior!" a voice called out. "Savior!"

Fecir's ears perked.

"The savior! He comes! He comes!" a jaguar across the walkway roared. He paced back and forth in his cage with his eyes lifted upwards and his voice loud in the darkness. Fecir watched him curiously. *Savior?*

"The white cat!" the jaguar snarled in a powerful voice. "He'll free us all! He'll come for us, he will! He will!"

White cat? Fecir suddenly thought of the white giant.

"Shut it!" the hungry jaguar on Fecir's left huffed, turning his attention to the preaching cat. "He won't come. Panthera has abandoned us, you moron!"

"He'll come!" the jaguar argued. Then, directing his voice back to the ceiling: "He'll save us all! When the full spring comes, he'll free us! He'll free us!"

"We'll never be free!" the hungry jag snarled acidly. His yellow eyes blazed. "Panthera has forgotten us! The jaguars will never be free! The Dark Place is where we'll all die!"

"Trust him! Trust him and he'll come!"

A loud clang suddenly sounded, and many of the animals hushed for a moment. The hungry jaguar retreated to the far corner of his kennel to drool and fume. The preaching jag's voice lowered to a mutter. All the cats began to shiver in fear.

"The choosing ... they're back ... they will choose ... will die." Hushed whispers hissed through the cages as the dim light flickered on. Two men suddenly appeared around the corner and walked down the aisle of cat cages. The cats snarled and hissed at them as they passed, but they were ignored. Fecir recognized Ángel as he came near, but the other man was unfamiliar. He looked much like Ángel, expect for that he was taller and his face was clean. As he came closer, Fecir saw the horrible pink gash on his left leg, a gnarled permanent scar. Both men stopped in front of Fecir's cage.

"Is this the new cat?" the man with the scar asked.

"Yes," Ángel answered, looking at Fecir. "This is him."

The scarred man peered inside. "That isn't a cat. That is just a little cub. What the hell is a kitten doing in here?"

Ángel shuffled his feet. "Well, I figured…. I thought that since he was a two-month-old, we could put him in here. I thought we didn't sell kits over two months."

"*Idiota*," the scarred man snarled. "If it fits in a cage, it sells. Get him out of there." He stalked away.

Ángel gave an exasperated sigh, unbolted the door, and stepped inside. Fecir didn't move when Ángel reached down and grabbed him roughly, holding him at arm's length as he carried him out of the kennel.

As they walked down the aisle of cages, all eyes were on the cub. When they passed the cage of the preaching jag, he looked up at Fecir and whispered gravely, "Panthera protect you."

Fecir squeezed his eyes shut and tried to block out the eyes.

They walked out of the Dark Place and into the light. The metal door closed again. And the animals began to scream in darkness.

The next place Fecir found himself in was a nice, cool, air-conditioned building. Inside this small building were stacks of both metal and glass cages lining the bright pink walls, and in the middle of the room was a desk with a cash register and a few pieces of paper. Sitting at the desk was a young she-human, and perched on her shoulder was a blue macaw.

In the metal cages were an assortment of small animals, the majority of them native birds – parrots, macaws, orioles, and even a large toucan whose bill could barely fit in its cage. There were several small capuchin and spider monkeys that twirled in circles behind their bars. At the bottom of the stack were two larger cages; in one was an overweight capybara, and in the other was a very dry, very lethargic baby caiman.

At the front of the building was a window, and stacked against that window were the glass cages. Most of these tiny boxes contained birds and monkeys as well. The monkeys banged on the glass walls and shrieked, while the birds flitted about and whistled shrilly. Fecir found himself inside one of these transparent boxes.

He looked about himself in wonder, looked at the creatures around him. The largest animal was another jaguar, a four-month-old about the size of a border collie, with bright golden fur and a pale underbelly. He was too large to fit in a cage, and so sat on a blanket in the far right corner of the building, tied up by his neck.

Tied up next to him was another large cat: a three-month-old lion cub. The lion cub had a tag around his neck that said "SOLD."

Fecir tried to stand up and move, but he found that he could only just barely turn himself around. He tried to walk through the transparent walls, but only ended up bumping his nose on the glass. He snarled and swiped at it, and his paws left smudges on the surface. The four-month-old watched him with interest.

Fecir growled and roared. He began to turn himself in circles, twirling and pacing about his cage, furious at having been put here, furious and scared. He didn't know where he was. His mother had never said anything about a smaller, well-lit version of the Dark Place. Where was he?

Mother. He suddenly remembered her. He turned toward the window and peered out at the dusty world beyond. He could see the red truck still parked in the same place, but there was no sign of his mother anywhere. Where did Ricardo take her? Fecir looked frantically. "Mother!" he screeched loudly.

"Hey!" snarled an angry voice. Fecir was startled. In the glass box next to him was another jaguar cub.

"Do you mind?" she growled irritably, opening one eye. "Trying to sleep here."

The cub was tiny – no more than a month old, with a blend of yellow and tawny fur speckled with dark brown rosettes. She had been asleep, curled up in a ball on top of a dirty blanket.

Fecir was too panicked to be polite. "Where am I?" he demanded in a rushed voice.

"Take it easy," the cub yawned. "No need to lose your temper, now. Ask me nicely and I might tell you." She winked impishly.

Fecir thought a moment, took a deep breath, and tried again. "Tell me where I am." He paused. "Please."

"Much better. You know, if you ask nicely, you're more likely to get an answer." She smiled brightly at him and stood up. "I'm Paggick. What's your name?"

Fecir was caught off guard. "F-Fecir," he stuttered.

Paggick smiled again. "Okay, Fecir. Obviously you're new here. This is the Adoption Center. It's where small animals are put until a human takes them home."

A snort came from outside the box. Both cubs looked down at the four-month-old tied to the corner.

"What's so funny, Tecka?" Paggick demanded.

"Nothing," he chuckled. "It's just that you said that we stay until a human takes us home. You forgot to mention that if a human doesn't take us, we are thrown into the Dark Place to grow up and die."

Fecir flattened his ears, but Paggick just scoffed. "Yeah, yeah. We've heard it all before. You're just angry because the humans don't look at you anymore."

"I'm glad they don't look at me. I don't like humans," Tecka snarled defensively. "I wish they'd all just go away, and maybe we could be free."

"Where would you go then, if you were free?" Paggick challenged.

"Where else? The jungle."

Fecir's ears perked.

"The jungle? You wouldn't survive there. I hear that there are poisonous snakes and giant lizards. You wouldn't last a day."

"I'd last long enough. I'll bet those giant lizards would be delicious."

"What about all those tree-things? Wouldn't you get lost in them?"

"I'd mark a scent trail. *Duh*. Jaguars were made to live in the jungle. Do you really think a jag could get lost in his own home?"

"I've been there," Fecir said quietly.

Both jaguars snapped their attention to Fecir. Fecir looked down, suddenly embarrassed. Paggick's eyes went wide.

"You? You've been to the jungle? Really?" she asked incredulously.

"I ... I was born there," Fecir murmured. "I was there ... just this morning...." His voice trailed off. A twinge of homesickness suddenly struck his heart. The full weight of what had just happened in the last twelve hours finally set in. He closed his eyes.

"Ha! No wonder he was going crazy. He's never been in a cage before," Tecka jeered. But then the taunting act dropped when he saw Fecir's shoulders shuddering. The cub was sobbing. Tecka immediately tried to recall his words. "Hey, I'm sorry…."

"I want to go home," Fecir choked. "I want my mother."

Both Paggick and Tecka fell silent. Tecka looked away out of shame. Fecir shook with sobs and let his head hang low. Paggick put a paw on the glass, wishing that she could comfort him.

"Hey, it'll be okay," she said soothingly. "You'll go home someday. I promise."

Fecir looked up at her questioningly. The tears were still in his eyes.

"That's right," Paggick said, a spark of hope entering her eyes. "We all will go to the jungle someday. We'll all be true jaguars. My mother said so. She said that when Panthera comes down to the earth again, he will free all the cats, and then the full spring will come."

Fecir was confused. "But … I thought … spring…."

"Yeah, it did come. The Endless Winter is gone. But that was just the first part of spring. The season of spring." Paggick lifted her chin proudly as she explained. "Back in the old times, the jaguars had a belief that was different from the other cats. They said that spring would come in two parts. The first part of spring was the season of spring, and that already came. The second part was the symbol of spring, and that symbol, to them, meant freedom. Freedom, rebirth, liberation from the snows, warmth and new life. The second part of spring is still yet to come."

Fecir was listening intently as Paggick went on.

"They say that when the white cat comes, a new Pantheraseer will be born, and he must teach us all to trust in Panthera. Only then would he free all the cats. Only then would the cages open, and spring would come."

Tecka coughed.

"What now?" Paggick demanded, whipping her head around to face him. "What are you laughing about this time?"

"I'm not laughing," Tecka said seriously, his eyes dark with anger. "I just think your story is full of bull."

Paggick frowned. "How so?"

"For one thing, if Panthera was going to save us, then why hasn't he done it already? Why let us suffer at the hands of Man for so long? The season of spring came over a thousand years ago. Why wait so long for the second half?"

"Well, there's–"

"And another thing, what makes you think that he will come at all? What makes you think he even cares about us? Have you ever seen Panthera? Have you ever met him?"

"I...."

"If you ask me, I don't believe there is a savior," Tecka concluded darkly. "If Panthera really existed, why would he wait so long to help us? Why would he let his children suffer like this, if he truly cared? If you ask me, the legends are nothing more than myths and fables. Panthera doesn't even exist."

"That's not true!" Paggick exploded desperately. "We have to trust him! Trust that he will come!"

"Trust?" Tecka scoffed and licked his lips. "The only thing we can ever trust is that one day we are all going to die at the hands of Man. That, you can see in the future. That, you know is coming. That is the one thing you can *trust* will happen."

For some reason, Fecir found himself agreeing with him.

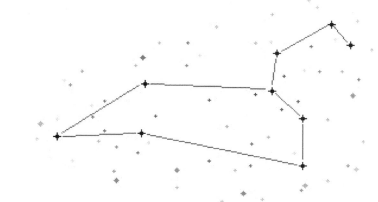

Chapter 10

Safe

The next few days went by in a blur.

At first, Fecir slept most of the time. When he was awake, he played with the stained blue blanket in his cage, tearing holes in it and teething on it. Once a day, the she-human at the desk would wipe his cage clean as well as fill his food dish with kibble, which Fecir refused to eat. His water source was a small bottle attached to the top of the cage, which dripped constantly. The water tasted moldy.

When Fecir could no longer sleep, he became restless and desperate for space. He started to pace in circles around his cage, twirling on his paws, unable to go anywhere. And the constant noise of the other animals was a horrible nuisance. Never ceasing, never fading, and only ever growing louder, the shrieks of monkeys and the trills of parrots were all he could hear. They became so loud that Fecir could hardly hear his own thoughts. The only time the noise was bearable was at night, when most of the animals went to sleep, and the moon shown bright through the window.

Daytime would treat the confined animals to a strange yet effective form of torture. At least ten hours a day, the adoption center was open to customers to come in and look at the animals. The people that came in stared at the animals with cold, hostile eyes. They judged them as they peered into each cage, judged them by their looks and the way they acted. Those strange, godlike eyes had the power over life and death, and held within them the promise of a most uncertain future. Fecir attracted much attention from these critical eyes, and he hated the stares. He could never hide from them within his transparent box, and so had no privacy. He grew sick under the constant, unfriendly gazes.

The children were the worst. They were ignorant of the animals and only wanted amusement. If Fecir tried to sleep, he was quickly woken by the palms of human cubs banging restlessly against the glass walls, wanting him to move for their enjoyment. Fecir wished that he could escape the judging stares, escape the bombarding children, but the only thing he could ever do was turn his back and chew his blanket, ignoring them as best he could.

While Fecir was miserable beneath the constant eyes of Man, the cramped conditions and the lack of sleep, he managed to find solace in his new friend, Paggick. Fecir enjoyed her spunky personality, and they soon became close as they spent their days together, often telling stories. Paggick enjoyed hearing about the jungle, and Fecir in turn learned a lot about her. He learned that she had been born in the Dark Place, just as Swana had been, and that Paggick's mother hadn't officially named her before they were separated. Because of this, Paggick decided to choose her own name, the jaguar word for "faith". When asked why she chose this name, she simply replied with, "I have a lot of it."

Fecir even started calling her by her preferred nickname: "Paggy".

The humans that came in would sometimes leave with an animal with them. Fecir saw many creatures come and go. Birds left in wire cages and monkeys left on shoulders. The lion cub with the sold tag left on the second day, early in the morning. He was walked out of the adoption center on a leash. Most of these transactions went unnoticed by Fecir. However, it was a sad day when Tecka left.

Tecka left for the Dark Place on the third day since Fecir's arrival. He had never talked much, but in their short time of knowing each other, Fecir had learned something of the moody cat. He learned that his past was riddled with scars. Tecka had also been born in the Dark Place. His brother had died in infancy before he could even walk, and then his mother was bludgeoned to death when she tried to protect Tecka from being taken away. Tecka had been traumatized by his ordeal, and so Fecir did not blame him for his moodiness.

When Tecka left, it was not because a human had bought him. It was because he had "outgrown" the adoption center. He had become too big to be adopted out. No customers ever looked at him like they did at Fecir and Paggick. When Tecka left, he was led away by Ángel to the Dark Place. Having already surrendered himself to his fate, Tecka walked quietly on the leash, out the door and toward the giant, menacing building. He did not say a word. Paggick and Fecir watched him silently, knowing his fate, and knowing that no words would bring hope to him now. For the rest of the day, Paggick and Fecir did not speak at all.

When night fell, and Fecir had closed his eyes to sleep, he was awakened by a quiet voice nearby. He opened one eye to see Paggick was up. She was facing the window and looking up at the night sky, her fur bathed in the light of the waning moon. She was whispering something to the sky. Fecir listened carefully. It was a prayer.

"Panthera, please watch over him. I know he has forsaken you, but please do not abandon him. I pray that you will lift his soul up to the stars with you, that you will protect him from all evil, even as he swims through rivers of blood. Please, Panthera … keep Tecka safe."

Fecir shut his eyes and went back to sleep.

Fecir lived at the adoption center for a total of two weeks. In that time, he grew very sick, becoming dazed and disoriented under the constant, relentless eyes. He began to pace endlessly about his box that seemed to grow smaller and smaller each hour. He barely slept, for he feared to close his eyes. In the darkness, his mother would come to haunt his dreams, and his ears would twitch with the warped sounds of rifle blasts.

Unable to eat his kibble, having not even been weaned yet, he became malnourished and emaciated. He grew weaker and weaker, and the staring eyes only worsened his condition. Without privacy, without space, not even the comfort of cheerful Paggick could cheer him up. And, as the days went by, even Paggick fell sick. She collapsed into an ever worsening state, sleeping for nearly twenty-two hours a day, unable to be woken up for anything.

Soon sickness merged with madness. Fecir's disoriented mind was now unable to make sense of his surroundings. His vision was blurred and warped, and his hearing became faint. He no longer made noise, having resigned to a mournful, weak silence. By his last day at the adoption center, Fecir could hardly even lift his head.

Unable to sleep and unable to move, Fecir faced the door to his box, watching as the she-human fed the animals. Within an hour, more humans would come in to stare. Fecir's eyes were glazed and dull – all that was visible was a blurred movement. His breathing rasped and his throat was raw with thirst. He tried to crawl over to the dripping water bottle, but he was too weak to move.

His head swirled, and his vision with it. Faintly, he became aware of a face looking into his box, watching him curiously. Two blue eyes. No hostility. Unbiased. No emotion. Fecir's head lolled to the side as he fell into a daze, and the face watched him.

The human cub peered silently into the glass box, studying the sick jaguar cub. Her blond hair went down to her shoulders, and her lips, withholding bright white teeth, were pursed together as she watched the sad animal. She made no movement, did not knock on the glass, did not demand movement from the poor creature – just observed, just watched with unique interest.

Suddenly, her lips cracked into a warm smile. "*Padre*," she said in a soft voice, as if afraid to disturb anyone. "This one here."

A man stood behind her, near the front desk. He was a thin man, dressed in newer clothes that revealed his sunburned arms. He approached the cub. "This the one you want?" he asked.

"*Sí*. Let's take him." She flashed her white teeth at him and returned her attention to Fecir. Fecir looked around with his eyes vaguely, not noticing or caring about anything around him. His eyes were almost white with filmy discharge – practically blind.

The man human, the she-cub's father, seemed nervous. Sweat beaded on his brow as he turned to the she-human at the desk. He spoke slowly and strained to understand her English. And the whole time he shuffled his feet and looked around himself, as if anxious to leave.

The human cub now turned away and looked into Paggick's box. Her eyes became sad as Paggick slept with her blanket, her sides rising and falling raggedly. The cub could tell that Paggy was sick, too, but she quickly turned away, and looked back at Fecir, who had closed his eyes, unable to keep them open any longer.

"*Pobre bebe*," she whispered sympathetically.

Finally the man human turned away from the desk. He had completed the exchange of currency with the she-human, and now he came to his daughter. He nodded to her and wiped his face with his arm. The cub smiled and opened the box.

Fecir barely noticed when two hands wrapped gently around his middle, lifting his limp, frail body out of the horrible box. He was then pressed protectively against a warm being – the she-cub cradled him against her chest. The warmth made Fecir open his eyes.

He still could not see, could not make sense, but he realized that they were moving. The motion was nauseating, enough to elicit a weak cry. A calm voice from above soothed him, and Fecir looked up, his delusional mind expecting to see his mother standing over him. Instead, his face was met with bright blue eyes.

Fecir's mind swirled. As his gut wrenched and sickness began to overtake him, he suddenly looked back at the box he'd lived in for the past two weeks. He saw Paggick, asleep in her box, her eyes squinted shut in dreams. A dim dawn rose up in Fecir's mind: he was leaving the adoption center. This was his goodbye.

He stared long after the sleeping cub, willing her to open her eyes and return his silent goodbye. She did not. She continued on sleeping, as sickly dreams enveloped her. Fecir turned away. Perhaps this was how it was supposed to be. Perhaps it would be best that she didn't see him leave. Perhaps it was best that she wake up later on and see that he was gone. She probably wouldn't even understand his absence.

Fecir said his goodbye to the spunky jag, as the man human opened the door for his cub. Warm air blasted Fecir's face as he committed the image of Paggick to mind, for he knew that he would never see her again.

Turning away, bright light greeted him. Fecir squinted as the she-cub carried him outside, out to his new life. As she cradled him gently, she bent her head down and whispered in his ear:

"You're safe now."

Fecir's mind seethed with nightmares.

It felt like there was no escape. The endless nightmares never ceased. He couldn't open his eyes. He couldn't wake from the images. And so he endured hell.

Fecir was in the forest, running; running for his life. Behind him trailed a pack of animals – dogs, the word came to him. The animals behind him were dogs, barking and snapping at his heels, their blue eyes focused and their white teeth vicious. Their black and white furs were stained with the blood of previous kills, and their jaws were hungry for more.

Fecir ran, ran and ran, but he couldn't get away. The forest tried to grab him, to hold him. Strange metal plants living beneath the leaf rot leaped up to snap at his feet as he ran over them. Vines snagged at his neck and thorns clung to his fur. He cried, yelped, screamed for help, screamed for his mother, but no one came for him. No one but the hunting dogs.

Fecir heard a screech above him and looked up. Through the branches he could see a flash of white – the white owl. The owl looked down at him as it flew over, lining up his shadow with

Fecir's back. It screeched again and flapped, pushing forward and suddenly wheeling left. Fecir swerved to follow it, his eyes on the canopy and the white owl.

As he was running, his head tilted upward, he didn't see the pit in front of him. He yelped as he found himself falling into a black abyss. The bird circled above him, screeching as the tiny opening of light slowly closed up as the jaguar fell deeper and deeper into darkness.

Fecir twisted himself around in the air, so that he faced whatever ground may rush up to meet him. *This is the end*, he thought as he saw a tiny dot of light steadily growing bigger. He realized, with a shock, that it was a face he was falling towards – the face of a white cat. The white jaguar opened his maw wide, and Fecir, with a horrified scream, fell into its throat. The jaws closed, and Fecir's consciousness slipped with the last remnants of light.

Fecir's eyes cracked open for what felt like the first time in months.

He didn't know how long he'd been asleep. It felt like it had been days. He felt so tired, and his vision was still blurred. He remembered, faintly, a pair of blue eyes and a warm, motherly touch. His stomach suddenly lurched, and his head dropped, and sleep overtook him once again.

When next he opened his eyes, it felt like even more time had passed. The blue eyes were there. Fecir could see them more clearly now. The blurriness was slowly receding, a fog lifting. Something smooth touched his muzzle, and without thinking he bit down on it. He was rewarded with a warm, milky liquid. Realizing how hungry he was, he sucked on the rubber, closing his eyes as his stomach filled with warmth. Within minutes he was asleep again, and the blue-eyed she-cub took the bottle away. She wrapped him in a heated towel and let him sleep.

Fecir woke up again hours later. He felt much stronger now: his consciousness no longer faded in and out, his mind no longer drifted, and his eyes were no longer blind. He was still disoriented and confused, but at least he could recognize one thing: he was hungry again. He began to cry out in a high-pitched voice. After a few moments, the she-cub appeared.

Fecir whimpered in hunger as she unwrapped him from the towel and gathered him into her arms. In one hand she held a warm bottle of milk. She put the bottle close to him, and he clawed at it, desperately hungry for the life-sustaining liquid. She put the rubber nipple to his lips, and he bit down on it and sucked, closing his eyes in bliss.

Only a few minutes later, what seemed like too soon, the she-cub took the bottle away and set it down. It was still half full. Fecir complained, staring at the bottle and crying at it, but he was still too weak and sick to crawl toward it. The she-cub held him gently in her arms, stroking him with her fingertips and whispering to him softly.

"You'll get more later," she said in a sweet voice. "Wait a while, Ferdinand."

Fecir could not understand her.

Eventually sleep took him once again, and the she-cub wrapped him in towels and let him sleep. Fecir was growing stronger in his sleep. In just two hours, he was awake and hungry again. Again, the girl came to his cries. Again, she let him drink out of the bottle. This time, she let him finish it, and then she held him until he dozed off in her arms.

As he slept, the she-cub stroked him softly and cooed him a lullaby. The soothing voice and the soft touch sparked dreams on his mother. He remembered her soft voice, her warmth, her love for him. He remembered her tongue rasping over him when she cleaned the firefly bits from his face, how she kissed him. How she stood over him during the thunderstorm, how she protected him from the sky's mighty voice. How the she-cub's touch was just like Swana's.

Fecir woke up again, expecting to see the she-cat there, standing over him as they lay in their kapok tree den, her warm voice growling softly in the night. But the den was not there. The forest was a distant memory. The girl with the blue eyes held him in her arms, and Fecir pressed closer to her, seeking the warmth of his mother.

For the next three days Fecir passed the hours in sleep, awakened only by hunger and crying only for milk. The human cub always came to him, nursed him back to health with the bottle. His strength returned hourly, his vision becoming clearer and clearer, until finally, he woke up and was able to see his world entirely. Finally, he could see more than the girl's eyes. Finally, he could see that he would survive.

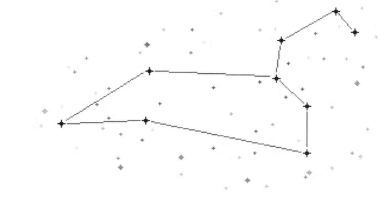

Chapter 11

The She-Cub

Sunlight shone onto Fecir's back, warming him filtered in through the window.

Fecir opened his eyes groggily, blinking away the grittiness. At first the light blinded, but after a few moments his eyes adjusted, and Fecir found himself inside a small room. He looked around for a moment, unable to understand, wondering where he was. The room was just like the adoption center, with one window that let in light, and a desk in the corner of the room. He lay at the foot of a bed atop a fleecy blue comforter.

There were no cages lining the walls, none whatsoever, say for one oddly shaped cage that hung from the ceiling near the desk. Fecir peered at it, his eyes still sleepy, and managed to make out the shape of a bird inside the cage. His eyes cleared a bit more, and he sat that the gray bird was also looking at him, as it sat completely still on its perch, not moving a muscle.

"Hello."

Fecir's ears pricked up at the croaky voice. He looked around, wondering where it had come from. The bird cocked his head as he watched Fecir's confusion.

"Hello."

Fecir stopped looking around. He looked straight at the bird, realizing that it was the only other creature around to have made that noise. He stared at the bird, watching for it to move its beak, and sure enough, it did.

"Here kitty-kitty!"

Fecir's head snapped back in surprise. The bird had made that noise. And what's more, it was speaking in human tongue.

The gray bird still watched him carefully, hesitant to speak. But the talkative animal soon spoke again. "Here kitty-kitty!" it said in the exact same tone as before, its voice croaky as it forced its throat to make those sounds. "Here kitty-kitty! Wanna treat?"

Fecir shook his head vigorously. *I must still be dreaming*, he thought. *This parrot is speaking human. I'm probably still asleep. This could only happen in my wildest dreams.*

Fecir tried to wake himself up by taking his hind foot and scratching his cheek. When he opened his eyes, the bird was still there, watching him curiously, tilting his head ever so slightly.

"Whatcha' doin'?" the bird asked innocently, its voice suddenly sounding more male than female. "Whatcha' doin', birdy? Whatcha' doin'?" The bird started to bob its head up and down, as if dancing. It shook itself and began to whistle some strange tune.

Fecir laid his head back down. *Nope, I'm definitely awake,* he thought miserably. He sighed as the bird started making an annoying buzzing sound; the sound of an alarm clock. The bird continued to screech that sound for several minutes until it interrupted itself by shrieking, "Pretty bird!"

"Shut up!" Fecir snarled, wishing he could go back to sleep. That was when the door opened.

"Hello!" the bird squawked as a figure stepped into the room. Fecir growled and squeezed his eyes shut, wanting everything to just be quiet.

"Hello," came a soft, gentle voice. Fecir's eyes opened at the new sound. He lifted his head and looked toward the doorway. And there by the door was the blue-eyed she-cub.

Fecir recognized her instantly from his dreams. He remembered her voice weaving through the nights of his sickness, her soft hands stroking his back, how she warmed him back to life. Fecir mewed in recognition as she stepped forward, closing the door behind her.

The girl smiled upon seeing Fecir awake and alert. Ignoring the bird's whistles and antics, she strode toward the bed and bent over Fecir, gently stroking his back. Fecir closed his eyes at the sensation and growled in pleasure.

"Good boy, Ferdinand. You're finally awake," the she-cub said softly. Fecir lifted his head as she scratched behind his ears. He couldn't understand any of the she-cub's words, and the fact was he couldn't care less, so long as she kept scratching his good spot with her long nails.

The bird suddenly screeched, seeking attention. The she-cub threw him a look, and the bird flapped its wings in annoyance. "Pretty bird," it muttered, turning away.

The she-cub smiled and patted Fecir's head. "I see you met Loro," she said, motioning to the cage.

"Pretty bird!" Loro squawked upon hearing his name. "Pretty bird! Here kitty-kitty-kitty!"

The she-cub giggled. "Crazy parrot."

As if to prove her point, the bird rolled its R's and started barking like a dog.

The she-cub smiled and turned back to Fecir. She stroked him for a few moments and then said, "Let's go outside. Some fresh air would do you good, I'll bet, now that you're well enough to stay awake. Come on, let's go outside."

She gathered Fecir into her arms and stood up, moving toward the door. The bird immediately noticed and began hopping up and down on its perch.

"Where're ya goin'? Where're ya goin'?" he squawked. The she-cub stopped at the door and turned to face the bird.

"To the barn, Loro. That's where we're going."

"*Nos vemos*," Loro said before whistling another tune.

The she-cub laughed as she closed the door behind her.

The property that the she-cub lived on was a large area of grassland surrounded on all sides by thick, green forest. The jungle was kept out by a tall chain link fence that was topped with loops of barbed wire surrounding the entire circular property. The humans' house was built in the middle of the area, on a rise that sloped gently downwards. Yellow grass grew up all around the white two-story house. A porch with an awning stood in front of the front door, and the cobblestone path leading up to that front door was fringed by a colorful flower garden.

A giant red barn stood nearby to the house, on a flat area near the bottom of the slope. A dirt path stemming from the cobblestones led to its giant doorway. This path to the barn also broke off to a second path that led to a wooden corral. The earth within this corral was trampled flat, with hoof prints visible in the loose dirt. Next to this corral and in front of the house was a small, two-seat swing set.

When the she-cub stepped out onto the porch, she was immediately greeted by two dogs that had been sleeping in the shade of the awning. One male and one female, the white sheepdogs bounded up to her, sniffing and wagging their tails excitedly. Fecir's claws came out when he saw their blue eyes and was reminded of his nightmare, but these dogs were different from the hunting dogs, especially in that they completely ignored him.

Sandra patted both of them, calling them by name. The smaller female with the pure-white coat was called Neva, while the larger male dog with black spots on his ears was named Bolero. They whined as she patted their heads, and she was petting one dog, the other shoved its way in, out of jealousy. They weaved around her legs, sniffing her and re-familiarizing themselves with her scent. Fecir's eyes followed, and he never retracted his claws.

"*Buenos perros*," the she-cub told them. "Good dogs. *¡Sientate, perros!* Sit for me."

The dogs heard her command and quickly placed their rumps on the wooden deck, their tails thumping against it as they waited for their next order. Fecir watched curiously, unsure of what these animals were doing.

"*Arriba,*" the she-cub said. The dogs lifted their front paws off the ground in a begging position. They held that pose for several moments.

"*¡Muy bien!* Very good dogs!" the she-cub praised, and the dogs immediately dropped their poses and came to her. The she-cub bent over to pet each one, then stepped down off the deck and onto the cobblestones. She walked between the flowers with the dogs trailing at her heels, and headed toward the giant red building that was the barn.

As they walked up the slope, the dogs ran ahead, Bolero leading. The she-cub cuddled Fecir as she walked with him, and though the experience of being touched by Man was new to him, he found that he was enjoying the she-cub's playfulness and her soft touch.

They walked up to the barn door, and immediately they were greeted by a sharp whinny. Fecir's eyes went wide, wondering what animal could've made that sound. There were three wooden stalls in the barn, and out of the closest one to the door appeared the giant head of a brown quarter horse.

The she-cub smiled as the horse greeted her, snorting and shaking his mane. Fecir dug his claws into her shirt at the sight of the animal. No deer or tapir ever had a head this big back in the jungle. What was this strange animal? As the she-cub walked toward it, Fecir's eyes grew wider and wider.

The horse clearly smelled him as the she-cub approached, but somehow didn't seem to mind Fecir at all. Unlike the dogs, he did put his muzzle close and sniff him a few times to get used to the cub's scent. He blew air out of two giant nostrils while the she-cub stroked his face, running her hand along his white blaze.

"Good boy, Alano," the she-cub said quietly. The horse nickered at her voice, lowering his ears and listening. Fecir reached out a curious paw and dabbed the horse's nose. Alano didn't seem to have any reaction at all, except that he turned his head away so the she-cub could pat his neck.

Two other whinnies now sounded in the next two stalls. Two more heads appeared, both pure-white horses. The she-cub went over to stroke each one, yet she did not name them. Fecir realized that these horses must not have names. When the white horses smelled Fecir's scent, they backed away uneasily.

The she-cub boosted Fecir up a bit so that he was riding partially on her shoulder. "These two horses aren't mine," she explained, even though she knew the cub couldn't understand her. "They're boarder horses. I'm training them for a client. They're circus horses. Their owner sent them to me for a few months so I could teach them some new tricks before they go off to perform. They have four months to go before the owner takes them back. Until then it's my job to train them."

She paused and frowned. "Actually, I should be training them right now." She placed Fecir temporarily on the straw-strewn floor. He looked up at her with a confused expression while she attached a lead rope to each of the white horses' halters. Then she led them out of their stalls, stopped to pick up Fecir again, and walked out of the barn with the horses in tow.

Fecir lay on the railing of the wooden corral, watching somewhat sleepily as the she-cub worked with the horses in the center of the ring.

At first Fecir was amazed at the tricks she got the animals to do. First she had them run around in circles for a while. Then, she called them over and raised both her arms. The horses immediately reared up. When they came back down, the she-cub twirled on her heels, and, mimicking her, the horses did the same, circling about themselves in a strange, synchronized dance. She climbed on the back of one horse and stood up with her arms out while the horse trotted around the perimeter of the corral. They repeated these tricks over and over to the point where Fecir finally started to get bored.

He now let his mind wander, going over everything that he had learned so far throughout the day. He had met Loro, the noisy, talkative African gray parrot that the she-cub kept in a cage in her bedroom. He'd met the two sheepdogs, learned their names, learned that they were well-trained and only responded to Spanish commands. He'd met Alano, the brown gelding that was also apparently well-trained, knowing far more tricks than what the she-cub was teaching to the white horses now. And he'd met the she-cub, finally, outside of his dreams.

The she-cub reminded him so much of his mother it was unbelievable. How a young human being, a completely different species, and a creature well-known for its violent nature at that, could be so caring to an animal of another kind was beyond him. This creature couldn't be the cruel Man that his mother had spoken of. This creature was the opposite of cruel – she was kind. She had saved his life. And now he was even starting to learn her name: Sandra.

He couldn't understand human speech. However, the word "Ferdinand" had been repeated to him several times throughout the day. *What meaning could it have?* he wondered. *Could it be a word for a cub? A simple noise, maybe? Or is it ... my new name?*

As Fecir watched, Sandra suddenly ended the training session, patting both horses and attaching their leads to their halters. She led them toward the gate, and as she did the two dogs outside the gate stood up to follow her wherever she went. Fecir watched her head up the slope to the barn and disappear inside it.

As he waited for the she-cub to return, he looked toward the fence and the jungle beyond it. He could hear the calls of tapirs and monkeys just beyond the chain link. At first he wanted to remain on the railing, but the call of the jungle pulled him to his feet, and, after making sure nobody was watching, he jumped down and scampered toward the fence.

As he approached the chain link fence, he breathed in the scents of his old home, the jungle that seemed to strangely distant from him now. He closed his eyes and smelled the ferns, the mud, the rotting leaves, the fruits, the tree bark – all the smells that he so fondly remembered. He put one paw on the metal links, just breathing, just remembering.

He remembered the burning smell of smoke and the thunder of gunshots ringing in his ears. He remembered the trees rushing by, abandoning him as he was whisked away from the forest. He remembered the meadow and the red monster rolling into its midst. He remembered the white giant, a wire cage. A spurt of blood. A furious roar. A piercing scream. Dead, yellow eyes.

Fecir's eyes snapped open and he leaped away, breathing heavily from the vivid horror of the memory. As he gasped for breath, he swore he could almost see his mother on the other side of the fence, her fur soaked in blood, her piercing eyes, forever angry, forever sightless, staring coldly at him from within the shadows. Fecir backed slowly away from the fence as those eyes bore into his own. *No*, he thought in horror. *No*.

"Ferdinand? Where did you go?"

Fecir looked away, ears pricking upon hearing the voice. He could see the she-cub looking for him around the corral, the dogs sniffing as they searched him out. He looked back at the forest, but his mother was gone. Her eyes were gone, and her face had disappeared into the shadows. Fecir peered at the trees, searching for her, when suddenly he felt hands underneath him, and he was lifted up into the air.

"Ferdinand! There you are," the she-cub said, holding him against her chest. "Bad kitty. You shouldn't run off like that. Bad Ferdinand."

The she-cub squeezed him in her arms before turning around to walk away. Fecir looked over her shoulder at the jungle again as she moved away from the fence. For a split second, he thought he saw his mother standing there again, half-hidden by the trees, her dead eyes watching him leave. A moment, later, she turned and disappeared into the deepening shadows, leaving not a sound in her wake. Fecir whimpered in fear and buried his nose in the girl's shoulder.

Sunset found the girl and her cat sitting together on the swing set.

The dogs lay around the wooden frame, their head on their paws, watching as the sun went down. Sandra sat on the plastic seat with Fecir in her lap, gently swaying back and forth while she kept one hand on his back, to keep him for falling. At first, Fecir didn't want to stay on her lap. When the swing started moving, he fought the urge to jump off. But the she-cub's soothing voice had relaxed him, and now he found the idea of gently swinging to be quite enjoyable.

Sandra sang softly as she watched the sun disappear over the canopy, blanketing the sky with a gradient of twilight. Stars started to pop out randomly, the brightest ones first, then the fainter ones as the sky grew darker. The jungle music switched from day to night, as birds went to sleep and frogs rose to take their place. As Fecir sat in the girl's lap, he listened to this music and her pleasant singing, and thought that he never wanted to get up.

Of course, he soon had to leave, for Sandra's father called her in for dinner. She scooped Fecir up into her arms and walked up the way to the house, the dogs following steadily behind.

After the she-cub had eaten her dinner with the man-human, she gave Fecir half a bottle of warm milk to help him sleep. Fecir was already exhausted from the long day, and the bottle was enough to make his eyes droop. As he sat on the bed and waited for Sandra to get ready to sleep, he tried to keep himself awake by watching the parrot as it preened its feathers before bed.

Sandra soon came into the room, dressed in her pajamas. Her blond hair was pulled back in a ponytail, and she yawned, cupping her mouth with her hand. She sat on the bed and said a quick prayer, bowing her chin to her chest. After a few words, she gently picked up Fecir and tucked him under the covers. Then she slipped in beside him, turned off the light, and kissed his forehead.

"*Buenas noches,* Ferdinand," she whispered as she lay with her arm around him. Pretty soon she fell asleep. Her eyes drifted closed and her breathing became deep and regular. A little while later, and she was dreaming.

Fecir closed his eyes but found he could not sleep. He was tired, but his mind seemed restless. Every time he tried to fall asleep, a single thought stopped him: the image of his mother in the forest.

Eventually Fecir gave up on sleep. He stood up and gently wriggled himself out from beneath the girl's harm. He padded on top of the covers over to the open window, through which he had a clear view of the moon and stars.

Fecir looked out onto the night world beyond. From the forest came the faint nightly song, the sounds of crickets and frogs and ocelots growling in the dark. Down in the flower garden and floating among the yellow grass were the fireflies blinking steadily in the cool air, and above the canopy was Panthera, his nine stars perfectly visible among the black-water sky.

Fecir suddenly growled when he spotted him. His eyes went dark and a shadow seemed to pass through his heart when he saw that constellation above the forest, when he saw the fireflies, the forest guardians, dancing in the flowers. He flattened his ears and bared his teeth at the sky.

"You lied to me," he growled coldly. "You lied to us, to me and my mother. You told us that the forest was safe. You let the fireflies dance and you told us that nothing would do us harm. You lied to us, Panthera. The forest was never safe. You lied."

Fecir turned away, scorn and hurt etched across his face. It was as if all he had ever believed in was shattered, all his loves and dreams thrown away to the wind. Never before had he felt so angry, so in pain. And so he made a vow to himself that night: he vowed to never return to the jungle, and to never place his trust in Panthera ever again.

Chapter 12

Sandra's Circus

The next three years went by without Fecir even noticing it.

Most of the days spent with Sandra went about with much the same routine: the she-cub would wake up in the morning and let the dogs and Fecir outside to "do their business." Then the animals would come in to get their morning meals. For the dogs, it was kibble, which they wolfed down like savages. For Fecir, at least for his first two months with Sandra, it was kitten formula from a baby bottle. As he got older, she eventually started to wean him off of milk and introduce him to meat. By the time he was two years old, he was eating over four pounds of pure raw meat every day.

The next item on the agenda was to feed the animals in the barn. Sandra would feed each horse a scoop of pellets and throw a pile of fresh hay from the loft into each stall. Then she would take all three horses out to the corral to run around for a bit while she mucked out each stall, scooping all the mess into a barrel and dumping it into a towering pile right behind the barn. One morning when Fecir was just three months old, Bolero unknowingly pushed him into the pile while Sandra was emptying the wheelbarrow, and that little incident prompted Fecir's first ever "bath" which he immediately associated with "fear". Fecir learned to avoid the dung pile at all cost.

Over time, Fecir also began to explore the barn. He climbed the ladder up to the loft and discovered plenty of interesting things. Old toys, saddles, halters, a chest, farm equipment, woodcutting tools, spider webs, a rat's nest, bags of feed, and piles upon piles of hay. Fecir even dug himself a nest inside one of the hay bales and would often hide up in his little burrow while Sandra fed the horses. When the she-cub would go up to the loft to find him afterwards, he would wait in hiding and pounce on her shoes.

After Sandra finished with the barn chores, she would usually take the two boarder horses out to the corral for a morning training session while the cool mist was still wafting around them. Fecir would jump up or be placed on the top railing so he would get the best view. He would watch as the horses danced within the white fog, their manes billowing behind them as they trotted and reared, their bodies fading until they were little more than gray shadows moving within the vapor.

After working with the boarder horses, Sandra sometimes brought Alano out to practice his tricks. Alano was a much older horse; not yet lame, but definitely old, yet when he trained with Sandra it was as if he had gone back in time to his colt years. The old gelding would prance on request and even let Sandra stand on his neck. He was very tolerant and patient, and willing to do almost anything for Sandra.

Normally by the time the horses were taken care of, noon had already arrived, and the man-human would be calling Sandra in for lunch. Fecir and the dogs would follow her in and would all three be waiting under the table for scraps, which she gave often. Fecir learned as a cub that if he put a paw on her leg, she would instantly reward him with a slice of ham or a piece of cheese. The dogs' method of begging was a bit different from Fecir's – they whimpered softly and pleaded with their eyes, and sometimes Neva licked Sandra's feet.

After lunch, Sandra took the dogs out to the porch to practice their tricks. Her dog training method was different from the horses in that she rewarded the dogs with biscuits. Fecir would often watch them work from the comfort of a rocking chair that sat out on the porch. He saw the dogs stand up and twirl on their back legs, like ballerinas pirouetting on their toes. He saw Bolero play dead, in which Sandra pointed her finger at him and said sharply: "¡*Bang!*" Bolero would fall on his side and dramatically whine.

Neva knew some interesting tricks as well. She could walk on her front paws and even perform a back flip, on a good day. There were days when she wouldn't do certain tricks, even at Sandra's command. She was more stubborn than her male counterpart, but Sandra loved working with her for just that reason. Teaching Neva a new trick was a huge accomplishment given the dog's attention span's tendency to wander away from the task at hand. Fecir enjoyed quietly watching these sessions and seeing something new each day.

When Fecir was four months old, he was introduced to a brand new phenomenon completely outside of the ordinary routine. Every six months after Sandra received two boarders, she would put on a show in which she would demonstrate the horses' progress through performance. She called it a "final exam" for the animals, for their owners would come to see the performance and see if the horses' training was satisfactory enough for proper payment. And more than just the boarders' owners would come to see the show – Sandra's neighbors would come, too, and add to the audience. The dogs and Alano and even Loro would perform their tricks in the show alongside the boarder horses, which made the recital very appealing. The she-cub referred to this popular performance as "Sandra's Circus".

The first time Fecir saw this performance, he did not understand fully what was going on. The first thing he noticed was several trucks appearing in the driveway, and several humans milling about the property. When the people first arrived, Fecir went and hid in his hay burrow up in the loft, but Sandra found him and convinced him that it was alright, that there was no need to hide. When Sandra brought the horses out and lined them up by the corral, Fecir took his place on the railing as he always did, thinking that the she-cub was doing another training session. As he watched from his perch, he tried to ignore the fact that there were other people watching the performance alongside him, standing on the outside of the fence and looking in with excited, anxious eyes.

When the show started, Sandra came out to greet the other humans. She spoke loudly, introducing herself and the show. Then the first animal appeared for his performance: Loro. He stood on Sandra's outstretched arm and went through his verbal tricks of singing and sound effects. This started the crowd laughing, but all Fecir could think was how annoying that bird was.

The next two performers took the stage: Bolero and Neva. Their doggy prowess wowed the crowd. Neva even did her back flip trick, and the crowd laughed when Bolero played dead. The audience was enticed by the sight of Neva walking on her front paws, and while most of the people could understand Sandra's Spanish commands, the English-speaking men were awestruck at the dogs' ability to understand and perform to a bilingual master's requests.

When the dogs finished their act, Alano came in to set the stage for the two boarder horses. He would go through his patterns, running in his circle around the perimeter of the corral and only coming to the center when called. He reared up and whinnied when Sandra raised both her arms. He followed her with his nose touching her back when she walked around the corral, stopping when she stopped, walking when she walked, even kicking out his leg when she kicked. Each trick was rewarded by a loving scratch on his forehead, and his performance ended with him kneeling on one front leg, taking a boy. The audience clapped for Alano as he was led out of corral, but Fecir just yawned. He'd seen it all before.

The final two performers in Sandra's circus were the boarders, the moment that the horses' owner had been waiting for. He now paid close attention as the magnificent white animals were led into the center of the corral. Sandra clicked to them, sending them both running around the corral. With a simple whistle she separated one white horse from the other and called him to the center. That horse performed a trick while the other ran, and then she set them both trotting around, now in the opposite direction. The other horse was called to perform a trick, and the process was repeated. Finally, both horses were called out to show their newfound menagerie of skills, rearing up and coming back down, twirling about themselves, even rolling over and allowing Sandra to sit on their chests. The audience was amazed at the end of the performance, and the boarders' owner was greatly pleased.

At the end of that day, Fecir watched from his place in the swing set seat as Sandra led the white horses over to their owner's trailer and helped to load them up. Sandra was sad to see the horses leave, but she knew that they weren't hers to keep. After a tearful goodbye and a firm, thankful handshake from the owner, the horses were on their way, and Fecir never saw them again.

Sandra then came and sat with Fecir on the swing set, placing him in her lap as she'd done every evening. Fecir had come to look forward to this sunset ritual, to the point where he jumped up into the plastic seat and waited for her to finish her evening chores. She would swing gently back and forth and sing softly, as they watched the sun go behind the trees, abandoning the world to darkness.

A month after the first Sandra's Circus, the she-cub received a new pair of boarders to train. She also began to train Fecir, as now he was finally weaned off the bottle and eating a mostly meat diet. Every afternoon after working with the dogs, she would take Fecir out to the corral to practice some basic tricks. At first, she kept him on a leash throughout the whole session to keep him from wandering away. After a few weeks, he started to get used to the routine, and soon Sandra took away the leash entirely and allowed him free roam about the corral during a session. She used bits of ham or chicken as rewards for good behavior, and sometimes bits of milk as a special treat at the end of each session.

She started him off with the more basic commands: sit, lay down, shake hands, and speak. Fecir's voice had steadily grown deeper and so he learned that speak meant that he should growl or cough to get a reward. These tricks took a while for him to learn, as being a cat his attention span was limited. But within a few months he had mastered the basics, and Sandra graduated him to the intermediate tricks.

These tricks included stay, come, roll over, sit pretty, and circle. Now that Fecir was used to receiving instruction, he caught on a lot quicker, learning to turn about himself when told to "circle" and to sit up on his haunches in a begging position when told to "sit pretty". He became so accustomed to the verbal requests that even Loro could give him a command, and he would do it.

However, Sandra did not want him to rely solely on verbal cues, so she made sure that he learned to do these actions on just hand signals alone. They worked on each trick for hours at a time every single day, until Fecir could perform all of his skills on just a simple hand movement. The dogs were trained the same way, answering to both hand and verbal commands. Soon the dogs would start to train with Fecir in the corral, and while Fecir was starting to learn the advanced level tricks, Sandra was making sure that he practiced the previous level tricks by teaching him to perform combinations of tricks with the dogs. This combination training and choreography would prepare Fecir for what was ahead.

When Fecir turned a year old, he participated in his first ever "Sandra's Circus".

At first Fecir had no idea what was going on. He thought it would be another show, and that he would be allowed to watch from the railings like he always did. But then he was lined up with the dogs near the gate, as the people gathered in a semicircle around the outside of the corral, chattering like excited capuchins. Then Sandra walked out to the center of the ring and began talking. The crowd clapped and the show quickly began.

Fecir watched from behind the fence as Loro and the dogs went through their performances. Alano did not perform in this show, since Sandra was waiting on him to be re-shoed. The boarder horses came out and strutted their stuff, showing off their manes and tails as they danced around the she-cub. After the horses' performance ended and they were led out of the corral, Fecir saw himself being shoved into the ring. He instantly became confused, but then he saw the she-cub waiting there with a bit of meat in her hand. She whistled to him, then threw it on the other side of the corral.

Fecir immediately ran after it at full speed.

The crowd was greatly surprised. After witnessing household and farmyard animals performing for the first twenty minutes, they were not expecting to see a half-grown jaguar come charging into the ring. Many people backed away from the railing, but Fecir paid no attention, as Sandra kept on throwing small chunks of meat into different corners of the corral, enticing him to run after them.

Sandra talked as she tossed the meat, introducing Fecir and explaining his weight, size, and habits. She educated the audience on his diet and his past, as Fecir showed off his speed and muscular legs through running. Finally, after the she-cub had finished her introduction, she called Fecir over, and he came, just as if they were in a training session.

Sandra had him go through his tricks, starting with some of the basics and then moving onto the advanced. She had him sit, roll over, sit up, and jump up to catch a piece of meat. She brought out a hoop and had him at first run through, then jump through it as she held it off the ground. She had him circle around himself both left and right, and the crowd reacted with pure amazement. They had all known that Sandra was a skilled animal trainer, but never had they seen such a young girl tame a beast such as the mighty jaguar.

Fecir paid absolutely no attention to the crowd, only focusing on pleasing Sandra and earning his treat. This was pretty much a training session for him, except that there was an audience watching. At the end of the performance, both Sandra and Fecir took their bows, Fecir crouching down and stretching his front paws out in front of him at the command. The audience stood up and cheered. The sound was a bit frightening to Fecir, yet he also took some pride in it, knowing that he had pleased the she-cub and had completed his first live performance flawlessly.

Fecir lived a pretty easy life on Sandra's property. The routines normally did not change – every day he was fed, let outside, played with, and trained. Every morning he would watch Sandra work with the horses, and every evening he'd enjoy an hour on the swing set. His time spent with the she-cub on the swing in the waning moments of daylight was still his most favorite memory.

Fecir quickly outgrew Sandra's lap. By the time he was a little over a year, he could no longer ride the swing with her. And so he learned to sit on the top of the swing set, climbing up to the wooden plank to which the seats attached and laying on it as if were a branch. From there he could hear Sandra singing beneath him as she swayed back and forth gently while he watched the sun setting over the canopy. From this high rise he could witness the night enveloping the property, the shadows of the forest creeping up to touch the windows on the house, until they consumed the whole land. From here, he could be the first to say hello to the waking stars.

Fecir continued growing, becoming larger and heavier, under the she-cub's care. Being fed every day ensured he would reach his full weight, and even become a little overweight, thanks to the table scraps Sandra still snuck to him. He still slept in her room, lying at the foot of her bed, and she managed to put up with his snoring. Fecir was now three years old – a fully grown, mature adult jaguar.

He no longer thought of the jungle. He hardly remembered his mother anymore. He had suppressed his memories of her, just as she once suppressed the Dark Place. He sometimes still saw her in his dreams, but not often, and always when he woke up, the she-cub was there to comfort him.

Fecir still remembered the vow he had made that night as a cub. He never looked for Panthera in the sky anymore, and he made sure to force the thought of the Star Lords out of his mind. The only thing he thought of was Sandra now. That was the only thing.

One morning, when Sandra let him and the dogs out to "do their business" in the grass, Fecir was trotting along the chain link fence, looking for a suitable spot to relieve himself, when suddenly he noticed a large hole at the bottom, a tear in the chain links. The chains were rusted and weak, and must've broken at some point, creating a hole big enough for him to fit into, a hole that led out to the jungle beyond. Fecir stared at the hole for a very, very long time.

He looked around, looked at where the dogs had gone, looked toward the house to see if anyone was watching him. He sniffed at the hole, stuck his paw through it, but quickly took it back and shuddered. He looked long and hard at the hole, at the jungle beyond it, just remembering.

He remembered being born in the jungle and chasing the fireflies in the meadow. He missed those times, missed the cries of birds and the chatter of monkeys that were parts of his soul. But he also remembered his mother's death, how she died in the jungle, how her blood stained the green leaves a dark crimson. How she still seemed to haunt the forest, how her yellow eyes seemed to watch him from the trees. Fecir stood up and shuddered. He looked at the hole one last time. He then turned around and walked away from it. He thought nothing of it after that day. The vow still held in his mind: he would never return to the forest.

Fecir hoped he would spend all of his days with the she-cub he had come to love and cherish. But this was not to be. A wind began to blow through the jungle, rustling the leaves and sending shivers through the creatures of the canopy. A strange omen rode within that chilling wind – a sign, a forecast of terrible change ahead.

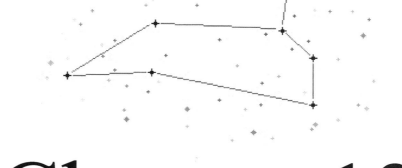

Chapter 13

Betrayal

"And now I would like to introduce you to our two boarder horses, Adriana and Alona!"

The two horses trotted into the corral, swishing their tails behind them and tossing up their heads. They immediately began to trot around the perimeter of the ring, as they were trained to do, with the black mare in the lead and the white mare trailing behind, as Sandra stood in the center of their dance.

"I've been working with these horses for six months now," Sandra said to her audience. Among that crowd, the two men that owned the horses were watching, their arms folded and their faces serious, as they noted the animals' posture, stride, position, and elegance. They watched to be sure that they would perform to their standards, and they scrutinized Sandra like owls preparing to swoop down upon a rat.

Sandra was used to these kinds of looks, and so ignored them, focusing on the audience as a whole, as she continued explaining to them about the horses and the time she'd spent with them. Then she fell silent, allowing the animals to speak for themselves through their performance. The crowd, too, fell silent, as they watched the strange equestrian dance before them.

Sandra called the black mare out of the circle first. She made her rear and hold her position, standing on her hind legs and balancing her weight. She came down and Sandra let her run back to the circle. The black mare fell in step behind the white one, and they both trotted around for a few laps, reducing speed and accelerating at Sandra's request. Then the white one was called out to perform the same trick as the black one. The running repeated, but this time in the middle of a lap Sandra whistled, and both horses instantly changed direction and started galloping side-by-side around the corral.

The two men looked on, slightly amused. So far, so good. They were cooperating well and had learned the desired tricks. The taller man leaned over to the shorter and whispered in his ear.

"What do you think, Juan?" he asked. "*¿Son buenos?*"

"So far," Juan answered. "What's your opinion, Tomás?"

"They look pretty good," he observed. "Girl has done a good job."

"We got her pay?"

"Yeah, in my pocket."

"Good. Hold onto that. Show's almost over."

The horses had both been called out now, and were twirling about themselves. Sandra made them both rear one last time, and then she sent them out of the corral, and the audience clapped at their performance. Juan and Tomás both cracked a smile, and Sandra let out a sigh of relief, knowing that she had pleased them.

Now she grinned widely, for the show was not over. The two men started to leave, but she stopped them with her loud, sudden voice.

"And out last performer, ladies and gentlemen. Please put your hands together for Ferdinand!"

The men returned to their spots, clapping but slightly confused. Wasn't the show over? They had seen what they came here for. What more was there to see?

A loud, feral roar reached their ears, and instantly the men's eyes bulged.

Fecir came charging onto the scene, running after the bits of meat that Sandra threw, just as she always did at the beginning of a show. He roared and charged, shocking the crowd into silent awe of the magnificent animal. Juan's jaw dropped, and he looked at Tomás, who had the exact same expression. They had not been expecting a jaguar to be performing alongside their horses.

Sandra continued to toss bits of meat, all the while looking at the crowd's reaction and smiling. She decided to introduce him them, drawing the people's attention with her loud fence.

"This is Ferdinand here. He is a three-year-old, adult male Amazonian jaguar. He weighs almost one hundred and twenty kilograms, which is about two hundred and sixty-five pounds, if my math is correct."

The crowd chuckled a bit as Fecir continued to run. Sandra also chuckled and continued on, explaining his past.

"Ferdinand came to me when he was about two months old. We found him at a canned hunting reserve, where they were trying to sell him off as a pet. He was severely malnourished, dehydrated, and emaciated when we rescued him. We actually didn't think he would make it through the night. But he survived the ordeal, and now he's here to show you his tricks!"

The crowd clapped. Juan and Tomás leaned forward against the railing, watching intensely, as Sandra called Fecir over.

Fecir went through his routines. He performed his basics, first sitting down and putting his paw in Sandra's hand, which induced an *awww* from the crowd. Next he rolled over and let Sandra rub his belly. He stood up immediately when he clapped her hands, and then sat up on his haunches in a begging position, for which Sandra rewarded with a piece of raw meat.

The men looked on, amazed, yet as they watched there were thoughts going through their minds. They looked on as Fecir stepped into his advanced level tricks.

He jumped through hoops, stood up on his hind legs, spun around, and jumped straight up into the air. He played dead, sat up and twirled, roared on command, and even sneezed when Sandra told him. The crowd watched on, eyes wide in amazement. Juan looked at Tomás, and Tomás looked back at him. The exact same thought was going through their heads. That cat is valuable.

Fecir finished his act by taking a bow. Sandra then closed the show with a wave goodbye to the audience. The people began to leave, moving towards their vehicles parked in the driveway while Sandra praised Fecir and the dogs for a job well done. The two men brushed off their pants and approached Sandra as she was patting Fecir's head.

Fecir saw them approaching from behind, and an involuntary growl suddenly rumbled in his throat. These men ... they didn't smell right to him. Something was wrong. Fecir could sense something about these two humans, something sinister and dangerous. He nearly hissed.

Sandra put a calming hand on his forehead, and Fecir's growl stopped before it became louder. She greeted the two men with a smile and shook both their hands. Fecir fought back a snarl when he saw this exchange. He didn't want Sandra anywhere near these strange humans, much less touching them. He pressed his whole body against her leg, as if trying to push her away.

"*Hola*," Juan said, shaking Sandra's hand firmly. "I'm Juan. And this is Tomás." He motioned to his partner.

"Hi," Tomás said, reaching forward for the she-cub's hand.

"Nice to meet you both," Sandra said pleasantly.

"That was quite the show," Juan said with a shark-like grin. "Your cat at the end blew us away."

"Oh. Why, thank you. How did you like the horses?" Sandra blushed.

"They looked great. You did an amazing job with them. We'll be taking them home now, I guess."

"Awesome. They're in the barn. I'll go get them for you." Sandra turned to walk toward the barn.

"Now, wait just a minute there, *chica*." Juan reached forward and grabbed Sandra's arm to stop her. Fecir instantly snarled, and Juan quickly released his grip. Sandra turned around and patted Fecir's head to calm him, frowning a bit at his odd behavior.

"Is he dangerous?" Tomás asked while Juan shuffled his feet, slightly unnerved.

"No, not at all. I don't know what has gotten into him," Sandra said, directing a disapproving look at Fecir. He flattened his ears.

"That is a bit strange," Tomás observed. Juan looked up and put his hands in his pockets, eyeing Fecir suspiciously with cold, black eyes. Fecir fought back a growl.

Juan then turned to Sandra and smiled a bit overly pleasant. "Before you go and get the horses," he said in a voice like syrup, "we'd like to talk to you about something first."

"About what?" Sandra asked, a bit skeptical now.

"About your jaguar."

"What about Ferdinand?" Sandra's voice was starting to take on a protective tone.

"Well, we were wondering if you were going to sell him."

"Ferdinand is not for sale," the she-cub said in a flat voice. Her voice almost had a hint of threat in it.

"Are you sure? Because we would be willing to offer..." Juan pulled out his wallet and dug into it. He turned up a wad of green paper. "Eight hundred U.S. dollars for him."

"I wouldn't sell him for a thousand U.S. dollars," Sandra said angrily. "I saved his life and raised him from a kitten. I wouldn't part from him for anything." She was almost snarling at them. She abruptly turned around. "I'm going to go get your horses. Wait right here, please. Come on, Ferdinand."

Sandra started walking toward the barn. Fecir hesitated, eyeing the men warily, before trotting off after her.

Juan groaned in frustration and Tomás spat in the dirt. They cursed under their breaths as the smaller man kicked a clump of dirt.

"She won't sell it, but we really could use that cat," Tomás complained, staring at his shoes. "Our own cats are barely trained. A cat like that could really bring up a performance!"

"That cat could easily be worth *two* thousand U.S. dollars," Juan spat. He groaned again and shoved his hands into his pockets.

"What are we going to do, Juan? We won't find another animal like that anywhere. What are we going to do if she won't sell it?" Tomás asked.

"*No sé. ¡No sé!* I don't know!" Juan snarled.

Sandra suddenly appeared in front of the barn, leading the horses down the slope. The two men quickly hid their frustration behind fake smiles. Fecir's eyes narrowed when he saw that the two men still had not left the property.

Sandra handed over the horses to Tomás, putting their lead ropes in his hands. "Here you go."

"*Gracias,*" Tomás nodded, taking the leads. He tugged the ropes sharply, startling the horses a bit, and then led them both away to a trailer parked by the fence.

Juan dug around in coat for a bit before coming up with a white card. He handed it to Sandra along with a roll of cash for training the horses. Sandra looked at the white card carefully. "What is this?"

"That's my phone number," Juan said with a grin. "In case you change your mind about Fernando here."

"Ferdinand," Sandra corrected.

"Whatever," Juan said, reaching out his hand. After a moment of hesitation, Sandra shook his hand. Juan smiled and gave her a mock salute before walking away toward the trailer.

Sandra watched them until their truck pulled out of the driveway and passed through the gate. The sun was just starting to set now. Sandra looked down at Fecir. She was still a little unnerved by the men's question, but still she smiled when she saw Fecir looking back up at her with his bright yellow eyes.

"Come on, let's go swinging," Sandra said, and Fecir immediately took off toward the rickety set, all memory of the two men instantly forgotten.

Juan and Tomás walked through the back alleyways of the old town, their hands in their pockets, their heads low, pacing through the city streets as they looked for a store from which they could buy cheap meat. It had been two weeks since they took their horses back from the Sandra, and already those two animals had been put back on the circuit, performing in shows as far away as Panama. However, the two men still could not stop thinking about that girl's jaguar, how valuable that animal could be to their business. How if they could somehow acquire him, they would surely be given a huge cash bonus, or even a raise in their monthly paycheck.

They had tried to put the cat out of their heads. The girl had already said she wouldn't sell it. And they weren't about to stoop so low as to steal it, and then end up having to face charges. And besides, neither of them knew how they would ever manage to steal two hundred-plus pound jaguar.

They were just about to give up on trying to find a way to acquire Fecir. But it was then, on that afternoon, that something caught Juan's interest.

They had been walking for several minutes, looking for a store, when they noticed a ragged blanket set up on the ground next to a dumpster, and an equally ragged man sitting on top of that blanket. The man had a dirty awning set up to shade him from the boiling sun. He sat cross-legged on the torn blanket, scratching his scraggly beard and looking out at the people walking around. But it was not the homeless man that Juan noticed – it was his product.

Behind the man sat three wire cages. And in each cage sat a tiny, scruffy, big cat kitten.

Juan stopped Tomás and pointed to the scraggly man. The man noticed their pointing and waved at them, motioning for them to come closer. As they did, they saw a very small sign lying next to the man's bare feet. The sign read, in barely legible letters, "GATITOS EN VENTA – kittens for sale".

Juan peered at the cages behind the man after he read the sign. In each one was a big cat cub – one was a tiny, eight week old lion cub. The other was a barely breathing cougar. And the third cub, the one that really caught his eyes, was an eight week old jaguar cub with pure white fur.

"*Hola*," the ragged man said. "You like my cats?"

"Where did you get that white one?" Juan demanded in a flat voice.

"*¿El blanco?*" The man looked over his shoulder. "I don't know. I just found him. You like him?"

"*Where* did you get that animal?" Juan demanded again, his voice seething. The tiny cub raised his head and blinked his eyes, eyes that glowed a bright spring green. He yawned, revealing his tiny teeth, before closing his eyes and going back to sleep.

The scraggly man sweated. He scratched his beard nervously. "Look, I just sell kittens," he tried to explain with his limited English vocabulary. "That is all I do. I sell. Will you buy?"

Juan thought for a bit, as he kept looking at the white cub. As he looked, Tomás looked around nervously, wondering if anyone was watching them. After a few moments, an idea slithered into Juan's mind, and he smiled a toothy grin.

"Yes, actually," Juan said amiably. He reached into his pocket for his wallet. "I will buy the white kitten. How much?"

"Juan, what are you doing?" Tomás hissed.

"What does it look like I'm doing? I'm buying me a cat."

"But, we are supposed to be buying–"

"*Cállate,* Tomás. Trust me for a moment."

Tomás instantly grew silent as Juan turned his attention back to the scraggly man. "How much?"

"Two hundred," the man answered. Juan grudgingly dug through his wallet and pulled out the wad of cash. The man took it and immediately began to count the money. When he was satisfied, a toothless smile spread across his face, and he reached behind him and grabbed the white cat's cage. He carefully handed it to them.

"*Muchas gracias,*" Juan said, taking the cage. He and Tomás then walked away, looking down at the kitten in the cage. The cat looked around with wide eyes, surprised to be suddenly moving. Its coat was a startling white hue, and its rosettes were a warm cinnamon.

"Juan, why on earth did you buy that cat? We don't need a kitten right now. That money was supposed to be for–"

"Shut up, Tomás. I have a plan in mind."

Fecir lay on the top plank of the swing set, panting in the humidity, his paws hanging slightly off the edge of the platform. The setting sun cast its red light over his pelt, bathing the magnificent feline in warmth and sunrays. Fecir closed his eyes, listening to the sweet sound of Sandra's voice and feeling the soft caress of the evening air on his fur.

As he sat up there, his ears suddenly detected a sound, and his eyes opened. His whole body grew tense and alert, and he looked toward the fence, at the gate leading up to the driveway. Sandra must've heard it, too, for she stopped singing and stood up off the seat. She quickly ran up to the house and disappeared inside, leaving Fecir to sit atop his perch, watching the gate.

A truck pulled up to the gate and honked the horn a few times. Sandra's father quickly came out of the house and ran down the slope to open the gate, all the while the truck honked impatiently. Fecir stood up on the platform and growled deep in his throat. He recognized that truck as it pulled up the driveway and stopped near the house. The side doors opened, and the two men jumped out.

Fecir snarled and jumped off the swing set, recognizing that same sinister smell from nearly a month before. He quickly trotted up to Sandra and sat beside her as she stood at the doorway, watching the two men from the porch. Fecir growled low in his throat as the two strange men greeted Sandra's father, and then walked up to the porch. Fecir's growl deepened and grew louder, but the she-cub's gentle touch on his neck calmed his threatening voice.

"*Hola, chica,*" Juan greeted, politely reaching out his hand to Sandra. Sandra refused it, and the hand retreated. She eyed the two men suspiciously.

"*Hola,*" she returned their greeting. "What are you two doing back here?"

"Well, we just thought we'd pay a visit," Juan said innocently.

Sandra sensed that he was withholding information. She raised her eyebrows. "And?"

"And we wanted to see if you had changed your mind about selling your cat."

"No, I haven't," Sandra said, her voice starting to sound vicious. "Ferdinand is not for sale."

"Are you sure about that? Because I'd be willing to make a trade," Juan smiled. Behind him Tomás also smiled.

Sandra seemed dubious. She crossed her arms over her chest. "A trade? What kind of trade?"

Juan looked over his shoulder at Tomás, and they exchanged knowing grins. She was falling for their trap. He made a motion with his head, and Tomás stood up and started walking toward the truck. Juan turned his head back to Sandra.

"A trade that you cannot refuse," Juan said. "I remembered you saying that when you rescued Fabio here–"

"Ferdinand," Sandra corrected irritably.

"Ferdinand." Juan nodded. "You said that when you rescued him, he was very sick and near-death, am I right?"

"Yes," Sandra said skeptically. "I rescued him from a canned hunting farm. What about it?"

"Yes. So see, you rescued him, right? You couldn't help but feel that you needed to save him?" Juan's smiled was growing ever more devilish.

"Your point?" Sandra growled.

"Well, we just found a kitten that doesn't look so good, and we were wondering if you would like to look at it."

Sandra fell completely silent. At that moment, Tomás came back with a wire cage in his hand. Inside that cage was a very weak jaguar kitten with pure white fur.

Fecir's eyes went wide when he saw the cub. White fur. Cinnamon rosettes. Bright green eyes.

Panthera.

Sandra's breath caught in her throat when she saw the cub's condition. Its body was just skin and bones, and the poor cub couldn't be much younger than Fecir when she rescued him. His fur was grimy and there was discharge coming out of his eyes. The tiny cub could barely lift his head.

Fecir could smell the cub's scent from where he sat at Sandra's side. He smelled ill, of death and blood and poison, it seemed. The tiny cub was dying of sickness. Fecir turned his nose away from the god-awful smell.

Sandra leaned forward to take the cage out of Tomás's hands. But before she could touch it, he yanked the cage back, smiling evilly.

"Sorry, but this cat is ours," Juan said.

"That cat needs help," Sandra said, trying to keep her emotions under control. "Where did you find him?"

"We found him on the road. Looked like his mother had abandoned him. He looked like this when we got him," Juan lied through his teeth.

In reality, the two men had actually kept the poor cub for almost two weeks after they bought it from the peddler on the street, and during those two weeks they purposely underfed it so that it would grow sick and weak, just for this purpose.

"He needs treatment," Sandra said in a firm voice. "He's very sick. He needs to get help right away."

"Well, maybe we don't want treatment," Juan said impishly.

"If he doesn't get treatment soon, he'll die!" Sandra said desperately. "You don't understand. Look how weak he is!"

"Remember what I said about a trade?"

Sandra was silenced. She quickly stepped back, her lips quivering, fighting back tears and still staring at that poor kitten that could be dying as they spoke. "Yes, I remember," she said in a small voice.

"Well, this is my offer. I let you have this cat, and you can treat him and nurse him back to health and do whatever you want. And in return," Juan's voice seethed, "you give me your cat here." He pointed at Fecir.

Sandra was shocked at the horrible offer. But she thought about it for a moment. She knew that the white cub needed help immediately, and she was the only one who could provide it. On the other hand, she couldn't imagine parting with her Ferdinand. She was torn. The offer was completely unfair. A baby's life for an unbreakable friendship. Sandra took a deep breath and closed her eyes. She made a decision.

"Give me the cage," she said.

"Good choice, *chica. Muchas gracias*," Juan praised triumphantly. Tomás handed over the wire cage, and Sandra took it. She hid her face as tears began to stream from her eyes.

"I'll go get his leash," she sniffed.

"Good, good. And don't you worry. He's going to a good home," Tomás reassured her. Sandra turned and took the cage into the house. She came back a moment later with Fecir's leash and collar. She slipped the collar around his neck and clipped the leash to it. Then, to Fecir's horror, she handed the leash to Juan.

Juan smiled cruelly and took the leash in his fist. "It was great doing business with you. Have a nice day now."

Sandra didn't answer, just looked at Fecir with tears rolling down her cheeks. Fecir looked back at her in disbelief. *After all we'd been through, you're giving me away? And for a cub?*

Fecir could see the cage sitting on the floor just beyond Sandra's feet, with the sick white jaguar cub lying inside. His eyes narrow and flamed with anger and betrayal. *You monster,* he thought acidly. *You stole my Sandra from me.*

A harsh tug on his leash brought his attention back to the two men. He snarled, but Sandra touched his forehead softly, soothingly. Fecir looked up at her with pleading eyes, but hers had already grown indifferent to his. However, she still leaned down and took his head in her hands.

"Don't worry," she said softly. "Everything will be okay. Be a good boy, Ferdinand. Be good."

"Come on, cat! Let's go!" Fecir felt the yank on his neck, and he jumped up to follow. As he trotted behind the two cruel men, he looked back and saw Sandra go into the house. She came back out with the white cub cradled in her arms.

Fecir turned away, disgusted and heartbroken. The men led him to the tailgate of their truck. They lowered the gate, and Fecir saw the large metal cage in the back. His heart began to race as he thought of the metal trap, and he started to back away from the truck.

There was a sudden pain in the back of his neck, and Fecir snarled. He whipped his head around and saw Tomás with an empty syringe in his hand. Moments later Fecir began to feel woozy. He started to stagger, and within minutes he had passed out on the ground.

The two men loaded him up into the cage and put up the tailgate, then started up the truck and drove away. Sandra watched them drive down the driveway and through the gate, as she held the sickly white cub in her arms. When the truck was out of sight, she turned around and went back into the house, shutting the door behind her as the sun's last rays disappeared behind the canopy, and darkness fell over the empty swing set in the yard.

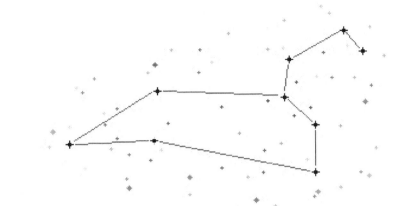

Chapter 14

The White Giant

When Fecir woke up, he immediately groaned from what felt like the worst headache he had ever experienced in his life.

He was incredibly groggy, so much so that he nearly fell back into sleep. The ground was hard and covered sparsely with bits of hay and straw. Had he fallen asleep in the barn? He forced his eyes to open.

Blurry. He blinked his eyes a few times, but they wouldn't clear. He let his eyelids droop shut and groaned again, putting a paw over his head. Bright yellow light was shining down on his, and the vivid color only seemed to worsen the pounding in his head. He growled low in his throat, cursing the light, and tried to go back to sleep.

"Hey. Hey, kid. Wake up."

Fecir's eyes popped open. He looked around, not bothering to lift his head, his drowsy eyes seeing nothing but a blur. Although it sounded like it was close by, he couldn't see where the voice was coming from, and so groaned and closed his eyes again.

"You okay, kid? You don't look so well."

Fecir opened his eyes again, but still could not see. He refused to lift his head.

"Up here, fella," the voice said above him.

Fecir, with a low moan, finally lifted his head and sat up, though he staggered a bit, unable to keep his balance as an aftereffect of being drugged. He yawned and nearly fell over, barely catching himself before his chin hit the hard floor.

"Whoa, buddy. Careful there. Don't hurt yourself," the calm, friendly voice said. Fecir looked around, but still couldn't see anything. He could barely even think straight what with his head aching so much.

"Where are you? I can't see," he whimpered.

"Right next to you. Just give yourself a moment there. It'll pass."

Fecir waited a few moments, and sure enough the voice was right. His vision slowly began to clear. First he could see the ground beneath his paws – concrete, with thin straw bedding – and then what was directly in front of him: metal bars. Fecir's eyes became wide, and he whimpered in sudden fear.

Where am I? Am I back in the Dark Place? His heart began to race and he flattened his ears. His lip involuntarily curled up to reveal his teeth.

"Easy, buddy. You're alright. Don't panic now, or you'll hurt yourself."

Fecir blinked, and his eyes suddenly cleared completely. He looked around himself now, and saw that he was in a cage raises slightly off the ground. The cage had a solid black roof, and beyond that roof the sky was covered by a red-and-white striped fabric – the ceiling of a large tent. A few yellow light bulbs hung from wires attached to the ceiling. The ground within the tent was dirt, and also covered in bits of straw.

Fecir breathed a sigh of relief. *Not the Dark Place*, he thought. *But still ... where am I?*

Fecir moaned, still confused as to how he ended up in the cage in the first place. Looking about the tent in the dim light, he tried to recall everything he could. He remembered doing a show with Sandra, and two strange-smelling men approaching her. He remembered the swing set and a truck coming up the driveway. He remembered Sandra crying and putting on his collar and giving the leash to the men and–

The white jaguar cub. He remembered the white cat, the one that took his Sandra away from him. He growled low in his throat, realizing that the two men had put him in this cage, beneath the weird, giant tent. And it was all the white cat's fault.

"I guess your vision is finally cleared up a bit. Good. It takes a while for the eyes to adjust after waking up from being drugged. Believe me, I'd know."

Fecir turned his head to the right and saw that there was an identical cage right next to his. And inside that cage was a black jaguar.

Fecir was dumbstruck for a moment. He hadn't seen an adult member of his own kind in almost three years. It was strange to see another jaguar, and what more a melanistic jag, after such a long time that he almost did not recognize that the cat beside him was one of his own species. As Fecir stared at him strangely, noting his dark fur and very faint but visible rosettes, he saw the black jaguar smile.

"Like the view?" he chuckled. "My name's Tarunaq – old jaguar word for 'shadow'. What's your name?"

Fecir hesitated. It had been so long since he heard his own language. For a moment he was afraid he wouldn't be able to speak it. He remained silent.

The black jag frowned and tilted his head. "What's the matter? Don't you have a name?"

Again he hesitated. Eventually he stuttered out, "Y-y-yes."

Tarunaq smiled. "Then let's hear it. What's your name, fella?"

Fecir was a bit bolder now, and did not hesitate, finally remembering how to form words. "Fecir," he said confidently.

"Ah. The word for firefly, if I'm not mistaken, right? Well, then. It's a pleasure to meet you, Fecir," Tarunaq said cheerfully, when suddenly he erupted into a violent coughing spasm. Gasping for breath and whistling through his teeth, the cat had to turn his head away. He hacked and wheezed for several long minutes. Fecir's ears perked up.

"Are ... are you okay?" he asked in a concerned voice.

"Yeah. I'm ... fine," Tarunaq choked out between coughs. "I'm just getting old, that's all." He continued to cough for yet longer. The spasm finally subsided after a long while, and Tarunaq could clear his throat. He sat up and shuddered, bristling his fur, then looked at Fecir with old yet playful eyes. A tendril of drool hung from his lip, left over from the spasm.

Fecir hesitated for a moment, as if waiting for another spasm to start, before speaking again. "What is this place?" he inquired, looking around curiously. "Where am I?"

Tarunaq cleared his throat again before answering. "This place? This is the circus, rookie. A traveling animal show, you could call it," he said. He smiled brightly. "Welcome to life on the road, kid, the life of a traveling circus performer!"

He laughed, and his laughter evolved into another fit of coughing. He turned away again to gag, and Fecir flattened his ears.

A circus? he thought. *Like Sandra's Circus? What exactly is this cat talking about?* He cocked his head, still very confused. He waited for the old jaguar to stop coughing before he spoke again.

"What do we do here at this circus? I mean, what happens here?" he demanded.

The black jaguar opened his mouth to speak, but before any sound could come out, a loud metallic clang slashed through the still air. Fecir started, but Tarunaq just rolled onto his side, sighing in annoyance. He muttered something under his breath. Fecir barely heard it: "Here we go again."

A door had suddenly opened in the cage across from them. As they watched, the sounds of men reached their ears, as they shouted and whooped in short, quick bursts of sound. There was a low, catlike growling, too; and a lion suddenly jumped up into the cage and began pacing about in it furiously. The door clanged shut behind him, and the sounds of the men went away, leaving just the lion to stalk around, teeth bared, yellow eyes glowing with fierceness, and gruff voice huffing out low, angry snarls.

Fecir watched, fascinated. Not even when he was in the Dark Place had he seen a full-grown male African lion. He had always had an idea as to what they looked like based on his mother's descriptions. This lion, pacing in anger, had a glorious reddish mane extending from his neck all the way to between his front legs. This bushy hair shivered and rustled as he stalked about, placing his paws heavily in front of each other, and snarling like a rabid dog.

Tarunaq, still lying beside Fecir, squeezed his eyes shut and covered his face with a paw as the lion began to roar loudly, sending out his voice toward the opening in the tent. Fecir continued to watch in awe of the magnificent creature. But as the lion returned to his pacing, his yellow eyes unexpectedly locked onto Fecir's. Fecir's body went rigid under the look of those hostile orbs.

The lion suddenly lunged himself at the bars, ramming his skull into the cage at full force. Fecir flinched at the sound of the impact. The lion fell away and scrambled back to his feet, huffing and snarling like a horrid, ravenous monster. Fecir backed away until his rump touched the back of his cage.

"You there! Jaguar!" the lion roared in a harsh, guttural voice. "What the hell are you staring at?"

Fecir's ears twitched. He found that, somehow, he could understand the lion's language. Though his accent was thick and exotic, he could still hear his words clearly. Fecir's mouth hung open, but no sound came out of it. He did not know how to answer to the lion's anger. Its yellow eyes, bloodshot from unprovoked rage, narrowed dangerously.

"Speak up!" he barked. Fecir flinched. "Speak up now, you cur!"

"Cool it, Mahkuu," Tarunaq muttered loudly, in a half-hearted attempt to diffuse the hostility. He didn't even open his eyes. "Lower your voice. I'm trying to sleep."

"Shut up, you old fool!" the lion snapped at him. He roared at the jaguar, but the old cat gave no reaction. Mahkuu's eyes then flickered back to Fecir, who stiffened again under the cold gaze.

"You," he snarled acidly. His voice was lower now, and seething with threat. There was an unspoken dare in his tone. "Talk. What is your name?"

Fecir hesitated. Mahkuu growled, and suddenly body shuddered, shaking and convulsing as if he were having a seizure. He shook his head violently, splattering the metal bars with saliva. He bellowed furiously, "SPEAK!"

"F-F-Fecir," Fecir stammered quickly, shaking in fear.

"There," the lion muttered, his voice suddenly lowering to barely audible. "There." As if a switch had been flipped, the lion turned around and went back to pacing, muttering and growling quietly to himself, foam dripping from his jaws. Fecir cocked his head in confusion at his sudden change in temper.

"What's with him?" he whispered wonderingly, leaning over to Tarunaq but still keeping one eye on the pacing lion.

"Just ignore him," the black jag growled through gritted teeth. "He's always like this."

"What do you mean?"

"I mean, his mood swings are completely terrible," the old cat sighed, finally opening his eyes. "Mahkuu is a very vicious cat. Even his name means angry. But don't worry. Just keep your distance and you'll be alright. He's always threatening others, but he can't hurt you."

"You're dead wrong, old jag!" the lion suddenly snarled, ramming the bars again. Fecir jumped in surprise as the lion roared, spraying saliva.

"I can kill you with only one claw. One claw! I'll rip your face off, you crippled half-wit!" he raged.

Tarunaq just smiled as he hoisted himself back into a sitting position. He looked at Fecir with an impish expression. "See? Empty threats."

"My rear," Mahkuu grunted. "Open this cage and I'll show you a threat. Fight me, you coward!"

"Nah," Tarunaq said mockingly, lying back down and rolling onto his back. "I'd much rather take a nap in my nice cage."

That sarcastic tone threw Mahkuu over the edge. With a roar, he again attacked the bars again, thrusting his paws between the metal cylinders. He grasped at Tarunaq's cage, but couldn't quite reach far enough across the aisle. Realizing this, his hooked claws retracted and he brought his arm back into the cage. He resigned back to pacing, muttering swear words beneath his breath and cursing the old jaguar. Fecir watched this whole exchange in awe and bitter amusement, wondering what kind of world he had been thrust into.

A loud, strange snort caught all three of the cats' attention. They looked over to the left where the tent opened up to a large ring with a skylight above it letting in pale moonlight to brighten the stage. Inside the ring of dirt was a large pedestal – an overturned water tub, really – and two men, one with a whip and the other with a vicious bullhook. The man with the whip snapped the coil and shouted angrily at an opening in the tent. As he shouted, a giant creature entered the ring.

Fecir's eyes grew wide as the enormous beast walked into view, swaying his great head as he lumbered toward the pedestal. His legs were like tree trunks, head like a battering ram, ears like wings, and nose like a snake. Upon his head was a red headdress, and his skin was pure white.

The giant flapped his wing-like ears, lifted his nose up to touch his forehead, feeling the golden tassels and the red fabric adorning his massive skull. Holding his head high and his mouth open, he stood still say for his swishing, ropelike tail, as the men circled around him like hungry wolves. The man with the hook hooted a command, coming around to the giant's side to jab him with the sharp end of the weapon. The white animal groaned and flapped his ears, placing one massive foot on the pedestal.

Now, as the three cats looked on and the men continued to circle, the giant put his other foot on the tub and hoisted himself up onto those two front legs. Fecir's mouth dropped open and Tarunaq smiled knowingly as they watched the colossal animal stand on the pedestal with his hind legs in the air, his front legs supporting him, and his nose still fondling the tassels on the red headdress.

"Magnificent, isn't he?"

Fecir almost didn't answer. He swallowed and glanced over his shoulder, unwilling to look away from the creature for more than a second. "Yes, he is," he said quietly. "What is he?"

"An elephant, I believe it's called," Tarunaq said. "Said to be the largest animals on land."

"Elephant, huh?" Fecir said. He looked at the white animal with a new admiration for it, an admiration brought about by knowing something's name.

"The humans tend to call him *elefante*. I figured it means the same thing," Tarunaq said. He grinned when he saw Fecir's keen interest. "He really is something. An amazing animal."

"No kidding," was all Fecir could answer. He was at loss for words.

The man with the whip again snapped the coil, and the elephant flapped his ears and carefully lowered his hind legs back down on the ground. When they touched, the second man with the bullhook snarled fiercely and stepped behind the elephant, taking his hook and stabbing it into the behemoth's white ankle. Fecir winced at the dull smack of the hook on the creature's touch skin. The elephant gave a blatant snort and lifted his legs up again, this time placing all four on the pedestal.

"They say that elephants are from a place called Africa. They roam the yellow plains with a multitude of other creatures, animals that you'd never see here," Tarunaq went on.

"And my kind, too," Mahkuu added quietly. "The lions walked with the elephants on the African plains."

"They also say that the elephant used to be extinct."

"Extinct?" Fecir's ears perked. He suddenly remembered the list of tigers his mother had told him were extinct. "How could they be extinct if one is standing here?"

"Like I said, *used* to be extinct. Back in the time of the Endless Winter," Tarunaq elaborated. "There were no elephants around a thousand years ago. But they came back when the snow melted, along with many other creatures. The herbivore with the long neck, the laughing dog, the singing whale...."

"The giraffe, the hyena, and the humpback whale, you mean," Mahkuu defined. "Also from Africa."

The black jaguar ignored him. "Some even say that the Siberian tiger is making a comeback," he said with a smile, "returning from the dead."

"Really? The tigers are coming back?" Fecir turned around to look the old jag in the eyes, to see if he was being truthful.

Tarunaq nodded gravely. "As winter is death, spring is birth. Perhaps that is why the animals that died during the Winter are coming back. But hey, these were only rumors. No one is sure that the tiger is coming back. But I'll believe that the animals are reviving. Elefante over there is living proof, isn't he?"

"Yes. I guess he is," Fecir said ponderingly, turning away. His eyes darkened as he became lost in thought, watching as the elephant slowly twirled around in a circle atop his pedestal. At the end of the movement, he raised his head and opened his jaws, lifting one foot into the air and letting out a long, droning groan. The whip cracked, and the elephant released the position and stepped off the water tub.

"He really is amazing," Fecir commented in wonder.

"He is quite something. See that nose of his? He can use it like a man's hand. I've seen it. I've even see him open cages," Tarunaq blabbered. "And his tusks are strong enough to stab holes through metal. He's a really powerful animal, but what I don't understand is why he doesn't use what the Star Lords gave him."

"What's that?" Fecir asked.

"His strength. You see how big he is. He could step on a human and squash him like an insect. He could use his tusks to impale a man, his trunk to squeeze the air out of their lungs. But he never uses them." Tarunaq's eyes grew dark and he bared his teeth, suddenly angry. A low growl started deep within his throat. Fecir's ears flattened.

"He never fights back. That's what bothers me," the black cat spat. "He's the strongest of all the circus animals, yet he's the most pathetic one here. He has never bared tooth or raised trunk against Man. He has never roared or bellowed at them. Even with all they do to him, he never tries to defend himself. It's sickening."

The black jaguar began to cough and hack again. Fecir turned to look at him in confusion, watching as the old cat gasped for breath. When he was done, his yellow eyes opened again, and the glowing orbs were bitter and hard.

"You asked me what happens here at the circus," he said, his acid voice seething with some intense inner anger, kept at bay only by his gritted teeth. "You asked me what we do here. Well, look at the elephant. Look at what he's doing. Look at what Man is making him do."

Slowly, uncertainly, Fecir turned back with ears still flat against his head. He watched the white elephant slowly walk around the pedestal, heading back toward the opening in the tent. As he walked, the whip snapped behind him, and the man with the bullhook repeatedly jabbed his back legs to keep him moving. The elephant's eyes narrowed slightly with each raw stab, yet he did little more than grumble in pain as the man drove him out of the ring.

"The humans control us here," Tarunaq said behind him. "And that is how they do it. Pain is our tutor, our warden, and we must all suffer at the hands of Man. He will force us all to perform, one way or another. He will kick, stab, electrocute, and murder, all for his own sick, twisted pleasure. That is what the circus is. That is what happens here."

Fecir let these words sink in, as the elephant wandered out of the ring without putting up any sort of a fight. The two men followed him out, and they could still hear the whip cracking outside the tent, and the elephant's guttural groans. Fecir couldn't help but feel deeply sorry for the majestic creature.

Tarunaq grunted and turned away, curling his lip up over his teeth. "Disgusting," he growled darkly, before lying down to sleep.

Fecir continued to stare out at the ring for a long, long time.

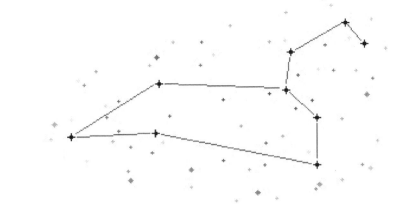

Chapter 15

Bullhook

That night, Fecir's nightmares returned again for the first time in three years. And they returned with a vengeance.

In his cage beneath the red and white tent, he writhed on the hard floor. His lips growled and curled over his teeth, and his paws twitched and jerked. Groaning and whimpering, he rolled over onto his back, as a strange yet somewhat familiar voice echoed in his dreams.

"Savior!" the warped voice called. "Savior!"

"Who's there?" Fecir asked sleepily.

He could see nothing but darkness, only hear his surroundings. Behind that strange voice were more voices, fainter and more distant. They sounded like they were moaning in agony.

"The savior!" the voice cried out again. "He comes! He comes!"

"Who's saying that?" Fecir asked again, but no answer came to him. The moaning continued in the background, and Fecir couldn't stop thinking that somehow he knew that strange voice. He'd heard it somewhere before, heard those exact words, but he couldn't remember where.

"He'll come!" the voice continued. "He'll save us all!"

"Who?" Fecir growled, becoming angry. "Who's coming? Save us from what?"

"He'll free us! When the full spring comes, he'll free us!"

"Who!" Fecir demanded.

"The white cat!" the voice answered. "Trust him and he'll come!"

Suddenly, Fecir remembered where he had heard that voice. It was the voice of the preaching jag, the one he'd heard during his short time in the Dark Place. He remembered the cat now, pacing around his cage, shouting to anyone that would listen to him, trying desperately to spread some hope. Fecir remembered.

"Trust him!"

"Wake up!"

Fecir was suddenly jolted awake by a sharp pain in his thigh. He leaped up with a snarl. His threat earned him another sharp poke, as his eyes found the face of a man standing outside his cage, looking at him. He bared his teeth at the man's cold stare.

The man's voice was gruff, and as equally cold as his eyes. He held in his hand the same sharp hook that he had used on the white elephant. As Fecir snarled and flattened his ears, the man stuck the hook between the bars and jabbed him with it. Fecir jumped up and began to pace around angrily.

"Come on, you cat," the man growled. Suddenly a part of the cage behind Fecir lifted away, revealing an opening to a chain link chute. Fecir froze when he heard the loud clang of the door lifting away, but a sharp stab at his rump made him roar and leap into the chute.

"Get going! Go! ¡Vas!" the man snarled, waving the bullhook as he ran around the cage to stand by the chute. Fecir flattened his ears and hissed at him as the man banged the top of the chute with the hook. Fecir growled and trotted down the chute, afraid and not knowing where it led, yet forced onward by the harassment of the hook.

The chute led to another ring in another ten, one with a high metal cage around it. A man stood in the middle of the ring – the man with the whip, and he uncurled the coil and snapped it menacingly. Fecir backed away, growling, not wanting to run into the ring, but a sharp bang on the chute was enough persuasion to cause him to leap out of the chute and into the ring.

The gateway to the chute was closed, leaving Fecir trapped in the ring with the man and his whip. The jaguar quickly found a corner and crouched into it, curling his tail and baring his teeth. He was frightened of that weapon, as the man continued to snap it, walking closer to him. He didn't know what the whip would do, but its loud crack made him shudder in fear. He shrank farther and farther into the corner as the man came closer and closer.

Too close. When he made a step too far, Fecir decided that his corner wasn't safe. Leaping away from the corner, he ran to the other side of the ring, hugging the chain link wall. In response, the man gave a loud shout and raised the whip above his head. With a crack, he brought the whip down, aiming it at the jaguar. Fecir yelped when he felt a sharp pain in the middle of his back, and a cut opened up above his spine.

He went sprawling, for he hadn't expected the pain. As he struggled to get up, the whip snapped again, and another sharp pain in his shoulder made him screech. A few drops of blood dripped onto the dusty floor.

"Get up, *gato*," the whip-man snarled, raising the coil above his head again. "*¡Levantense, ahora!*

The whip snapped again. What were they doing to him? Fecir couldn't understand. They were hurting him, but what had he done wrong? Never had Sandra raised a hand to him, never had she purposefully tried to hurt him. Never had he ever been abused in this way. Why? He couldn't understand. He moaned in pain.

Then, just moments after it began, it was over. The gateway to the chute opened again, and the man rolled up the whip. He stepped aside to the cage wall, allowing a clear path to the chute. At first, Fecir hesitated, unsure of what to do, wondering if maybe he was being tested. He watched the whip-man with careful, wary eyes for several seconds, neither of them making a sound.

The second man with the bullhook, who had been standing outside the cage, shouted loudly, jabbing the hook through the chain links. With a snarl, Fecir leaped up and shot into the chute. He ran down the corridor all the way back to his cage. There, he leaped onto the concrete and lay there, panting, his eyes watching and his ears back, a threatening growl prepared in the base of his throat. With a clang, the door closed, locking him out of the chute, and returning him permanently to his small confinement once again.

Fecir was quiet for a long time, still watching for the men, until he realized that they had gone. He finally breathed a sigh of relief, and twisted his neck around to examine himself. His bout with the whip had left several bleeding cut on his back and shoulders. He quickly began to lick the wounds, stemming the blood flow with his rough tongue.

"You okay, Fecir?"

The voice startled him. He leaped away, smashing his back against the ceiling of his cage. He pressed against the bars, shivering and hissing hysterically.

"Take it easy, Fecir! I'm not here to hurt you," Tarunaq said in a calm voice. His eyes were just as wide as Fecir's, for he, too, had been startled by the outburst. He hadn't expected Fecir to be so skittish.

Fecir instantly calmed down when he saw that it was only Tarunaq talking to him. He breathed a sigh of relief. "You scared me," he said breathlessly.

"*You* scared *me*," Tarunaq retorted. "Are you okay?"

"No," Fecir said, his voice still shaking. "I'm bleeding. What the heck happened in there? Why were they cutting me with the whip?"

"They were trying to break you," Tarunaq said calmly. "It happens to everyone when they first arrive."

"Why? I don't understand. What did I do wrong?"

"You did nothing wrong, Fecir. This is just how Man does things around here. They were trying to kill your spirit and make you fear them, that way you'd more readily obey their commands."

Fecir thought back to Sandra, how she rewarded him for performing his tricks well. He had been trained using positive reinforcement. This abusive mastership was entirely alien to him, and he fought to understand it. "But why? Why do they hurt us? Why not teach us a trick and reward us when we do it?"

"Because they know that we are so much stronger than they are, that we can easily kill them if we really wanted to," Tarunaq explained, stretching out his legs to lie down. "By beating us, they create the mindset that *they* are stronger than *us*, that if we tried to hurt them, it would only hurt us more. It's reassurance for them, but torture for us."

Fecir's ears flattened as he began to understand this horrid method. Tarunaq rested his chin on his paws, watching Mahkuu pace around his cage.

"We've all had our spirits broken," he said quietly. "Even Mahkuu over there. Man knows that he could hurt them, but he doesn't because they broke him when he was just a cub. And the same with me. We grew up abused, always kept in line by whip or bullhook. Though we talk of rebelling against Man, we know that nobody will ever try. We all fear Man's power too much to ever rise against him."

Fecir listened gravely, looking out at Mahkuu and wondering about him. His first impression of the lion had been of scorn – he had originally thought of him as just a bully, angry at the world for no reason at all. But now, he could see why Mahkuu was vicious. His childhood had been written in letters of his own blood.

Fecir whimpered, a terrible fear suddenly striking his heart. He knew that if he were to stay at the circus, eventually he would end up just like Tarunaq and Mahkuu – spiritless, angry, and miserable. He pined for his home with Sandra now more than ever. He wanted to feel safe and warm again in her arms.

"I want to go home," he said sadly.

"This is your home now," Tarunaq growled, lifting his head. "Whether you like it or not, you live here. Whoever your master was before, he's probably done with you, or else you would've never ended up here."

"That's not true!" Fecir growled. "Sandra loves me."

"Humans cannot love us cats," Tarunaq snarled harshly. "You will learn that here. If she truly loved you, do you really think she would've sent you here, to be beaten?"

"She loves me," Fecir said firmly, refusing to believe him. His eyes suddenly darkened as the image of the white kitten jumped into his mind. He growled deep in his throat and bared his teeth slightly in hatred for the tiny kitten that stole his Sandra away from him.

"It's all his fault," he whispered to himself. "He made her betray me. He stole her from me. It's all his fault."

Tarunaq grumbled and rolled onto his side, letting out a few tired coughs and clearing his throat. "They will probably try to break you again later on," he sighed. "They'll keep whipping you until you learn to fear them, until they know that they can control you. Until the mere sight of the bullhook makes you whimper and beg for mercy. So be prepared, Fecir. They'll be back." The old cat closed his eyes and slept.

Fecir sat up and stared blankly for a long time, thinking about what Tarunaq had said. He kept repeating to himself that Sandra loved him, but after a while he wasn't so sure of himself. And so he created a plan in his mind to find out if the black jaguar was telling the truth about humans. The first chance that comes, Fecir would escape, and find his way back to Sandra.

Over the next couple of days, a routine began to form for Fecir, just as there was a routine with Sandra. Every morning, the animals were fed – the cat's received only half a pound of meat per day. Fecir began to lose weight quickly on his reduced diet, and he found himself feeling hungry at all hours. His stomach, which was not accustomed to the smaller portion sizes, growled incessantly, and Fecir suffered from it.

About an hour after food was given, Fecir would be once again forced into the ring to undergo torture by whip and hook. These sessions normally lasted no more than ten minutes, and always left Fecir bleeding and terrified. These sessions would occur up to six times a day, and under the constant stress and pain, Fecir was broken by day three.

After he was deemed broken, the men began to train with him. Remembering some of the tricks that Sandra had taught him and using some of the same verbal commands, they worked him to get him ready for show. When Fecir refused to perform a command, he was beaten until he complied, until his spirit broke again. Most of the tricks he performed were acrobatic – walking on a beam, jumping from platform to platform, and leaping through hoops were the three most practiced tricks.

Eventually, as he became used to the whip and the training method, though he continued to hate every minute of it, the other cats began to join him in the caged ring for sessions. When Tarunaq and Mahkuu entered the ring from the chute, there was an instant change in both of them. Calm, wise Tarunaq became savage and angry at the sight of the whip, hissing and snarling and constantly being beaten for his threats.

Mahkuu, on the other hand, turned into a sniveling kitten, quiet and shy unless the whip was turned on him. He carried out orders to the best he could, trying desperately to avoid punishment, and only upon returning to his cage did he finally let his vicious nature show, only talking tough when Man wasn't around to hear him.

During the time between training sessions, the few men working for the circus usually ignored the cats, as they spent their time licking their wounds, pacing, or sleeping. At different times throughout the day, the other circus animals were either driven or led into the cage-less ring to be trained with as well, as the cats watched them from their cages. These animals received the exact same abuse, even the two boarder horses, who had to be re-broken after their time with Sandra.

There were many different animals at the circus that Fecir saw. These included several monkeys, a few small-breed dogs, one black bear, the horses, two zebras, and the white elephant. Fecir saw him most often, for he was chained inside the ring when it wasn't in use. He was too big to fit inside a cage or stall, and so was kept in one place by a tight chain around his front left leg that was staked deep into the dirt.

Fecir often found himself staring at the white elephant, watching as he rocked back and forth on his tree-trunk legs, rocking for several hours and swaying his trunk. This behavior was stereotypical of elephants, apparently, and he did this so often that when he was made to move again, he rocked as he was walking, once stumbling and nearly falling over after spending more than a day chained to the stake.

The giant creature, just like all the animals, also suffered at the end of the bullhook and whip, but a curious thing that Fecir noticed was that his white skin bore no marks of abuse. Though the elephant was stabbed many times, Fecir never saw his blood stain his white skin. It was a strange thing indeed, and at once it reminded him of something his mother had once said, about how a spirit could not bleed. But Fecir eventually put off the thought, telling himself that the elephant just had really thick skin.

Thick skin, and a very large brain, Fecir would later add. Within his first week of watching the white elephant, he learned of the creature's unique intelligence. He saw this intelligence firsthand one morning, when Man wasn't around. The elephant made sure no one was watching, then carefully pulled the stake out of the ground, freeing his chain and allowing him to roam as he pleased about the ring. And roám he did, moving in circles around the perimeter of the ring, stretching his sore legs after hours of standing still. After he had thoroughly stretched, he returned to the exact spot he had been standing in and replaced the stake back into the ground. And there the giant stood, once again rocking on his legs, a majestic creature reduced to a prisoner.

After a few days of watching this sad animal allow all this kind of abuse on himself, Fecir began to adopt Tarunaq's mindset, that the giant was pathetic. He looked upon the beast with scorn, seeing him as a magnificent animal, capable of doing many things – defending himself included – and yet does nothing but stand there and rock. Fecir soon found himself turning away from the sorrowful sight of elephant rocking, and abhorring him for his broken spirit.

For the most part, during Fecir's first week at the circus, the giant completely ignored him, and Fecir was content with that. But something did continually bother him about the creature – he felt like he had seen him somewhere before. The years of living a quiet life with Sandra had blurred his memory of the jungle a bit, and so Fecir could not remember where he might have seen the white elephant. This puzzled him greatly, as he stared at the white giant all day, wondering about him.

The everyday routine remained the same throughout the week. But things would change, however, when the first show came around. Fecir did not perform in this show. All of the other animals did, including Tarunaq and Mahkuu, but Fecir was still new, and thus still, for the most part, "untrained". Therefore, in order to still make a profit off of him, he was put on display, and crowds of people came to stare at him in his cage. Fecir couldn't help but be reminded of his days at the Adoption Center, and once again, he wished the eyes would go away.

When the show began, the people dispersed to find seats, and Mahkuu and Tarunaq were taken by chute to the caged ring. Fecir could hear the music and the crowd cheering, and, during times of silence, Mahkuu's mighty roar that brought about cries of joy and awe. The noise and loud music lasted for what seemed like an eternity. After a long, twenty minute act, the cats were finally allowed to come back to their cages, and both were too exhausted to speak. Tarunaq ended up in a coughing fit that lasted for several minutes.

At the end of the first show, as soon as all the guests had left, Fecir also experienced his first "move". The tents above him were taken down, and the fabric was folded into giant squares and loaded up onto the boxcars of a train. The animals, too, and the people were put into cars to be transported via train. The cats' cages were lifted up onto wheels and rolled up the ramp onto their designated car, while the train engine at the end of the line whistled and belched out steam. Fecir was the last to be loaded.

Before his cage was wheeled up the ramp, he noticed the white elephant being loaded onto a boxcar a few cars down the line, nearer to the engine. As he watched the elephant rocking on its legs and swaying its head, waiting to be loaded, their eyes suddenly locked, and dark brown found bright yellow. Though for only a second their eyes had met, it seemed that the elephant was reassured somehow, and it stopped swaying just before the men came around to load him into his car.

Fecir also seemed a bit reassured by those warm brown eyes, though he didn't know why. As soon as the spell between them had broken, he'd curled his lip in disgust of the giant, as the pathetic animal allowed himself to be stabbed and forced around. With heavy chains on all four of his legs, the elephant stepped slowly up the ramp, the bullhook driving him on. Fecir was loaded up after, and an hour after being loaded, the train released a loud, high-pitched, shrieking blast of steam. The boxcars jerked forward, and the train began to move, taking the animals far away from anything they had grown used to. And Fecir was taken farther away from Sandra.

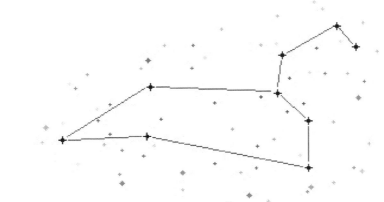

Chapter 16

Promise

Immediate chaos followed their arrival at their new location.

The cats had been traveling for several days without making many stops. The boxcar was hot and reeked of manure, and water was hard to come by, and so the cats sweated and panted in the heat. It was just like the Dark Place, Fecir decided, only not as loud.

When the train finally came to a screeching halt that lasted more than an hour, the cats knew that they had reached their destination. The sliding doors opened, and the men came in to wheel the cages down the ramp. The tents were set up, and the cages pushed inside. The animals were fed, and once all the equipment had been set up and everything has been taken care of, things finally began to settle down to silence.

Except for Tarunaq. In their short time together so far, Fecir had noticed that the black cat's coughing spasms had become progressively worse, lasting longer and leaving him constantly out of breath. The coughs sounded watery, and he often had to clear his throat. And he no longer sat quietly without a tendril of drool hanging from his jaws.

A couple days after the tents were again set up and the cats had resumed their training sessions, the old jaguar began giving off a peculiar smell. Fecir couldn't explain the scent – it was faint but distinctly vile, and it wafted straight from Tarunaq's skin. It was incredibly distracting during the training sessions, for he smelled so strange that both Mahkuu and Fecir went out of their way to avoid him in the ring, if the whip-man allowed it. And at night, the horrible scent haunted Fecir's dreams.

A change was coming over the old black cat. Fecir and Mahkuu could plainly see it. His eyes were no longer cheerful, and he snarled less often during training sessions, as if his heart was no longer beating for defiance. His movements were becoming slow, and he was beaten more often for stopping to cough. The smell became increasingly worse, and Tarunaq increasingly distant.

His spasms just kept getting worse. Soon the trainers could no longer work with him, because he hacked and gagged all the time. He began to vomit mucus in his cage, and when he slept his breathing was shallow and ragged. Neither Mahkuu nor Fecir could explain this odd change that had come over their friend. The change progressed so much that Tarunaq lost his voice and could no longer speak, and he stopped caring or listening to things around him. He even stopped curling his lip when he saw the white elephant enter the practice ring – he now just looked on blankly, as if the giant wasn't there at all.

He stopped eating. He slept all the time. He woke himself coughing. He drooled. His eyes dulled. He wouldn't drink. And the smell became worse and worse, to the point where even the humans could smell it. They began to avoid Tarunaq, refusing to go near his cage for more than the time it took to through cuts of meat at his paws.

Fecir was worried about his friend. Though he had only known Tarunaq for a few days, he had become attached to the cheerful jag. Having not been around his own kind for so long, he felt a physical need to be near to the cat, to have his elder comfort and lead him – like his mother would've done as he grew older. The black cat was a like a fatherly figure to him – a grandfather would be more accurate, but a figure of guidance nonetheless. And so, one afternoon, he spoke to Tarunaq in a deeply concerned voice.

"Tarunaq," he said quietly. He was hesitant to speak at first, for the old jag was asleep. But he mustered up his courage to speak louder. "Tarunaq, wake up."

The cat's ears twitched, and he lifted his head, looking up at Fecir dully. He said nothing.

Fecir looked on, in awe and wonder, at the shriveled old animal before him. He was not the same cat he met when he first woke in his cage. Looking at him curiously, he whispered, "What has happened to you?"

The jaguar continued to stare, his grayish-yellow eyes looking past Fecir. Then, with a low moan of despair, Tarunaq dropped his head and let it loll on the concrete, a few short coughs shaking his body before closing his eyes and letting sleep take over.

Fecir watched him for a long time. He knew, somewhere deep in his heart, that something was desperately wrong with Tarunaq. He couldn't understand it, but the cat was sick. His lungs were filled with infection that labored his breathing and drowned his throat with drool. Tarunaq was dying.

The next morning, when Fecir awoke to the sound of the men moving around the tents, and the elephant snorted as usual when pulled from his dreams, he opened his eyes and looked over at Tarunaq, who lay on his side in his cage, unmoving. At first, Fecir stared for a while, thinking that the old cat was just sleeping, but when he looked closer, he saw that his eyes were open and staring coldly upwards, and that his sides were not rising and falling with the steady rhythm that indicates breath. There was a spatter of blood around the black jaguar's jaws.

Tarunaq was dead.

At first, Fecir didn't want to believe it. He stuck his paw through the bars and gently nudged the cat's leg. "Hey," he whispered. "Wake up. Hey Tarunaq, get up."

The cat's limbs were already rigid. He had been lying dead for hours, staring with wide eyes out at the world beyond his cage.

Fecir growled, nudging him harder. "Wake up!" he snarled. "Wake up, you lazy old cat! Wake up!"

He continued to push on the dead animal, trying desperately to make him open his eyes. He knew that it was no use, that his words were a lost cause. But still, he refused to believe that his friend was gone. After already having lost his mother and Sandra, losing another parental figure was almost too much to bear. Angrily, he shoved the rigid cat so hard that he heard a snap – the sound of Tarunaq's frail bones breaking beneath the force of his shove. Tears began to stream down Fecir's face.

"Wake up!" he roared in agony.

His roar woke the heavily sleeping Mahkuu. His head jolted up with a snarl, and his eyes narrowed when he saw Fecir crying. He was about to scorn the young jaguar, growl a threat to him that if he didn't shut up he'd rip his ears off, or something along those lines, but then he noticed the black jaguar lying motionless and staring off into space. The old cat's eyes no longer had the light of life in them. The lion's anger and annoyance melted into pity.

He heard the cry of the young jaguar, and, even though he had scorned Tarunaq throughout their time together, he too felt a sharp pain in his heart. He let a low whimper escape his throat, as he watched Fecir's desperate attempts at making the dead return to life.

"Please wake up!" He was pleading now. "Don't leave! Please wake up!"

He hooked his claws into the old cat's broken leg and dragged him closer. Mahkuu immediately stood up, barking in alarm.

"Don't!" he said quickly, and Fecir's eyes narrowed on him. The lion stood his ground.

"Don't touch him. Don't do anything to him," Mahkuu threatened coldly. "Just … let him rest awhile. Let him sleep."

"He is dead." Fecir's eyes blurred with tears.

"Yeah, I know. But he's in a better place now. He's hunting with Panthera, chasing the comets in the night sky. He is young again," the lion said gravely. He seemed wise now, older, and more mature than ever before. "Just leave him be, okay? He's lived a long and hard life. The least he deserves is not to be disturbed. You understand that, right?"

Fecir sniffed. "Yes."

The lion nodded. "Don't worry. He's better now. He's in a better place."

Fecir nodded and turned away, pondering this for a while and fighting to control his sobs. After a while, Man came around with the feeding bucket, and as he tossed in bits of meat into the cages, he stopped and saw the dead, staring eyes. He stared for a while and then shook his head in disappointment. A little while later, three men came, and then opened the cage and took the body away, out the opening and into the sunlight. Mahkuu watched Tarunaq leaved, but Fecir closed his eyes, the image of his and his mother's eyes haunting his thoughts. He shuddered uncontrollably.

Fecir and Mahkuu were still made to train, even with Tarunaq absent. Fecir was beaten more severely, for his thoughts were elsewhere the entire session. He was grieving, mourning the loss of a good friend, and though the fact that he was being punished for his emotion bothered him, at that point he simply did not care. He was distant and disobeying up until the chute finally opened back up, and he returned to his cage. And the empty cage next to his was still stained with the blood spatter of Tarunaq's last dying cough.

Mahkuu was quiet that whole day – he was mourning as well, for he had been raised with Tarunaq. Though the black jag was much older than he was, he had known him all his life, and had even looked up to him, though his words contradicted his feelings. He did not pace or growl or snarl once that day – just sat and looked at the empty cage with dull eyes, seemingly in a daze, and mourning quietly in his heart for the black jaguar.

That night, as Mahkuu slept and the yellow lights were dimmer than normal, Fecir found that he could not sleep. He lay with his head on his paws, trying to force himself into unconsciousness, but he was restless. And so he sat up, glaring out at the world with his yellow eyes, unable to think of anything anymore, except for Sandra.

It had been about two weeks since she gave him away, and yet he still loved her. Her motherly touch haunted his dreams, and her singing voice during their times on the swing set echoed throughout the day. He longed to go back to her, even if it meant meeting the white cat face to face – the kitten that stole his Sandra from him.

Fecir bared his fangs. He couldn't stand to think of that horrible cat. How it could just waltz right in and steal Sandra's heart. Who did it think it was? He absolutely loathed that disgusting white cub. But after all that had happened to him, he just wanted to go back to someplace safe. If he had to bunk with the strange white kitten, he figured he'd get used to it. If only he could get out of his cage and escape.

He looked at the lock on the metal door. It was a padlock, requiring a key to open. For a while he chewed on it, trying to figure out how to make it unlock, without any success. And so he resigned to pacing in agitated circles, eyes glowing furiously, glittering in the dim.

There was a sound. Fecir froze, and looked toward the practice ring. The sound had come from the tent opening on the side of the ring. Fecir watched that opening, that dark square of outside world, when suddenly a giant white foot stepped into view.

The white elephant carefully shouldered his way through the narrow opening, holding his stake and chains in the wrap of his trunk. He stepped quietly into the ring and stopped for a moment, flapping his ears and blinking in the light. His deep breathing was the only sound heard.

Fecir curled his lip and turned away. *What's* he *doing here?* he thought quietly, growling in disgust. *Stupid animal.*

The elephant flapped his ears a few more times, looking around. He spotted Fecir's cage and stepped quietly toward it. When the giant animal was close enough to reach out and touch the cage, Fecir turned back around. His eyes widened at the proximity of the giant, and with a hiss he jumped to his feet and backed away to the rear of his cage. The elephant just stared.

Fecir eyed him cautiously, hardly daring to breathe, as the elephant searched for his eyes. Fecir snarled then, showing his teeth.

"You," he growled angrily, narrowing his eyes.

The elephant stood quietly with his ears spread wide.

"What do you want, you pathetic beast?" Fecir snarled scornfully. "You've never approached me before. Why did you come in here?"

The elephant just stared, barely moving at all.

Fecir scoffed and turned away. "Stupid, disgusting animal. Go back outside where you belong."

Elephant still remained silent. Then, slowly, carefully, it unrolled its trunk, laying the chains and the metal stake quietly on the dusty ground. Then it was still again, content to stare at the jaguar forever with his strange brown eyes.

Fecir bared his teeth and unsheathed his claws. "Did you not hear me?" he snarled, his voice rising in pitch. "I said go, you coward. Go away and leave me alone." He turned away again, not wanting to look at the sad, weak elephant. He looked directly into Tarunaq's cage, looked directly at the blood that still stained the cold concrete. His eyes began to tear up, and he hung his head in grief.

The elephant finally broke his silence. From his throat came a strange, almost purring sound, a thrumming groan that was calming to both him and to Fecir. Fecir's ears instantly perked, and he turned around, staring curiously at the giant's face. He'd heard that sound before.

He squinted, trying to remember, trying to recall where he'd heard that sound before. As he scrutinized the elephant's face, it reached up slowly with its trunk and fondled the golden tassels hanging from his headdress. It was then that Fecir's eyes lit up. He remembered.

"You're the white giant, aren't you?" he whispered in awe. "The one from when I was a cub?"

The elephant lowered his trunk and slowly nodded his head. He flapped his ears and shifted his weight over. Fecir looked down at his paws, suddenly embarrassed.

"I ... I'd forgotten about you," he admitted. "I had tried to help you. And then ... something happened. I don't remember what, but I ran away. I ran away and left you behind, abandoned you to the trees."

The white giant purred slowly, soothingly, as he fondled his headdress.

Fecir looked up and smiled sadly. "But I see you got away. You were able to break the rope, weren't you? That's a good thing."

A low rumbled came from the white animal's throat as he shifted his weight again. He started to rock from side to side, swaying his head slightly, as was so incredibly common of him.

Both were silent for a very long time, as they listened to Mahkuu growl in his sleep, snoring loudly. Eventually, Fecir broke the spell.

"You did something to me," he said, almost accusingly. "Back then, when I met you in the forest. You did something to me that made me run away. What did you do?"

The elephant stopped rocking and was still. Then, without making a sound, it slowly lifted its trunk. It carefully snaked its way between the bars of the cage, moving hesitantly toward Fecir's left forepaw. Fecir eyed it cautiously but did not move away. The white giant blinked its eyes, then lightly touched Fecir's toes with the tip of its trunk.

Fecir's eyes went wide, and his chest instantly seized. His neck curled backward and his mouth dropped open. A wave of images suddenly entered his mind and started flashing right before his eyes.

He heard the roar of thunder and saw the flash of lightning. He saw rain pattering onto the green jungle leaves as they rustled in the howling wind. He saw a rope tied to a tree, a rope that was chewed halfway through. Rain had softened the remaining tendrils of coil, and when it was pulled taught, the whole line snapped in half, and the tree moved away, fading into darkness.

The images released Fecir, and he gasped loudly for breath. His fur bristled and his eyes were wide. His head started to throb dully. After a few hard breaths, the jaguar looked up at the elephant, and his yellow eyes were met by warm brown.

"Is that ... is that what you did?" he said between gasps.

With a low grumble, the elephant nodded gravely.

Fecir took a moment to catch his breath, before straightening his back and sitting up tall. He looked the giant directly in the eye, and his face was nothing less than confident in the gaze of the strange white beast.

"Now I remember," Fecir said softly. "I remember that you did that to me, and I was scared. I ran away from you. But I'm not scared anymore. I know you. And I know that you didn't try to hurt me back then, just like you didn't hurt me now." Fecir paused and flattened his ears. "All these years, when I could remember you, I thought that you had broken our promise. But now I realize that *I* broke the deal. *I* ran away. I didn't help you, and for that, I am sorry."

The elephant purred and flapped his ears. His voice seemed forgiving and it soothed Fecir.

For a while both of them were silent again. Fecir looked around for a bit, as the elephant just stared and rocked back and forth. He noticed the elephant's blood-red headdress, smelled the sharp metallic scent that covered the familiar grassland smell of the giant's skin. His lip curled up a little bit.

"It's funny, isn't it?" he asked. "That we would both end up meeting each other again? Only this time we meet in Man's realm. I guess not even a strong elephant like you can outrun Man's rage."

The elephant slowly shook his head back and forth. He then tilted his head back and opened his mouth, revealing the massive molars in his jaws. Fecir flattened his ears, until he saw something wedged in the elephant's cheek. It was small and shiny. With a growl, the elephant reached his trunk in and carefully plucked it out. He closed his mouth, then held up the object for Fecir to see.

It was a small metal rod, with an oddly shaped, flattened end to it. It was the key to his cage.

"Where did you get that?" Fecir growled in amazement. He had seen Man use that key on his padlock before. That key would open the door to his cage, allow him to go free. He stared in shock, wondering as to how such a massive animal could steal and hide such an object.

The elephant groaned softly, twisting his trunk and delicately inserting the key into the padlock. He jiggled it and turned it clockwise, and the padlock clicked. The elephant then carefully slid the golden lock off of the metal bars. The door creaked open slightly.

    Fecir stared at the open door in astonishment. He looked at the elephant, then at the door, then back at the elephant. He was completely at loss for words. He just stared as the white giant hid the padlock in his cheek and stepped back, dragging the chains with him, allowing Fecir room to jump down.

    "You're...," Fecir breathed in astonishment. "You're ... helping me escape?"

    The elephant groaned, flapping his ears like wings and nodding his head.

    "I don't understand," Fecir shook his head. "Why are you doing this for me?"

    With a sigh, the elephant stepped forward again. He lifted his nose and touched it to Fecir's paw. Fecir prepared himself as another blast of images came to him. In a flash, he saw, through the giant's eyes, that fateful day when they first met, and he saw himself, the rambunctious cub, stepping forward to chew through the rope. He saw the rope cut half-through, with tendrils hanging off of it, the coil thin and feeble. The image then skipped ahead to later that night, to the thunderstorm, and Fecir once again saw the rope snap in half.

Fecir's vision quickly swam back. "I see," Fecir growled. "An eye for an eye. I helped you escape, so now you're helping me."

The elephant nodded and stepped back again. Fecir stepped toward the door and pushed it open with his head. Then he jumped down to the dusty floor, where the white giant towered over him, flapping his ears.

Fecir smiled up at him gratefully. "Thank you."

The elephant purred, then reach out with his trunk one last time. He touched Fecir lightly on the shoulder, and there was a flash of white light. He saw, in this final vision, a great orange cat lying on her side, and snow stretching out to all horizons. He saw her body decomposing, and from her flesh sprouted tiny little buds of life. They were flowers – the first flowers of spring, growing on the dead body of a tigress

The image instantly jumped away, and Fecir saw what looked like a white tiger with stunning blue eyes. As he watched, the tiger's body started to morph. A new creature took its place – a smaller animal, one with a bigger head and a stronger jaws, and powerful forelegs. Black stripes morphed into cinnamon rosettes, and the eyes turned bright green. The white tiger had turned into a white jaguar.

The images vanished, and Fecir looked up at the white giant in confusion, as the animal retracted its trunk and lifted it up to fondle the golden tassels once again. Warm brown eyes met Fecir's yellow ones, and the jaguar's brow furrowed.

"I don't understand," he whispered. "What were you trying to tell me?"

The elephant made no sound. Gently, it wrapped its trunk around the stake and chains on the ground. It lifted them up and started to turn around.

"Won't you answer me?" Fecir growled.

The white giant stopped and flapped its ears. It turned its head back to look at Fecir one last time. Then, still without making a sound, it turned and walked slowly back to the ring. It stepped toward the opening in the tent and disappeared through it. Fecir watched him go, and stared after the white giant for a long time.

There was a loud, tired yawn beside him. Fecir started and looked up at the cage to his right. Mahkuu smacked his lips and blinked open his weary eyes, looking around himself strangely. He saw Fecir on the ground and leaped to his feet.

"You!" he snarled. "How did ... how did you get out?"

Fecir did not know what to say to him. He didn't know how to explain that the white giant had freed him. So instead, he simply turned and started padding toward the exit.

"Hey, wait!" Mahkuu roared, pawing the bars. "What about us? What about the rest of us stuck here? Please don't go!"

Fecir stopped at the tent opening, turned and looked back at the vicious lion. Mahkuu's eyes burned with rage, and he bared his yellow teeth.

"You coward!" he snarled hysterically, foaming at the mouth. "You wretched mongrel!"

Fecir simply smiled and stepped out into the darkness of night. As he walked away from the giant circus tent, heading toward the brush and trees, he heard the lion roaring after him, his voice growing fainter and fainter as Fecir moved deeper and deeper into the shadows.

"Panthera comes! Save us! Save us all!"

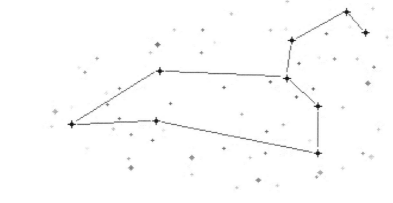

Chapter 17

Chak

Fecir trekked his way through the trees and their shadows, putting as much distance as he could between him and the circus as possible. His paws padded over soft jungle floor and he dodged vines and leaves as he trotted in darkness. His eyes, glowing bright yellow, illuminated the night for him, guided his way beneath the moonless sky. He had only one thing on his mind: Sandra.

It felt strange to him, to feel the rotting leaves between his toes once more after over three years. Strange, yet pleasant as well. He had missed this feeling, the soft whisper of vegetation as he passed through them, the endless music of birdsong and bug chatter.

As he ran, he did not once look back. He didn't dare stop to see the towering circus tent slowly fading into darkness behind him. That part of his life was over now. That part of his life was a memory. That part of his life was nothing but ancient history.

Sandra, though. She wasn't a memory. Fecir had to find her. His heart yearned for her, yearned to find out if she had really loved him. Yearned to see if she would take him back, if she would let him lie atop the swing set and grace him with her sweet, angelic voice once more.

The Star Lords watched over him as the jaguar moved through the night. His elusive instinct, having long been suppressed by the bounds of captivity and Man, was subconsciously resurfacing, and the cat made sure that he was hidden in the shadows, as he moved in the direction he hoped was right, he hoped would lead him to Sandra.

Many animals saw Fecir as he moved past them. A blur of shadow, he was, and the shadow frightened the forest creatures. And they should be frightened, for the jaguar was the king of the jungle, although Fecir did not consider himself royalty. He hardly thought of himself as a magnificent beast. His mind was that of a pet, and that was why he was so drawn to the simple girl who had tamed him, who had culled the wilderness from his very blood. He needed her to survive.

He ran for a very long time, until his muscles strained to move and his tongue lolled out of his mouth. The sun was just starting to rise, banishing the darkness back to Hell where it originated. And the Star Lords faded into the growing light. Fecir found himself a small hollow at the base of a tree and curled up within it. With the daytime humidity choking the air around him, he fell into a fitful, tormented sleep.

In his dreams, he heard the calls of a white owl, felt the whisper of its silent feathers as the great bird skimmed over him. He looked up at the creature, saw its feathers silhouetted against a black sky. In its talons it carried a small, simple yellow flower. The owl wheeled away, and Fecir collapsed into a field of silver grass – the white meadow.

When Fecir woke as night was falling, he felt as if he hadn't slept at all. Hearing the calls of night birds and insects, he dragged himself out of his hollow, wincing as every muscle protested against the movement. With a growl, he shook his pelt, and continued on his trek through the night, moving in silence as was his nature, elusive and invisible to the world.

In a week's time, Fecir found himself in familiar territory. Though he still moved through jungle, he noticed that the wild smells were changing and becoming more familiar. There was a sharpness in the air, a metallic twinge when he scented the breeze. This forest belonged to Man. He was home.

Excited to see his beloved Sandra again, he bounded forward, ignoring his exhaustion and ignoring how his body demanded food. In the week it had taken him to find his way back, Fecir had survived on insects and nothing more, for he had never been taught how to hunt. He had tried though; tried his luck on egrets in ponds and streams he passed by, tried stalking capybaras and peccaries while hiding in the brush. But always his prey had spotted him before he could leap, and Fecir had to make do with butterflies and beetles.

As he raced through the quiet jungle, he soon came upon the familiar chain link fence, with the barbed wire loops at the top. He saw the yellow grasses of his home, the hill upon which the house sat, and next to it the red barn that smelled sweetly of manure. He saw the black truck in the driveway, the flower garden and the dirt path, the corral; and next to it, the swing set. He was home.

His eyes lit up and absolutely joy. He could barely contain his excitement, as he reared up and put his paws on the fence, shaking it with his weight. He huffed in his low, growling voice, coughing and roaring as jaguars do, in hopes that Sandra would hear him. She should be awake by now – it was early morning, time to feed the dogs and let them out to "do their business." She should be coming out at any moment.

Fecir waited for her, but as he sat down to watch the front door, a strange feeling suddenly came over him, and he stood up and backed away with his ears flat against his head. *What if* ...

what if she doesn't want me back? What if she sees me and turns away? What if what Tarunaq said was true? What if she never loved me?

Fecir was overcome with this new fear, this nervousness, and so he slunk back into the shadows, hiding himself among the ferns. There, he waited, watching the door, and shaking uncontrollably.

The door opened. The two dogs burst out, yelping and barking as they charged out onto the grass. They scampered over the cobblestone path and out onto the dirt, racing around behind the house to "do their business" out of sight. But on the porch, a figure stood. Fecir's eyes lit up. Sandra.

She was holding something in her arms, a little white ball it seemed. She was cradling it like a baby, and she gently rocked it back and forth. Fecir's eyes narrowed, and he growled in hatred. Not a ball. It was the white kitten. The one who stole his Sandra from him.

As he watched Sandra hold the housecat-sized cub, she suddenly stooped over and put the kitten on the porch. She said something to it, then turned towards the front door. Fecir stood up. This was his chance. All he had to do was call out to her, and he would find out her true feelings. He would find out if she would take him back. But for some reason, he hesitated, unsure of himself, and Sandra went inside the house.

Fecir snarled. He'd missed his chance. Oh well. At least it was safe to come out of hiding now. He would wait until she came out to feed the horses. Then he would call out to her. Then he would find out the truth.

As he stepped out into the open, he saw – quite suddenly – the white cub plodding over the cobblestones between the towering stalks of flowers. His giant floppy paws and scruffy ears were a signal to his young age, which appeared to be only three months, at least. He seemed healthy, having been nursed back to strength by Sandra. His white fur was glossy over his filled ribs, and his faded cinnamon rosettes shimmered in the sunlight. His bright green eyes were alert to the plants and the insects buzzing around him, and as he stepped onto the dirt path, those eyes suddenly locked onto Fecir's.

Fecir froze. The cub froze. For a moment, the two stared at each other, as they stood on opposite sides of the fence. As they stared, Fecir almost thought he heard a voice inside his head, speaking to him: *"Trust him."*

The cub broke the spell. With a happy mew, he came bounding over on his floppy paws. He dove into the tall grass and made his way over to the fence, eyes bright with glee. Fecir's lip curled slightly, as he was unsure of the cub's approach. He backed away with ears flat.

"*The savior,*" the voice said. It was the voice of memory – the memory of the preaching jag whispering into his ears. "*Trust him and he'll come.*"

"Hello!"

Fecir's ears perked up. The white cub was standing at the fence, looking up at him with his bright green. Fecir hesitated, for a moment unsure of how to respond, as he stared into those deep pools of green. Eventually he swallowed and stepped forward. "Hello."

The cub's eyes lit up in delight upon hearing Fecir's response. With a happy bark, he spun around himself and put his paws on the fence, white fur shivering with excitement.

"I'm Chak!" the cub declared joyously. "What's your name?"

Fecir hesitated again. He glanced toward the porch, but Sandra had still not returned. He looked back at the cub.

"My name's Fecir," he growled. "It's … pleasant … to meet you." He felt awkward.

"Fecir. That's the word for firefly, isn't it?" Chak mewed.

Fecir's ears perked in surprise. "How'd you know that?"

Chak looked to the side; a bit humbly, one might say. "I know a lot of words," the white cub told him with a twitch of his ear. "I know that my name means 'white' in the old language, and that your name actually has two meanings. 'Firefly' is the more common meaning, but it is also the word for safe haven. It is a very special name, in my opinion. The name of a protector, a guardian, or a messenger."

Fecir was listening intently. His ears flattened at the way the cub spoke – it was as if he were older than he actually was. He sat down, looking at the cub through the chain links, thinking him quite strange, and yet, interesting as well.

The cub turned his head back to him. "I can also tell you the names of all the Star Lords in the sky. Would you like to hear them?"

Fecir's ears perked. *All the Star Lords? Most cubs at his age couldn't name four. I can barely name more than five.*

Chak took Fecir's silence as a signal to continue. He began reciting the names off one by one. "There's Panthera, Hydra, Cancer, Corvus, Ursa Major, Ursa Minor, Cetus, Gemini, Lupus, Pheonix, Pisces...."

"Okay, I get it. No need to tell me all of them," Fecir muttered in annoyance. "You certainly know a lot for your age."

The cub giggled gleefully. Fecir had to admit that he was impressed, but he looked away. His eyes darkened as he wondered, *who is this cub?*

Chak smiled up at him, twitching his big, triangular ears. His voice suddenly became very grave and humble. "It's great to finally meet you, Fecir."

Fecir's head whipped around at the sound of his name. He looked at Chak with complete confusion. He twitched his whiskers.

"What do you mean by 'finally'?" he demanded.

Chak's ears flattened for a short moment. He said innocently, "Well, I've been waiting for you to find me. Panthera told me you would come."

"Panthera?" Fecir was alarmed for a short moment, but as he looked at the white cub, an old, dark hate starting bubbling up in his blood, replacing his surprise. Panthera, the god who had ruined his life, who had lied to him. Fecir's lips twitched as he tried not to bare his teeth. "Explain this to me."

Chak took his paws off the fence and sat down, curling his tail around him. "He came to me in a dream," he said, "and told me that someone would come to meet me very soon. He told me that it was his destiny to find me."

"And Panthera told you this?" Fecir challenged skeptically.

Chak nodded indifferently. "Yes."

"And you're saying I'm that 'someone' he told you about?"

Chak shrugged. "Well, you're here, aren't you?"

Fecir fell silent. He grunted and turned away, somewhat frustrated by this cat. *Something is wrong with him,* he decided. *Kittens should not be talking like that, shouldn't say things like what he's saying. Perhaps his mind is sick.*

The white cub continued on, ignoring how Fecir had turned away. "And I'll bet you've been visited as well," he growled. "In your dreams, as Panthera has come to mine."

"Excuse me?" Fecir whirled around, snarling.

"If you're here, that means that Panthera must've–"

"What on earth makes you think I've had dreams?" Fecir hissed furiously. "What makes you think that I'm that someone that Panthera told you about – if he told you at all?"

"He did tell me!" Chak growled defensively. "I'm not lying! He did tell me. He told me that the cat who would come to me would be the Pantheraseer, the one to bring spring, and that it was my purpose to guide him. My destiny, as it was yours to find me."

Fecir turned away, huffing in disbelief. *Who is this child to just suddenly say stuff like that? Just who does he think he is?* He gritted his teeth in anger. *He really must be deranged, the poor cub. His mind must be twisted, must be sick and dying, making him say weird things. Sad little cub. But still....*

Fecir's eyes darkened as a memory floated to the surface of his mind. A memory of a dream he'd had as a cub, where he'd woken up in a field of silver grass and white flowers – the White Meadows. And above him a constellation – Panthera – had come to life, had taken the shape of a great white jaguar with green eyes. The cat had roared and shattered the dream. Could that have been the Star Lord seeping into his mind, communicating through dream? Could the white cub be telling the truth?

"*Trust him,*" the voice in his head whispered again.

Fecir snarled. No, it was impossible. He wasn't going to believe it. *And besides, it doesn't matter. I didn't come here to listen to him. I came back for* her. *For Sandra.*

Fecir turned back, baring his yellow teeth at the little cub. "Panthera lied to you, cub," he seethed. "I am not the Pantheraseer, for I did not come here for *you*. I came for *her*. The girl. Sandra."

Chak's ears perked in surprise. He cocked his head. "The human cub?" He glanced toward the porch. "Why her?"

"Why?" Fecir's anger suddenly returned to him, and his eyes became full of hatred for the strange white cub. "Why?! Because you stole her from me, you wretched fiend! You stole her!"

"Stole her from you?" Chak flattened his ears in confusion.

Fecir was radiating anger. "You made her betray me," he bellowed furiously. "You made her give me away. She used to love me. She raised me, fed me, trained me–"

"She tamed you." Chak's eyes widened in horror.

Fecir roared. "Silence! How dare you? She saved my life!"

"She took the wild from you," Chak breathed. "She raised you away from the jungle. She changed you. You're a pet."

"Shut up!" Fecir banged the fence with his paw. The chain links rattled and the whole fence swayed from the strength in that mighty paw. Chak flinched.

"We were living happily together. Just me and her. And then you showed up. Because of you, she gave me away, gave me to the circus, where I suffered hell on earth – pain you couldn't imagine. And it was all your fault! You made her betray me! You stole my Sandra from me!"

Chak was shocked by the accusation. But he stood up and snarled in his own defense, his own fury rising up within him.

"You think I had a choice?" he growled, enraged. "You think I asked for this to happen? You think I wanted to see my mother and siblings shot, one by one, to watch the life flee from their eyes? You think I asked for men to come and tear me from their lifeless bodies, stuff me into a bird cage to be stared at and sold? You think I wanted to be here?!"

Fecir stopped snarling, stunned by the cub's outburst.

"I never wanted anything to happen," Chak continued. "I never wanted to end up here. I accept what happened to me in the past because I know it was part of Panthera's plan for me. But that doesn't mean that I enjoyed it. That doesn't mean that I don't miss my mother and sisters. That doesn't mean that I wanted to be with Man. That doesn't mean that I wanted to leave the jungle. I never wanted any of this to happen!"

Chak was sobbing now. Fecir just looked on in silence.

"I only wanted to be a true jaguar!" Chak cried, losing steam. "I just wanted to live as the wild jaguar should, no matter what my fur color was, no matter who I looked like. I just wanted to be free. As you are now." He looked into Fecir's eyes.

Fecir shook his head, still stunned by what he'd heard. He'd never considered, in his weeks of being away, the possibility that the white cub could be just like he was: an innocent victim.

Chak hung his head again. "So you see," he said in a low voice, "I never wanted to be here. You think I stole the human cub from you; well, you can have her back. I don't want her. I never did."

Fecir did not know what to say.

"I'm sorry for falsely identifying you as the Pantheraseer," Chak continued meekly. "Even though I was so sure you were the one. I guess I was wrong. But even so, you did come here, so may I at least ask for your help?"

Fecir's throat felt raw, but he forced it to form words. "My help?"

"Yes. Help me get out of here. Help me get to the other side of the fence. I don't want to stay here any longer. Please, can you help me be free?"

Fecir hesitated, as he looked into the cub's eyes and heard his desperate plea. He looked up, toward the porch, where Sandra still had not come out. He realized that she could come out at any moment. Time was of the essence, and so he decided to help the cub.

He turned to Chak and uttered a low growl. "Follow me."

He started trotting along the fence, with Chak on the other side keeping pace. They moved through the tall grass and shadows, and Fecir's eyes narrowed as he tried to remember where it was. He hoped it was still there. He sniffed the ground, searching, until he found it, just where it had always been.

The hole.

Fecir directed Chak toward the small opening, and the cub's green eyes lit up with delight when he saw the rusted, broken links.

"You can squeeze through here," Fecir said quietly. "Quickly, now."

"Thank you," the cub whispered breathlessly. He dove into the opening, scrabbling his paws in the dirt, until he had successfully pushed himself through. He stood up on the other side and shook his fur, before giving a wild whoop of joy.

"I'm free!" he rejoiced before turning to Fecir with grateful eyes. "Oh, thank you! Thank you! I owe you one!"

"Yeah, don't mention it," Fecir grunted, dipping his head toward the hole. He put one paw through it.

"You're not going back in, are you?"

Fecir looked back at the little white cub. "I am," he said defensively. "Sandra is my home. I've come all this way to find her. Of course I'm going back in."

Chak's eyes betrayed his disappointment. He lowered his head. "I can't stop you," he said gravely. "But I can tell you this: captivity is no place for a big cat. No true jaguar would call a fenced property his home, for cats and Man are not meant to be together. Sandra is not a home."

Fecir's whiskers twitched, but he did not interrupt.

"It's your choice," Chak went on, "whether or not you want to be true. But whatever you decide, I give you this message: Panthera has come down to earth, and if you trust him, he will free all the cats, and spring will come."

Fecir snorted. "Are you done?"

Chak gave him a reproachful look before turning away sadly. "Good luck," he said. "I go to seek the Pantheraseer. Live happily, my friend, and thank you. Farewell."

The little cub scampered off into the trees.

Fecir stood there for a long time, with one paw in the opening and the others in the jungle. He pondered the white cat's words for a long time. Was it really better to be true? Were cats and Man truly not meant to live together? Was he right about Sandra not being his home?

Has Panthera really come?

At that moment in time, though he hated to admit it, Fecir's curiosity for the white cub was greater than his love for Sandra. And so he made a fateful decision. He turned away from the fence, and looked to the forest with new eyes. The forest was his home, for he would be a true jaguar from then on.

And so Fecir broke his vow to never live in the forest. He darted into the ferns, moving quickly away from the fence. He never looked back.

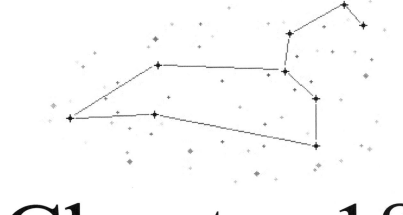

Chapter 18

Fate

"Fecir! So you did decide to come. I'm so glad you changed your mind."

Fecir had just caught up to Chak, as they walked beneath a ceiling of leaves. The sun peeked in through breaks in the thick canopy, and so their pelts were dappled with spots of golden light. And all around them, the song of the jungle rang out for as far away as the mountains; a symphony of birdsong and bug chatter, and the occasional groan of a howler monkey in the trees. It was a welcoming sound, calling the two cats to their true home in the shadows of the trees.

"Shut up, cub. I didn't do it for your sake," Fecir grunted, although he knew he was lying. "I just … needed a change in scenery, is all."

Chak cocked his head to the side and smiled a knowing smile, for even though he was incredibly young, he had wisdom beyond his years, and he could easily see through deception. Even so, he said nothing about it.

"So, where are you headed?" he asked curiously.

"No idea," Fecir growled. "My priority now is just to find shelter. I have no real destination in mind."

"Can I come with you?"

"Why? I thought you were off to find the Pantheraseer."

"Have you not noticed how small I am? It would be too dangerous for me to walk alone."

"Well then, that's certainly a dilemma. But unfortunately for you, cub, I don't have the means to take care of you. Or of myself, for that matter. Remember, I was raised in captivity, so I don't really know how to survive."

"We'd have a better chance if we go together."

"A better chance? Ha! There wouldn't be enough food for the both of us. You'd starve if you went with me."

"Well, better to starve in the company of another than to starve all alone. Am I right?"

Fecir sighed. This cub put up a pretty convincing argument, and after all the traveling Fecir had done previously, he was too tired to continue on. He growled in exasperation. "Fine, cub. You can come with me. But don't complain about anything."

"I won't! Don't worry. We'll learn to survive together," Chak yelped gleefully. "As Panthera would have it, I will walk with you. Fate at its finest."

"Alright, would you knock it off with all the Panthera-fate-destiny crap? You're giving me a headache," Fecir snarled.

"Why? Don't you believe in Panthera?" Chak cocked his head.

"Of course I *believe* in him. It's just really annoying when you won't shut up about him," Fecir huffed. "Also, Panthera and I are not on the best of terms, so I'd rather not think about him, if you don't mind."

"What do you mean? Why don't you like him anymore?" Chak asked innocently, as he walked at Fecir's shoulder.

The jaguar sighed as his eyes clouded over with memories. "There are things he's done to me in the past that I don't think I can ever forgive him for," he growled darkly. "There. I said it. Will you stop talking about him now?"

"Well, what has he done?"

"Give it a rest, cub."

"My name's not cub," Chak suddenly snarled. "It's Chak, and I prefer to be called by that name."

"Whatever, *Chak*," Fecir sneered. "Give it a rest."

"That's much better." Chak smiled brightly. "See? You're learning my name. Perhaps we are meant to walk together."

"Didn't you hear what I've been saying? I said, shut up!" Fecir snarled. This cat was definitely starting to get on his nerves.

"But I like talking to you. You're fun to talk to. Would you like to hear a story?"

That's it. Fecir stopped in his tracks and whirled on the cub, shoving his face right into Chak's, and snarled. The white kitten flattened his ears and cringed away from his foul breath. Fecir looked Chak straight in the eye and growled in a low voice.

"Here's the thing, Chak," he said. "If you want to continue following me, then I'd better not here one more word out of you for the rest of the day. Got it?" His voice seethed with threat.

"Got it," Chak nodded obediently.

"Alright. One word, and I'm chasing you off. So be quiet," Fecir warned. "Let's go find a hollow."

Chak was silent.

In the forest beneath the endless skies, the nocturnal creatures awakened to the darkness of night and blinked in the absent of light. Their glowing, nocturnal eyes saw their world as brightly as in the daytime, and they scuttled out of their burrows and caves, scurried off into the shadows, took wing into the dark. Their cries mingled with the music of the forest night, as the frogs chirped and the insects sang beneath an audience of glowing stardust.

As bats flitted about through the trees and a leopard cat prowled through the underbrush, watching with her yellow eyes, Fecir found a den beneath the roots of a tree. Growling as mosquitoes bothered his ears, he shook his fur and squeezed himself into the tight opening. Once inside, however, the burrow was quite roomy, and Fecir found that he had space to sleep soundly and comfortably.

Behind him, an exhausted Chak also nosed his way into the entrance. Without saying a word, he climbed down into the hollow and trotted up to Fecir lying on his side. Growling tiredly, he tried to curl up next to him, but the bigger cat pushed him away with his hind legs.

"Don't touch me," Fecir warned, baring his teeth. "You sleep on your side, and I'll sleep on mine."

Chak looked at him meekly before silently retreating to his designated sleeping spot. His white fur glowed in the shadows as he curled up in a ball on the other side of the spacious den. Once comfortable, the tired cub quickly fell asleep.

Fecir also closed his eyes to rest, but it wasn't long before Chak was awake again, and restless. Having forgotten his deal with Fecir, he spoke for the first time in hours.

"Fecir?"

The older jaguar groaned in his sleep.

"Fecir? Are you awake?" Chak asked in a small voice.

Fecir's eyes snapped open, and he snarled, "What do you want?"

"You told me earlier that Panthera did something to you that made you distrust him."

Fecir lifted his head and looked at Chak. "What about it?"

Chak seemed so small then, so innocent and insignificant, as he sat with his head down and looking at Fecir from the tops of his green eyes. He hesitated to ask. "What … what did he do to you?"

Fecir sighed and laid his head back down, closing his eyes in deep thought. He gritted his teeth as he remembered that night, his first night with Sandra, when he made that vow. When he opened his eyes again, they were angry.

"I'll tell you what he did," he growled. "He lied to me. He sent the fireflies to give a false message to me and my mother. And because we trusted him, believed his word and trusted his messengers, we let our guard down. It was Panthera's lie that killed my mother, and sent me down a path of flames and hell."

Chak was listening carefully. "Tell me," he said softly. "Tell me what happened to you."

Fecir sighed and stretched his front legs, still lying on his side. He looked up at the dark canopy outside the hollow, at the trail of ants marching up and down the roots of the tree, shining in dappled moonlight breaking through the leaves. He closed his eyes.

"Before I was born," he began, "my mother had lived in a horrible place. The Dark Place, the cats called it; a place of screams and death. Animals went there to await their end. They were held captive by Man until a human chose one of them, and then that cat was killed, and his head was taken as a trophy for the hunter."

His voice was disgusted, and his face cringed from the memory of the horrid building, of the starving, rabid creatures and the preaching jaguar. Chak patiently waited for him, listening quietly, as he sat in the dark.

"My mother escaped," Fecir continued. "She managed to break free of her cage, but in the process she killed a man. For a long time after her escape, she was hunted by Man, for they were vengeful. They hunted her for her blood, for her life, as punishment for the life she stole. But she managed to elude them, and the fireflies told her she was safe."

Chak's ears perked, and Fecir's eyes glowed brightly in the shadows as he stared straight ahead into darkness.

"A year later, she gave birth to me, and named me Fecir after the fireflies that had saved her," he growled. "As I grew up, I was taught the ways of Panthera and his messengers, how the fireflies' glowing lights only shined in a forest that was safe from

Man. And as I lived there, the fireflies would dance every night. But their message was a lie."

Fecir's eyes grew dark. "The forest was not safe. When I was two months old, I walked into a trap. My mother came to the sound of my cries and found me. She tried to break me free, but couldn't. And then she told me that Man would come and take us to the Dark Place.

"And the next morning, they came. They entered the meadow in a red truck. Four of them came for us. My mother attacked, and two of the men fell before her fangs but did not die. One shot her with his rifle, putting three holes in her, and she was dead before she fell. I watched her die."

Chak had grown rigid, as he remembered his own experience of watching his parent and siblings die by gunfire. The sound of the blasts seemed to echo in his mind.

"I was taken to the Dark Place," Fecir went on. "I saw firsthand where my mother grew up. I was put up for adoption because I was still young, and the humans stared at me all day long, stared until I grew sick. And that was when Sandra saved me. I would've died had she not come."

He took a deep breath, his eyes becoming angry again. "But it was all Panthera's fault," he seethed, grinding his teeth. "He told us that the forest was safe from Man. Well, it wasn't, and because of him, my mother died and I had to be raised by Man."

He paused and gave a long sigh. "So now you see, Chak," he said in a low voice. "This is why I don't trust in Panthera. Because he killed my family and took the wild from me. I can never forgive him for it."

Chak was quiet for a while, as he thought about those words. The silence between them lasted for a long time, as Fecir stared off into space and the white cub looked down at his paws. The night music swirled around them, taking the place of the silence, and a frog right outside the hollow chirped loudly in his quest for a mate. Finally, Chak spoke.

"Fecir," he said softly; almost sadly. "You are wrong."

Fecir lifted his head and looked at the little cub, but did not say a word.

"Panthera did not kill your mother," he said slowly. "And it wasn't him who took you from the wild. It was Man who did that, Fecir. Not Panthera. For Man did the same thing to me."

Fecir bared his teeth. "He still lied."

"Perhaps he didn't see." Chak lifted his head. "A Star Lord's vision is limited. He didn't see that Man had set a trap in the woods. Or maybe he saw it, but didn't have time to warn you."

Fecir laid his head back down.

Chak's voice became even lower. "Or maybe...."

"What?" Fecir growled, becoming irritated.

"Maybe it was your destiny, Fecir," Chak said. "Maybe Panthera had meant for it to happen, meant for you to have obstacles in your life, ones that he knew you would overcome. Maybe he played with fate because you are the Pantheraseer, and you're meant to play an important role. Like me. I know that what happened to me was his doing, but also that he had a reason for it."

Fecir growled and closed his eyes. "Goodnight, Chak."

"Fecir, please, just think about–"

"*Goodnight*, Chak."

Chak sighed, realizing that there was no argument. He curled up in his corner and made himself comfortable, before closing his eyes to sleep. "Goodnight, Fecir," he whispered before drifting off into dreams.

Fecir's eyes remained open, as now he could not sleep, and he stared restlessly into the darkness as he listened to the endless music of the forest night.

The next day, the two cats resumed their aimless wanderings, as they moved through the ferns and brush with no inclination of what direction they were headed, of what destination lie at the end of their path. All they knew was that they were traveling – and traveling was good, for if they kept moving constantly, they were unlikely to be followed by Man.

Chak did not talk as much today as he did the day before, even though the ban on his words had been lifted. He could speak freely, but oddly he chose not to. As a sensitive cub, he had quickly become attuned to Fecir's feelings and temper And so, while Fecir walked with his eyes darkened and his mind in deep thought, Chak sensed that his partner was in a bad mood, and decided it was best to leave him be.

This silence between them lasted for the rest of the day, and into the next night, during which they slept out in the open, having not found a suitable hollow to sleep in. And so, with vampire bats flitting over them and insects crawling in their fur, they did their best to close their eyes and rest.

The next day, the silence persisted until noon. It was then, while Fecir trudged wearily ahead and Chak followed at his heels, that the white cub suddenly stopped and perked his ears. He listened, looking deep into the brush, and his body became completely rigid. Fecir halted when he realized that Chak wasn't following him, and looked back at the cub.

"Why have you stopped?" he growled irritably.

Chak did not answer. Instead, he quickly darted into the brush, disappearing from sight.

"Chak!" Fecir barked in alarm, racing after him. He dove into the rustling leaves with a snarl. *What is this cub up to now?* he thought angrily.

"Chak! Chak, where are you?" Fecir snarled, as vines tangled around his neck and leaves slapped his face. He weaved his way through the thick forest brush, yelling for the white cub, but receiving no answer to his calls.

He began to panic, searching and scrambling in the thicket, roaring now for Chak. He couldn't really understand why he was suddenly so worried about the strange, annoying little cat. But at the moment, he didn't think about that. He had to find him. He called again and again.

"Chak!"

Suddenly he heard his voice. Fecir stopped and listened. It wasn't an answer to his calls, but it was Chak's voice alright, talking to someone, someone who wasn't speaking back. There was a clearing up ahead where Chak's voice sounded from. Fecir flattened his ears and crept forward to listen.

"Don't be scared of me. I promise I won't hurt you."

Fecir's eyes narrowed as he saw sunlight breaking through brush up ahead. He was going to throttle that cub for running away.

"Please come down. I didn't mean to scare you. I just wanted to give you some good news."

The innocent voice was louder than ever. Fecir nosed aside a large fern and was struck by bright sunlight. He blinked, blind for a moment, but his eyes quickly adjusted. And there was Chak, standing at the far edge of the clearing, peering up into the high branches of a tree.

"I just wanted to tell you," Chak said politely, "and I don't know if you can understand my words, but it is my duty to spread the word: Panthera has come, dear cat. He has come to save us all."

There was an angry hiss in the leaves above the cub's head. Fecir's eyes traveled up to the branches, and there he caught his breath. There were fierce yellow eyes peeking out from behind the leaves. The eyes of an ocelot, glowering angrily at the small jaguar cub that had him treed.

"Panthera is here! He's here for you, cat! Don't you see? We are saved!" Chak roared reverently.

"Chak!" Fecir snarled, leaping from the brush. He charged up to the cub, roaring in anger. With one quick swipe of his paw, he knocked Chak over onto his side. With a sharp scream, the ocelot leaped away, jumping from branch to branch as he scurried back into hiding. And Fecir stood over the white cub with fury in his eyes.

"What on earth do you think you're doing?!" Fecir demanded, his breath hot on Chak's face.

Chak was in a state of shock, but he shook himself out of it and bared his teeth. "Me?!" he snarled, narrowing his eyes. "What does it look like I'm doing? I'm spreading the word that Panthera had come to earth, that spring is almost here! I'm fulfilling my destiny! What are *you* doing?! Hindering the right of Panthera to have his message heard?!"

"That ocelot could've attacked you," Fecir snarled "He could've killed you. That was a stupid move, running off on your own. You could've been hurt, and I couldn't find you! And for what? To preach to a cat that can't even understand our language?!" He was clearly outraged.

Chak had grown silent. His ears were flat against his head, but not in guilt. It was in humbleness. He looked up at Fecir from the tops of his eyes.

"Were you ... really that scared for me?" he asked in a small voice.

Fecir stopped snarling, and turned his head. He stepped away from Chak and allowed him to stand up, while Fecir stood huffing with his back to the white cub. He realized that he had been scared for Chak. Was he really starting to care for the strange cub?

"I wasn't scared," Fecir said gruffly. "I was just ... wondering where you were off to in such a hurry." He shook himself. "Let's go. Come on."

He started walking while Chak pulled himself to his paws. He shook his pelt and scampered off after the jaguar; smiling to himself, for he had sensed the lie in Fecir's voice – he was beginning to care.

Fecir just didn't want to admit that Chak was growing on him, like a flower blooming on the decay of a corpse.

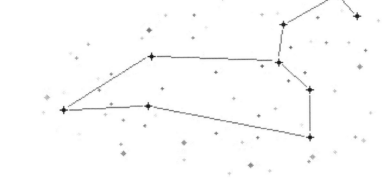

Chapter 19

The Pseudopanthera

That night, on the bank of a dry rivulet, the two cats lay within a little cave made by the flow of water during the rainy season. The crackling cakes of mud formed a strong ceiling above them, and little tendrils of grass and leaf rot fringed the top of the entrance. The grass roots dangled from the ceiling, and outside this cozy cave came the sound of frogs singing to their mates. It was the only sound heard, for this part of the forest was quiet, bereft of life, as it had fled with the drying of the creek, and left behind only the frogs to sing the midnight lullaby of the rainforest.

    Fecir lay near the front of the cave, with the moonlight shining onto his face and reflecting in his eyes. Chak was curled up in the back of the cave, his body bathed in shadow. As Fecir looked out at the dark forest beyond, he could not help but let his mind wander to the events of the day. Fecir had been thinking quite a lot more often lately, as many things now seemed to confuse and interest him. Such as what Chak had said to him before, about how his duty was to spread the good word of the Lord of all Cats. Was it really necessary for him to have tackled the poor cub and snarled at an action done in faith?

But Fecir hadn't been angry at Chak for what he was saying to the ocelot. He'd been angry because the white cub had run off to the ocelot, without giving a reason for his disappearance. This had scared Fecir – to think that he may not have found Chak, that he may have been separated from him forever.

He growled. He *was* starting to care about Chak. But as he thought more about it, he realized that it was not a bad thing, to have a companion. After all, it had taken two weeks to see the better side of Mahkuu. Perhaps he and Chak could become great friends.

He rolled over onto his side. Chak had called him a hindrance, growled that he had gotten in the way of his destiny. Fecir had been furious at him for running off, but he had to admit, it was pretty amazing for him to have heard the ocelot before Fecir had, and had immediately charged off to it just to share the news. He found himself wondering again, *Just who is this white cub? Could he really be the savior that the jaguars in the Dark Place had hoped for?*

Fecir lifted his head and looked back at the little cub, curled up in a fetal ball. He saw how his fur glowed in the shadow, how it was so pure-white that it seemed to repel the darkness. He could contain his curiosity no longer. He had to find out about Chak. He had to find out why he was here, where he had come from – why he looked so much like Panthera.

"Chak," Fecir hissed.

Chak's ears twitched, and he lifted his head. "Yes?" he said sleepily, and yawned in the darkness.

"I've been meaning to ask you something, Chak."

"What is it?" Chak blinked his eyes.

Fecir was hesitant to say. He worried of offending the cub. He took a deep breath.

"Why is your fur white?"

At first, Chak was silent in the darkness. Then, he smiled.

"I was wondering when you'd finally say something. I haven't met one cat who hasn't asked me the same thing," Chak said. "The answer is a bit hard to understand."

"Try me," Fecir dared, scooting closer to the cub.

Chak sighed and looked away, looked up at the earthworms wriggling as they hung dung from the cave ceiling. His whiskers twitched. "Do you know the story of the Pantheraseer and the Endless Winter?"

"Of course I do," Fecir said. "There isn't a cat alive who hasn't been told the legend. Why do you ask?"

"Do you know about the role that the white tiger played in the legend?"

"He was the spirit of Panthera," Fecir growled confidently. "He came down to earth and banished the snow with his touch."

Chak showed his teeth. "You're wrong."

Fecir growled and cocked his head. "Wrong?"

"The white tiger was not Panthera," Chak explained. "He had almost nothing to do with the actual forthcoming of spring. No, he was what I call a Pseudopanthera – the false Panthera spirit. He was born in the image of Panthera himself."

"That can't be true," Fecir snarled. "The white tiger was Panthera's spirit. Everyone believes that."

"The white tiger could not have been the spirit of Panthera simply because of one reason: a spirit cannot die. And the white tiger was killed by a bullet wound." Chak finally looked up, into Fecir's eyes. "The beliefs are incorrect. Thousands of years of storytelling and recitals have twisted the tale. Some parts of the legend have even been forgotten, lost forever to the flow of time. But the white tiger was a Pseudopanthera, and I tell you this because I, too, am like him."

Fecir had grown silent as this information sank in. It seemed like everything he'd ever been told was wrong. He looked blankly up at Chak and had no words to say. And so, Chak continued on.

"I am a Pseudopanthera. I was born in the image of Panthera. Panthera made me. He played with my fate, played with my fur and eyes while I was still growing within my mother's womb, so that I would be born white like him, and so that he could connect with me. I was made in the image that the jaguars believed in: a white cat with green eyes and spots the color of cinnamon. I was made this way so that the Pantheraseer would be drawn to follow me, just as Seragah was drawn to the white tiger."

Fecir's ears perked. He remembered that name. "Seragah?"

"Yes? What about her?" Chak asked.

"Who's Seragah?"

Chak smiled genuinely. "Seragah was the Pantheraseer, Fecir. She was the one who died for us all, and banished the Endless Winter from the land. Her name was Seragah."

Fecir looked away, a feeling of amazement washing over him. The Pantheraseer's name ... he remembered hearing that word in a dream before, and feeling that it was so familiar to him, that he had recognized the voice saying it. He could finally know who that name said belonged to. Seragah, the Siberian tigress; the Pantheraseer.

Fecir's eyes suddenly narrowed, and he turned to Chak. "Where did you hear that name?" he demanded.

Chak's smile grew even wider. "I am the Pseudopanthera, and so have a connection with Panthera. He told me her name."

Fecir growled and turned away again. "Of course he did."

"He told you it, too, didn't he?" Chak said. "In a dream?"

Fecir whipped around with a snarl, about to deny it, but he stopped and fell silent. He didn't know why he was unwilling to lie at that moment, to claim that Chak was crazy as was the easiest thing to do. His words seemed to make sense – he had heard that name in a dream. But was that Panthera's voice speaking to him? Fecir did not answer Chak's question.

Chak twitched his ears and shook his head as mosquitoes buzzed around him. He licked his jaws and continued on.

"Seragah was the First Pantheraseer, the tigress famed for bringing spring to the world and banishing the snows of the Endless Winter. Guided by the white tiger, she inspired belief in the cats and in herself, and even sacrificed herself for that belief, so that we could be alive today. Her death itself helped influence the spring, for her decaying body provided nourishment for the first flowers of spring, which grew straight from her fur."

Fecir's ears perked as he remembered the image of a dead cat with flowers growing from her pelt. So that cat had been the Pantheraseer. It was a strange realization, and he shuddered from the disturbing image.

"The white tiger was born to guide Seragah toward her faith, for when she began her journey she was doubtful of the very existence of Panthera. It was because of the white tiger that she finally found her faith at the very end, when Panthera revealed himself to her. I believe that I was born for the same purpose: to be the new Pantheraseer's guide toward trust in Panthera, and to help him on his quest. To help him bring freedom to the cats, just as Seragah once did on her journey, thousands of years ago."

Fecir blinked his eyes in the dark. Chak yawned and laid down on the ground, resting his chin on his outstretched paws. He looked up at Fecir and yawned again.

"So," he said in a tired voice. "Were you able to understand my answer to your question?"

Fecir also laid down and twitched his tail. He nodded at Chak. "Yes."

"Good," Chak said, closing his eyes.

"There is one thing that still doesn't make sense, though."

"And what is that?" The white cub's eyes cracked open.

"If the white tiger wasn't Panthera's spirit," Fecir said, "then who was?"

Chak smiled and rolled onto his back, waving his paws in the air. "In that time," he said, "Panthera came to earth in the form of a snowy owl."

"An owl?" Again, Fecir recalled his dreams, and he could see again those giant yellow eyes staring down at him, see the pure-white feathers of a magnificent bird silhouetted against the starry sky. "Panthera was a bird? Why?"

"Another part of the legend that was forgotten," Chak said with a yawn, "was that Panthera could come as any animal, not limited to just cats. He would be known by his white feathers, fur, or skin."

Fecir thought back to the white elephant suddenly, but he shook his head. It wasn't possible. He yawned and rolled over onto his side, resting his head near the little white cub.

"Chak," he whispered.

There was no answer. The cub was asleep.

"Chak!" Fecir hissed.

Chak still did not answer. He had fallen deeply asleep, exhausted from their long day of traveling. With a growl, Fecir, too, felt the weight of exhaustion bearing down on him. He closed his eyes, the final question he'd wanted to ask still echoing in his mind.

Do you really think that I'm the Pantheraseer?

The sky overhead was covered in a thick blanket of gray clouds.

The trees around him were completely bare, shivering in the bitter cold wind that swept flurries of snow into the air, heaping the white powder into large, round dunes, piling them onto the shaking branches, creating a thick fog of white through the forest. Fecir blinked his eyes. He could see nothing. The closest trees were mere silhouettes, shadows in the white. And the storm raged over him, dropping ever more snow onto the ground, as the wind howled into the air.

Fecir shivered. His thin, sleek fur was not made to protect him from cold. It was made for heat, for humidity – never for a blizzard. He stood stock still with his paws deep in the snow, paralyzed by intense cold. His breath came out as puffs of steam, and his blood felt more like sludge as precious heat seeped from his skin and was whisked away by the merciless wind, howling and attacking like a pack of wolves. He could not move for the life of him, for he was so incredibly cold. And so he shivered, unaware of where he was, unaware of how he got there, unaware of why he had come to this strange place.

Gritting his teeth against the frost and peering into the thick, swirling fog, he tried to see anything that could give him any sort of warmth or shelter from the bitter cold. But there was nothing – just the creaking branches swaying overhead, helpless to protect him from the terrible wind. His paws were going numb in the snow, and he looked up, searching for the sun in the sky, searching for that warm ball of light, but it wasn't there. The clouds had taken over it, swallowed it, killed it, and went on to blanket the world in freezing, icy white.

As Fecir looked around, he saw two lights appear in the turbulent fog. He squinted as they came closer to him. They were bright blue and they moved side-by-side. Behind them, a shadow started to appear; a shadow in the shape of a large, muscular animal. Fecir snarled, wondering if the snow itself had formed a beast within the white, and that the creature was coming to sink its icicle fangs into him, to finish him while he was too cold to move. His threats were swept away by the wind.

As the creature came still ever closer, Fecir began to recognize its shape. It was a cat, and as it stepped out of the fog to stand in front of him, Fecir saw the stripes appear on its white fur, winding and snaking around its legs and body, painting his face with ribbons of black, as the two blue lights – the cat's eyes – illuminated the face upon which they sat; the face of a white tiger.

The Pseudopanthera.

Fecir was frozen in place, not only with cold, but in awe of the white tiger, the legendary cat who aided the Pantheraseer. As Fecir stared up at him, the white tiger stared back, and their eyes met. Fecir felt a shock as he suddenly saw a message appear before his eyes, a message given by those blue eyes. *Move.*

Fecir flattened his ears and tried, but his paws felt detached from his body. He was completely numb, as his fur bristled against the wind. He looked back at the white tiger and shook his head. The tiger made no movement. The message again flashed across his blue eyes: *Move.*

"I can't," Fecir said plaintively. "I tried. I'm too cold."

The tiger chuffed and turned away, turned to face the blizzard. With a swish of his tail, he started to walk into the fog.

"Wait!" Fecir roared. "Pseudopanthera, stop! I need your help!"

Desperate to be near the white tiger, to be near any living body, Fecir found his frozen paws and lifted them. He lunged forward, his stiff limbs failing to catch him as he flopped face-first into the snow. He scrambled to his feet and bounded forward again, the movement bringing feeling back into his frozen body. And the white tiger waited for him as Fecir trudged over to stand at his side.

The white tiger chuffed in satisfaction – a strange sound, one that Fecir was not used to hearing. Then the white cat put his face close to Fecir's again. A message appeared in the tiger's blue eyes. *Follow me.*

Fecir nodded, willing to go anywhere with the white tiger so long as he brought them out of the blizzard. The tiger lead the way into the thick of the storm, and Fecir followed at his heels, as they disappeared into the white.

They walked in fog for what seemed like hours. Finally, Fecir felt the wind begin to die down, and the white begin to fade. The shadows of the trees became more prominent, until suddenly they were completely visible. The snow stopped falling altogether, and the clouds broke to reveal the reborn sun.

They continued walking through the skeleton forest. Fecir flattened his ears at the dead things around him, at the forking branches overhead and the silence throughout the white land. He stayed close to the white tiger, as the cat moved indifferently through this realm, leading him through the barren woods silently, with his glowing eyes guiding his way.

An owl flitted overhead, and its shadow passed over the two cats. The white tiger paused and looked up at it as it swooped down to land on a thin branch above them. Fecir stared up at the creature, stared at its white feathers and its wise, yellow eyes. The white tiger nodded at the bird and continued on beneath the branch. Fecir followed with his head down low, and the owl swiveled his head around to watch them go.

The white tiger finally stopped at a clearing and sat down, looking straight ahead. Fecir also sat down beside him, wondering what he was waiting for. The tiger chuffed loudly, startling Fecir for a moment, before standing up and turning to leave.

Fecir stood up behind him. "Where are you going?" he growled at him.

The white tiger did not answer as he trotted off into the trees.

"Wait!" Fecir roared, about to charge after him, until a sound behind him made him stop. The snap of a twig rang loudly in his ears, and with a snarl, he whirled around, baring his teeth to the world. But he froze when he saw that before him, in the middle of the clearing and with the sun shining onto her fur, was a beautiful Siberian tigress.

"Hello," the tigress growled in a deep, musical voice.

Fecir hesitated before growling back. "Hello," he said curtly, narrowing his eyes. "Who are you?"

"Who am I?" the tigress said. "I'm Seragah, Fecir, the one who died for you. Welcome to my world, in the time of the Endless Winter."

Fecir's ears perked. *The Endless Winter...? This can't be right! Where am I?*

"This is a dream," Fecir snarled. "I'm asleep and this isn't real. You're not real."

"I'm as real as the past, as your memories and experiences, Fecir," Seragah said slowly. "Yes, this is a dream, but that doesn't mean that I do not exist."

"You're dead. You died thousands of years ago."

"Yes, I did. And I would think you'd be more grateful for that, considering you wouldn't be here if not for me," the tigress growled dangerously. "So watch your tone, there, jaguar. Even though this is a dream, my claws could still really hurt if I used them. I could turn this world into a realm of nightmares and terror for you, if you don't show me some respect."

Fecir closed his mouth and flattened his ears, hearing the threat in her voice. He backed down to the bigger cat, and she chuffed with satisfaction.

"Much better," she sneered.

"Why are you here?" Fecir said in a small voice.

"Why?" she asked. "I thought it was obvious." As she spoke, the white owl suddenly appeared out of the trees and flew over to land on a tree branch behind the tigress. The bird folded his wings and sat on his perch, peering down at Fecir curiously. Fecir watched the bird out of the corner of his eyes.

"Apparently not obvious enough," he huffed. "What do you want from me?"

"Want? I'm dead. What could I possibly want from the living?" Seragah chuffed. "I didn't come here because I wanted something. I came to give you a message, Fecir. And you would be wise to listen to it."

The owl in the trees began to preen his feathers indifferently. Fecir focused his attention back on the tigress.

"What message?" he asked.

Seragah smiled. "You already know, deep within your heart, what I'm about to say. Just my presence here proves my words. You are the Pantheraseer, Fecir. As I once was. You have been given the eyes to see the truth in lies, to see Panthera's spirit when he comes down to earth, and he is here, Fecir. He has already come. He walks through the forest and watches for you, for he knows that you will come to his calls."

"You sound just like Chak," Fecir snarled. "But why should I believe you? If this is a dream, then why should I take what you say as truth?"

"You'll just have to trust me, Fecir," Seragah said. "Trust, and he will come to you. He will free the cats. You have to trust him." Her voice began to fade away as a harsh wind suddenly blew a flurry between them. The owl in the branches screeched and lifted away.

"Wait!" Fecir cried, but the tigress was gone, having been swept away by the mighty wind. The fog swarmed around him, swirling and whipping his fur, coating his face and whiskers in frost. Fecir braced himself against the force of the sudden weather, and as he did he heard a snarl within the swirling white. He looked behind him and saw the white tiger standing in the snow. Only his eyes were no longer blue. They were green.

With a roar, the tiger attacked him, lunging forward and pushing him to the ground. Fecir yelped as he was pinned beneath the weight of the white tiger. The cat snarled in his face, and Fecir cringed away from his foul breath, closing his eyes. The tiger raised his paw overhead, hooked claws glinting in the white. With a thunderous bellow, he brought the paw down, and his roar echoed into darkness.

Fecir gasped as he burst out of the dream. His eyes snapped open and he scrambled to his feet, huffing and panting for breath, as sweat trickled into his fur. His head throbbed as the roars of the white tiger and the howling of the wind still rang in his ears. *A dream. All a dream.* He shuddered as he leaned against the wall.

Chak was still asleep in the back of the cave, his paws twitching and his muzzle smiling with happy dreams. Fecir stared at him for a long time, stared at his white fur with the faded cinnamon rosettes. He slumped to the ground as his breath finally caught up to him, and he sighed in exhaustion.

Only a dream, he thought again. *Or was it?*

He peered out of the entrance of the cave, looked up at the night sky was just starting to turn gray in the east. Dawn was approaching, but the stars still glowed brightly in the darkness. And one constellation, shining brighter than all the rest, sat in the middle of the sky, looking down on Fecir in the cave. Panthera was watching him.

"Am I really the Pantheraseer?" Fecir thought aloud.

Chak snorted in his sleep and rolled over. Fecir flinched, turning away from the stars to look back at the little white cub. For the first time ever, he smiled at the Chak, smiled at how he slept so peacefully, with his tiny whiskers twitching and little tongue flicking out of his mouth. The strange cub had been right about him all along, he realized. He was the Pantheraseer. It had been his destiny to find Chak all along.

He couldn't deny his fate anymore. He wanted to wake Chak up and tell him about the dream, to apologize to the cub for his attitude before, but he decided against it. The little cat needed his rest. He would tell him in the morning.

Fecir yawned and stood up in the cave. Ducking his head beneath the low ceiling, he crept toward the white cub, padding silently so as not to wake him. He laid down beside Chak and curled up around him, allowing the cub to snuggle into his fur. And the two cats slept beneath the watchful eye of Panthera, as the morning sun began its long climb to greet the land, and its light announced the dawn of a new day.

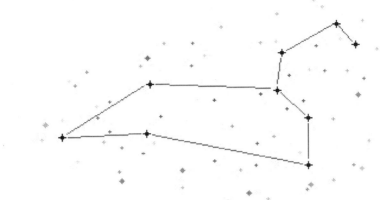

Chapter 20

Pit

Fecir and Chak quickly became the best of friends.

They grew close to each other after Fecir finally learned to accept who he was; so close that they began to call each other "brother". It was a strange thing for Fecir to feel as though he had a sibling, but Chak took it in stride. He looked up to Fecir and followed him at his side wherever they went, happy to be around him in whatever situation they landed in. And the two cats grew together as their partnership became stronger.

Fecir was the Pantheraseer now, and though he accepted his responsibility, he did not openly call himself the Pantheraseer simply out of embarrassment. He thought of himself as clueless in the field he was supposed to be teaching in. He did not preach the word of Panthera because he did not know much about Panthera at all. For that reason, that part of the job fell to Chak's jurisdiction, and the young cub took it upon himself to teach Fecir the ways of the Star Lords as well as every random cat they came across.

However, in the jungle it was quite rare to come across another cat. Jaguars, ocelots, and leopard cats were all very elusive, to the point where they even preferred to stay hidden from their own kind. Fecir and Chak felt this instinct to remain out of sight as well, but fought against it for the will of their god. Fecir often stood by while Chak called out to a hidden cat, telling him of Panthera's coming to earth, and how the Pantheraseer had come to make the cats trust in their Star Lord. How Panthera had arrived to free the slave cats from their suffering behind bars.

With those words said, Chak and Fecir would leave the stranger cat to his business. And that cat hidden in the shadows, having heard the words of the white cub, was often left with a sense of wonder of having indirectly met the Pantheraseer. A new hope will have also ignited within that cat's soul: Panthera has come. The savior is here. At last, we will be free.

While Chak preached and Fecir listened, the two cats continued to travel in an unknown direction toward an unknown destination. Fecir led the way, and as they walked he learned to hunt more than just insects. He taught himself to lie in wait for peccaries and capybaras, and even learned to snatch birds out of the sky, just as his mother used to do. He and Chak rarely went hungry after Fecir acquired this new knowledge, and so they walked in ease beneath a thick ceiling of leaves.

Eventually, many months after their first meeting, Chak and Fecir found a territory and decided to claim it as their own, ending their long, aimless march. They found a piece of jungle about eighteen square miles across, with several suitable dens to lay in and a trickling stream from which they could drink. By now, Chak was nearly a year old and was beginning to accompany Fecir on hunts. This territory had an endless supply of fish and peccaries to choose from.

And the fireflies danced every night in this land. Their glowing little tails blinked green in the leaves, in the brush and in the high branches of the trees. Those little beacons of hope and safety were what really sealed the deal for the cats when they decided to call this territory home. Although Fecir was still a bit weary and untrusting of the insects, Chak would not live anywhere else. And so, this land of fireflies, of food and water and shelter, became their safe haven, guarded by the watchful eye of Panthera in the stars.

As Fecir and Chak lived together, Fecir noticed the change that had taken place over the last several months. He was no longer the angry, self-centered cat he used to be, and he found that he no longer held a grudge against Panthera. Though he couldn't say that he completely trusted Panthera just yet, he could openly say that he completely trusted Chak.

When the two cats had first met, Fecir had found Chak annoying and peculiar. He had been incredibly reclusive around the white cub, whereas now he freely discussed every topic that came to mind with Chak. The white cub was so much like a younger sibling to him now that Fecir now began to think that he couldn't live without him. Chak was now a part of his family.

The two cats lived together for a total period of fourteen months. Fecir was now just over four years old, and Chak was halfway till two. The cub was half-grown and lanky, and filled to the brim with energy, to the point where his boundless spirit kept him from sleeping at night. It was now not uncommon for Chak to leave whatever den they were sleeping in to go on a midnight stroll. Fecir never worried about this, for the cub always came back every morning before dawn. This land was a safe haven, according to Chak. Nothing would ever happen to them so long as the fireflies continued to dance.

But one night, unnoticed by the cats, the fireflies stopped their dance. They opened their wings and flew away, for they sensed something on the wind. This land wouldn't be safe for much long. They left in a huge swarm under cover of night, and because the cats had been sleeping, they never saw the guardians go, and they never felt the sudden change in the humid air.

A new scent began to waft through the trees – a scent of metal, of blood. Of death.

The sky was just turning gray in the east when Chak's eyes opened in the darkness.

He lifted his head, yawned, and blinked a few times, flicking is tail and smacking his lips. He looked over at Fecir sleeping next to him and smiled. The large cat was twitching in his sleep, and his lips moved over his teeth, growling at some invisible foe. Chak knew that he was deeply immersed in his dreams, so deeply so that he wouldn't be waking up for a long while. The white cat twitched his ears and stood up to leave.

"I'll be back soon," he whispered, as he always did before going on a stroll before morning. And he would be, he knew. He always was back before Fecir woke. That grumpy old cat wouldn't even know he had left until Chak told him about his walk later – during which then, Fecir would enjoy hearing his stories of the forest night.

The white jaguar stepped outside into the starlight and lifted his head to feel the cool air on his neck. It was much better to walk at night than in daytime, for the humidity during darkness was much less. The crisp, clear air was ringing with the song of the rainforest, which was slowly morphing from nighttime to daytime as the night insects went into hiding from the light, and the day insects woke up to greet the morning. Chak listened to this song for a good while as he went about licking his fur, smoothing it over his shoulders and cleaning away the dirt. Once he was satisfied with his pelt, he stood up, shook himself, and bounded away into the darkness.

Chak's green eyes were wide open to catch the full glory of the nightly forest within their pupils. They glowed with the reflected starlight, shining like a mirror that illuminated the path before him. It was always a treat to Chak to see the land at different times of the day, for every moment hid a new surprise for him. A few nights before, he'd noticed a caiman that had waddled a bit too far from the water. A few weeks ago, he'd seen a rare bird: a Spix's macaw that had just woken up at the crack of dawn. Last month, he'd spotted (and eaten) a large turtle by the stream. Every night offered a new discovery.

And on this night, a strange scent was drifting through the brush. Chak immediately recognized it as a meat smell – a strange meat smell, but still a scent that made his jaws slaver with hunger. He moved toward the smell, powerful legs propelling him across the mud and through the brush, as the sky continued to grow brighter with the advent of dawn.

Another scent soon joined the meat smell, as Chak trotted closer to the source. Chak couldn't very well detect this smell, as it was masked by the delectable meat. He soon could distinguish the type of meat he was smelling – peccary. The thought of pork was too much to resist. He moved faster through the brush.

He soon came upon the meat, a bare leg of raw, red pork in the middle of the clearing. Chak's eyes narrowed on it. He was so focused on the bloody limb that he didn't noticed the ground around it, that it was littered with dead leaves that had not fallen from the canopy. The shape of the leaves was wrong, and the color – they were from an entirely different forest. But Chak did not notice, as he stared at the meat swinging back and forth over the strange, foreign carpet, as it hung from a thin coil of rope over the center.

Chak waited a few moments, looking about himself to make sure that no other predator was closing in on the meat. Again, he was so focused on his hunger that he didn't hear the silence around him, how even the insects had fled from this clearing. Chak flattened his ears, eyes returning to the hanging red leg. He crouched low, preparing to pounce. His rear wiggled in the air, and he leaped.

He missed the hanging leg, barely nicking it with his claws before falling back to the ground. As he fell, the strange brown carpet of leaves beneath him simply gave way to his weight, and collapsed into the earth. With a startled yelp, Chak was swallowed by the leaves, as the ground caved in beneath him, and he fell into a dark pit below.

He slammed hard into the ground as the leaves covered him. Instantly, he was back on his feet, shaking his head and snarling in fury and confusion. He looked around himself and saw vertical walls of dirt, nearly nine feet high, and a small circle of sky directly above him, still glowing with its sprinkling of stars.

Instantly, Chak began to panic, racing around the small hole and clawing at the walls, trying to climb his way out. But the walls were too steep to climb, and too tall to leap above. He was trapped at the bottom of a hole, and now finally he could smell the scent of Man around him – on the walls that he dug with his shovels, and the leaves he gathered to conceal the pit, and on the meat that still swayed mockingly above the white cat, taunting him with its red goodness as it hung on the manmade coil. Man had been here. Man had come for them.

Chak was stuck in a pitfall trap, with no way out and his only option being to wait for Man to come with his rifles. It dawned on him, quite suddenly, that the fireflies had left, that he had never seen them go, that he hadn't heard their warning that Man had come; the warning spread by the buzzing of their wings when they had flown off together in a swarm. Chak's eyes grew wide with fear. He did the only thing he knew to do. He began to scream.

In one of the many dens scattered throughout his territory, Fecir's eyes cracked open to meet the light of a new day.

Stubborn as always, he tried to go back to sleep, but the light would not make it so. With a growl, he opened his eyes again and yawned, standing up to shake his fur. Still sleepy and with eyes half-closed, he stumbled out of his den to sit and bask in the sunlight.

He noticed, as he stepped outside, that Chak was missing from the den. This, at first, was strange to him, as whenever Chak went for a walk, he always returned before morning. He was always there when Fecir awoke. This confused Fecir, and even worried him a little, but then he just brushed those thoughts aside. Chak was probably so caught up in exploring that he'd forgotten to come home before the sun rose. He'd be back before long.

Fecir smiled. He remembered when he was a cub, how all he wanted to do was go off exploring. He winced as he remembered where his curiosity had once landed him – behind metal bars. He shook his head. He hated thinking of the past now. He preferred to think of the present now, and smiled again, knowing that the Dark Place was a thing of the past. It would never come back to haunt him.

He had just started to groom himself when he heard a scream suddenly pierce the air, and a flock of macaws fluttered into the air with a chorus of startled squawks. Fecir's ears pricked and his eyes narrowed. Instantly, he knew what had happened. Chak was in trouble. With a snarl, he leaped forward into the brush, following the sound of the scream.

"Help!" the voice trailed into the air.

"Chak!" Fecir barked back. "Chak! Stay where you are! I'm coming!"

"Help me!" Chak cried. He wasn't far away. His voice was quickly becoming louder. Fecir snarled as leaves and vines smacked into his face.

"Chak! Hang on!"

"Fecir!"

"I'm here!" The clearing was just up ahead. With a roar, Fecir burst into the sunlight.

When he leaped out of the forest, he quickly discovered that there was no ground beneath him at all. With a yelp and a snarl, he tumbled headfirst into the pit. He hit the ground hard and was knocked unconscious by the impact.

When he awoke, the white cat was standing over him, staring down with concerned green eyes. Those eyes brightened when they saw that Fecir's had opened, and he sniffed his friend's ear.

"You're awake," he said. "Thank Panthera."

Fecir blinked as he looked around, still lying on his side where he had fallen. He saw the steep walls surrounding them and the earthworms wriggling in the dirt; the circle of sunlight and the dangling peccary leg. He flattened his ears and snarled.

"Where are we?" he demanded angrily, wincing as he tried to claw his way to his feet. Chak took a few steps back to allow him to stand up.

"We're in a pit," he said. "Looks like Man dug it out, and he set that leg up there as bait."

"And you were foolish enough to take the bait?" Fecir snarled.

Chak ducked his head guiltily. "I'm sorry, Fecir. I didn't mean to–"

"No use explaining yourself now. It won't get us out of this pit," Fecir growled. He was silent for a moment before erupting into a long string of cat curses, words that made Chak turn his head and cringe.

"How do we get out of here?" the white cat asked after Fecir had calmed down a bit.

"We don't," Fecir said curtly, swiping his paw over the vertical wall. The dirt crumbled away in his grip, revealing the wriggling insects beneath. "The walls are too steep and slick to climb up, and not even I can make a jump that high. We're stuck down here until Man comes."

With a snarl, Fecir began another round of cursing. Chak had never seen him so angry.

"What will happen when Man comes?" he whimpered.

"You and I both have been under the rule of Man before, so we should know what to expect. When I was trapped as a cub in a cage-trap, my mother told me that one of two things would happen. Either Man would kill us, or he'd take us to the Dark Place."

Fecir looked at Chak. "And I know I've told you about the Dark Place. It is not at all pleasant. That is most likely where we will end up, when Man comes. And there is nothing we can do about it." He spat on the dirt in anger.

"There is one thing we can do," Chak said.

"What?" Fecir snapped.

"We can pray."

The jaguar snorted. "And a whole lot of good that will do us," he hissed. "Words alone won't lift us from this pit."

"But it will give us peace of mind, if we are to face death or torture ahead. And hope."

Fecir thought a moment, then sighed. "Fine. Let's pray. You'll lead the words."

Chak smiled and bowed his head, while the sun rose ever higher above them.

Chak and Fecir spent two nights in that pit, praying and going over every option they could think of to climb out of the pit. They dug holes, scrabbled at the walls, leaped as high as they could, with no luck. At one point, Chak even tried to leap off of Fecir's back, to give himself a boost, but he was still feet short of the surface. They soon realized that escape was impossible.

But they never lost hope. At night they sent their words to the Star Lords, and at day they prayed silently in their minds. Fecir's prayers, however, were inconsistent, and his mind was a rage of tormented thoughts, conflicting once again over whose side Panthera was on. Part of him still did not trust the god, while the other devoted his existence to him. His mind was split into two different cats, and frankly, the angry, distrusting cat was the more prevalent of the two halves, and so Fecir began to think that this trap was Panthera's doing once again. He stopped praying at the beginning of the second night.

On the morning of their third day trapped, and with their bellies hungry and after having spent hours gazing dreamily up at the hanging pork, a sound broke the silence of the forest, and the cats readied themselves for what they knew was coming. For the sound was of giant paws crashing through plant and brush. Round paws, tires – the feet that could only belong to a truck. A putrid odor entered the air, the smell of exhaust fumes choking the atmosphere. And the roaring of the vehicle drowned out all other noise.

"They're here," Fecir hissed, unsheathing his claws. Chak cringed in fear.

Fecir's eyes were darkening with rage as the truck drew closer to the pit. He remembered, suddenly, his mother standing in front of the cage, shielding him from Man's view, and leaping forward to take bullets in a vain effort to protect him. Though Fecir could never know the love a mother has for her child, he felt that same protective instinct within himself now – the instinct to protect Chak, his young friend, his brother, from all harm rang loudly in his mind, and it was a strong enough emotion to make him forget his own life and snarl in the face of death by Man. His lips trembled threateningly over his massive teeth as a rumbling growl vibrated through his muzzle, arguing with the voice of the truck, challenging to battle.

The engine cut off, and the voice died down. The men now entered the jungle nearby and started moving toward the pit. They talked loudly, laughing as men always did, obnoxious and raucous. They knew they had caught a prize when they heard Fecir's mighty roar. Their feet crashed through the leaves as they ran, swinging and waving their arms over their heads.

A face appeared in the circle of sunlight. Fecir hissed a threat at the Man looking down on them. The man smiled and called the others to the pit. They came, and now two more heads appeared at the pit. Fecir snarled.

One of the men pointed at Chak. "*¡Mira!*" he said. "*¡Un gato blanco!*"

"*¡Vamos a ser ricos!*" a second man agreed.

"Get the tranquilizers ready," the third man said, in a voice and language different from his group. He spoke with authority and his eyes were cold. "Shoot them now so we can get them on the truck."

Fecir roared in anger and hatred of the men above as the two Spanish men departed for the truck, running back for what were no doubt their weapons. Chak whimpered in fear.

"Fecir," he said. "What are they doing? Will they kill us?"

"Not yet," Fecir growled through his teeth. "They'll have to kill me first."

"Panthera save us," Chak whispered.

Fecir snarled at the words.

The two men returned with their rifles at their sides, already loaded with darts of sedative. They stood up and pointed the barrels down at the cats, finding them in the crosshairs. Fecir roared defiantly, as would be his last word.

Not his last, for he would not die. The dart was fired, and it stuck into his shoulder. Fecir snarled and jumped up at the sight of the red dart, and the liquid draining into his skin.

Chak also yelped as a dart found the back of his neck. Instantly, the two cats began to feel woozy. The darts had been loaded with a fast-acting drug, and the two cats began to stumble as they clawed the darts out of their pelts. Fecir's chin soon hit the ground, and Chak's next to him. Though they fought the drug, it was a losing battle. Their minds clouded with strange dreams.

The last thing Fecir remembered seeing was the peccary leg swinging back and forth above him. And then, with the silence and speed of a ghost, a white owl swooped down to snatch the leg up. His eyes closed, and he surrendered to the drug, falling into a deep, undisturbed sleep.

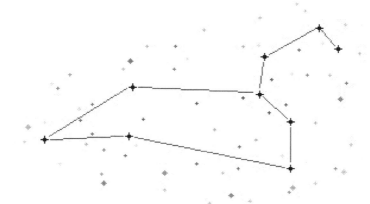

Chapter 21

Screams

Fecir lie motionless, dazed by the drug that was slowly wearing off.

The rumbling of the truck had stopped, and the tarpaulin covering his body was removed. Ropes were tied around his paws, and he was slid of the bed of the truck. He fell into the dirt hard, but could do nothing. He was paralyzed by dizziness.

The ropes were taken in hand by the men, and he was dragged toward the giant building. Fecir blinked sleepily at the blurry image, barely recognizing his surroundings. For a moment, he thought the building was Sandra's house, and that he was being taken back to Sandra. He closed his eyes.

When next they opened, he had entered the building. Still being dragged by his hind legs, his body left a trail in the dirt floor.

He passed the rope pens, the ones that had before contained the enormous beasts of the worlds. But now only one pen was full. Two brown eyes sought Fecir's out and locked onto them.

He passed beneath the nose of the white giant, reaching out to him. His giant ears flapped, agitated by the heat. The elephant tried to touch Fecir as he passed, but he was too far out of reach. And so the great animal stood behind the rope fence, watching Fecir as he was dragged away.

Fecir's eyes rolled up into the back of his head. He decided that he must be dreaming, or hallucinating, to see the white elephant now, of all times. He sighed as the drug overtook him again. He slipped into blackness and became unaware once more.

It was the screams that awakened Fecir to his nightmare.

Fecir's eyes cracked open, and he sniffed. Instantly he cringed, lifting his head and hissing with disgust of the god-awful smell that defiled his nose. And then he heard the screams, and his eyes began to adjust to the darkness around him. He picked out the bars in front of him, surrounding him; the feces heaped in the corners, the urine puddles on the concrete floor; the cats pacing angrily in the adjacent cages, their eyes glowing with hatred, fear, despair. Their cries echoed all around him. The Dark Place.

Fecir scrambled to his paws, shaking his head in disbelief. *Not again,* he thought. *Not here. Not ever again.*

The captive cats all around him roared and lunged at their bars, begging for freedom, for food and clean water, for escape from the unbearable heat. Stripped of their existence as cats, the savage animals snarled, speaking insane, gibberish words, as if they'd forgotten their own language. They paced about their stalls, growling to themselves; filthy, unhealthy, inhumane. They were mad with fear, rage, and misery.

As Fecir looked upon this sad imagery with mournful eyes, a thought suddenly occurred to him. *Chak! Where is he? Was he taken here, too?*

"Chak!" Fecir barked.

There was no answer to his voice in the darkness, other than the incessant screams. The darkness was blinding to him, but he fought to see.

"Chak! Where are you?"

"Who is that? Whose voice is that?" snarled a gruff, angry voice.

Fecir was startled. He recognized that anger from deep within his past. He squinted his eyes and looked toward the cage across from him. In the dimness, he could just make out a shadow of the cat, but that shadow was just the same size and shape. He was thin and lanky, and his matted, fuzzy mane was thick with dirt and grime, but it was him. Those cold, yellow eyes staring angrily at Fecir were of no doubt, his.

"Mahkuu? Is that you?" Fecir yelped.

"Fecir? What the hell!" the lion roared, lunging at the bars. "Imagine seeing you in this place, you scrawny cur!"

"Mahkuu! It really is you," Fecir growled. At the moment, he was unsure whether to be delighted or terrified, that the lion bully of his circus days was in the same situation as he was. "How did you end up here?"

Mahkuu's eyes took on a deadly light. "Your fault!" he snarled, slashing the bars with his paw. "After you left, the circus couldn't perform anymore. You crippled us! The acts were ruined! And so, all of us were sold. To here! Even the elephant! And it's your fault!"

"The elephant?" Fecir's ears perked, and he looked around in the darkness. He listened carefully, and as he did, he realized that he could hear a certain sound: the sound of chains rattling, of a heavy beast rocking back and forth on its tree trunk legs. So he really had seen the elephant earlier. It hadn't been a dream. He was there.

"We've been rotting in here for weeks!" Mahkuu raged on, pacing. "Weeks! Even worse than training sessions at the circus! We've suffered! Suffered because of you!"

"Be quiet!" snapped another voice. "Do you mind, lion? Trying to sleep here."

With a gasp, Fecir turned to the cage on his right. And there, lying up against the bars, furrowing her brow stubbornly as she slept, was a cat that Fecir had thought he'd never see again. My, had Paggick grown since they last saw each other, but he still recognized her, even in the blackness.

"Paggick!" Fecir said in surprise. "Paggick, it's you!"

The she-cat lifted her head and looked at him dully. "Do I know you?"

"You don't remember? It's me, Fecir!" Fecir roared, trying to be heard over all the other screams.

Paggick's ears perked, but she hardly blinked. "Fecir? Humph. A small world we live in. I thought you were dead. Guess not." She sounded as if she could care less as she laid her head back down to sleep.

"Paggick, I–" Fecir began, but was cut off by a groggy groan. Fecir flinched and whipped his head around.

In the cage on his left, Chak finally opened his green eyes to the darkness. At first, the white cat was startled by the sounds, the smells, and the lack of sight. He scrambled to his paws and backed against the wooden wall behind him, flattening his ears and cowering.

"Chak!" Fecir yelped, relieved to see that he was alright. His eyes were much more adjusted now, and he could see his friend's white fur. "It's alright, Chak. I'm right here."

"Where?" Chak whimpered. "Fecir, I can't see anything."

"You'll adjust. Give it a moment," Fecir growled. He pressed his face against the bars separating them. "I'm right next to you, so don't worry."

"Where are we? What is this place?" the white cat mewed, looking about himself blindly. "Is this the Dark Place?"

A snort came from behind Fecir, and he looked back to see Paggick chuckling. It was a cynical laugh, and Fecir bared his fangs at the sound, for it was not the kind of laugh he remembered Paggick to have.

"Of course this is the Dark Place, cub," the she-cat sneered. "Where else would you be if you heard screaming and saw nothing? Hell? Well, here we are, I guess. Welcome to fear. Welcome to hell." She laughed sinisterly.

Chak's eyes went wide as he heard her words. "Panthera save us!" he moaned.

"Panthera? Ha! What a lie he is," Paggick snarled, baring her fangs in disgust. "He won't save you, even if you look like him, for he's not here. He doesn't exist for us anymore. He'll never appear to save us." She laughed again.

Fecir looked at her strangely and growled. The Paggick he knew would've never said that. Her name itself was the jaguar word for faith. What had happened to her to make her denounce

Panthera? He snarled angrily at her, at the cat he once knew to be his "friend".

"What's the matter with you?" he growled. "The Paggick I knew would've never said that. You're talking more like Tecka now."

"Yes. Well, cats change over time," she mused, refusing to look at him. "And Tecka is dead. He was chosen. I watched him with my own eyes. I watched the dart go into him, watched him struggle on the floor, until he lost against the drug and fell asleep, and was taken away." Her voice was completely emotionless. It was like she didn't care about anything anymore. The name Tecka meant nothing to her now.

"I don't understand," Fecir said, trying to break through to her, to make her acknowledge him. "You named yourself after your faith. You used to talk of nothing but Panthera. Your hope was stronger than anyone I had ever known when you told me the legend of the Pantheraseer. Where has your faith gone, Paggick?"

"It went with Tecka," she growled darkly, "when he was dragged away to die."

Suddenly there came a loud clang, and the lights flickered on overhead. The cats and the other creatures momentarily fell silent, their voices becoming hisses and hushed whispers, their bodies shaking with fear. A collective murmur began to sweep through the stalls and cages.

"The choosing ... who will die ... fear ... they come...."

"They're here," Mahkuu growled, turning away to pace.

"They've come to choose," Paggick said tiredly, closing her eyes.

Fecir bared his teeth, and Chak shivered uncontrollably.

"Fecir, I'm scared," he whimpered.

"Hush, Chak. I'll protect you."

The white cat fell silent as a puddle of urine formed beneath him. Fecir unsheathed his claws, and a snarl rippled across his jaws, announcing his hatred for Man as his scent filled the barn. The metallic smell of death and weaponry burned the nostrils of the animals that smelled it, and as he walked between the rows of stalls, the creatures turned away in fear of his power to decide life and death. His footsteps were heard among the hushed voices, drawing closer and closer.

And another sound was heard, beneath the heartbeat of footsteps – the rattling of chains, the snorting of a giant beast, the purring growl of the white elephant.

Two men came into view as they rounded the bend and found the row of kennels containing cats. Immediately the animals became agitated upon mere sight of them. Mahkuu snarled and turned his back to them, feigning fearsomeness to hide his fear. Paggick didn't even lift her head. Chak still stood in the puddle of his urine, frozen with fear and pressed to the back wall, eyes wide open as he saw them enter the rows. And Fecir remained rigid in his stance, his teeth bared and his hatred for Man seething through his skin.

As they walked closer, Fecir's eyes narrowed on their bare legs – the only part of them eye-level to him. And, with a snarl, he saw the scar on the first man's brown skin; the ugly, pink slash that carved a rippling line from his knee to his ankle. He recognized that scar, and he recognized the man. They'd met before, many years ago, but the scar was still the same. This man was the owner of the canned hunting farm, and the one who ordered the deaths.

When the animals saw his scar, they knew exactly who he was. More often than not, he carried the rifle in his hands. He did so now, and behind him waddled an obese man with fair skin and a bad sunburn on his neck. This man was the client, and he would choose his prize.

"The choosing…," murmured the cats in fear. "Who will go? Who will stay? Who will die?"

"*Aquí están los gatos*," said the scarred man. "Here are the cats. Pick your favorite."

The obese man wiped the sweat off his brow and fanned his face with his hand. "It's hot in here!" he complained.

"Yeah, I know," the scarred man growled. "Choose."

The scarred man would walk no farther into the rows. He stepped aside and motioned the fat man forward. The pale man wiped his forehead again and stumbled forward, swaying with each weighted step. He moved heavily between the cages, receiving a quiet snarl from each cat, until he passed by Fecir's cage. And there he stopped, and peered inside.

Fecir snarled, about to lunge at the bars, attack his bloated face, until he heard Chak in the cage beside him. And then he realized that the fat man was not looking at him, but at the white-furred cat. The man pointed to Chak and smiled.

"Him," he said. "I like him."

"The white cat?" The scarred man walked over to stand beside him.

"That's the one." The fat man smiled.

"Oh," said the scarred man. "Are you sure? You see, that cat … he isn't very big yet. He's not full-grown, you see?"

"Don't care," growled the fat man. "I want the white cat."

The scarred man opened his mouth to speak, but stop. He was reluctant to give the man Chak, for business purposes. Chak was still a cub and so he wouldn't be worth as much as an adult. He wanted to keep the white cat for a year or so, that way he'd grow fully into his pelt, and be worth more to the next client.

He couldn't say this to the fat man, since it would also be bad for business to directly refuse a client's request. So he sighed, though his sigh came out more as a growl, and told the man the price. The fat man smirked and slapped the paper money into his hand.

"Great! Get him ready for me. I'm getting out of this heat," the fat man said with a grin. He strode heavily away, leaving the scarred man to stand alone, surrounded by the cages and the cats. He growled to himself in anger and took his rifle in his hands.

One of the cats down the line snarled, and his voice rang out loudly over the quieted growls. "The white cat has been chosen!" he roared.

Fecir gasped. Chak barely breathed.

Paggick lifted her head up. "Should've known," she growled. "With a coat like that, he was bound to go next. I would've called it."

"No!" Fecir snarled in disbelief. Not him. Not now. Not ever. Not Chak. He would not let it happen. With a snarl, he lunged at the bars and trust to thrust his arms between them. The scarred man jumped in surprise and snarled, reaching out an open palm to bang the cage. The rattling metal sent shudders down Fecir's spine, and he hissed viciously, refusing to move away from the bars.

The scarred man kicked the dirt with his boot and spat. "*¡Cállate!*" he bellowed. "*Estúpido gato.*"

Fecir growled deep in his throat, letting the threat reverberate on his teeth and vibrate on the roof of his jaw. He looked into the eyes of the scarred man, trying to frighten him with his gaze. But the man looked away and spat again. He would never understand the language of animals, the words of their eyes and the sounds of their throats, and he would never care to learn.

He lifted his rifle to his eyes and carefully nudged the barrel between the bars of Chak's cage. He took aim at the white jaguar, squinting his eyes as he lined up his crosshairs. Chak's ears flattened and he whimpered, but could not move away, for fear of Man had locked his limbs in place. Fecir and clawed at the bars furiously, roaring like a demon from hell as the other cats looked on in awed silence.

Then, they all looked away, even Mahkuu, for they knew what came next. The pop. The scream. The panic. The scarred man pulled the trigger and fired.

The pop was so loud that it silenced all the captives, even the white elephant in his rope pen. All noise stopped for a split second; all movement halted as the animals went rigid, went still. They listened carefully for the next sound.

Then, the scream. Chak roared in terror as a dart went into his shoulder. He fell to the concrete, clawing at it, rolling in the filth, trying to rip the needle out of his skin. His scream was the signal for the other animals to begin shouting and screaming all at once.

Fecir bellowed in horror, rearing up against the bars separating their cages. "Chak!" he roared. "No!"

Chak was scrabbling at his skin, but already his limbs were becoming numb. He started to twitch and moan. Foam formed on his lips as he convulsed on the floor. And the scarred man took his rifle and sauntered away.

Now, the panic. With the man gone, all the creatures snarled and flew into a flurry of angry howls. They ran in circles about their cages, ran in fear and horror of the sight they'd seen. Their words were incoherent as they moved excitedly about, unable to control themselves, and unable to watch directly as Chak twitched and writhed in the filth of his cage. But Fecir watched. He stood with his paws still on the cage, looking on in revulsion, snarling at Chak to fight the drug.

"Don't fall asleep!" he ordered sternly. "Stay awake, Chak! Don't you dare fall asleep!"

The convulsions were beginning to subside. Chak's eyes were becoming cloudy and dull. He looked blankly up at Fecir.

"Chak!" Fecir roared. "If you fall asleep, I'll never forgive you! You are the Pseudopanthera! You're not supposed to die like this!"

Chak opened his mouth to speak, but all that came out was a soft, tired moan.

"Get up!" There were tears in Fecir's eyes. "You need to get up! You need to walk with me, you need to guide me! That's what you were born for, wasn't it? That is your destiny! You said it yourself, right? Your life isn't supposed to end like this!"

It was already too late. Chak's eyes were closing. His limbs were relaxing, and his breathing was slowing. The drug was winning against him, coaxing him to sleep with the promise of endless dreams. Fecir wasn't going to watch him be dragged away. He leaped off the wall and began to ram it with his shoulders, trying vainly to break down the bars, but the sturdy rods wouldn't budge.

He snarled in fury, and his pain, his shock and anger of watching his closest friend be chosen and drugged by Man, was enough to make Mahkuu stop his pacing and stare, and Paggick stand up and watch. There was some resemblance of empathy in her eyes – the emotions that she had once buried beneath dullness and indifference in order to survive were resurfacing now, after having not been seen since the death of Tecka.

"You have to wake up! Please, Chak, wake up!"

"*¡Cállate!*" An open palm banged the bars of the cage, startling Fecir. The scarred man had returned, and in his hands he carried an orange nylon rope. Fecir hissed in rage.

"I won't let you!" he shrieked. "I won't let you take him!"

The other cats looked away in shame and sadness, for they knew that Fecir could do nothing while in that cage, and that they could do nothing to help him while in theirs.

The scarred man ignored Fecir and went to the door to Chak's cage. He slid the bolt and the door swung open with a sharp, metallic squeal. The man stepped inside and nudged Chak with his foot a few times. Fecir hissed each time he touched the white cat.

Satisfied with the drug effects, the man stooped over and looped the rope around Chak's hind legs. He tied the rope and then stood up to leave. He stepped out onto the dirt floor, dragging the sleeping form of Chak behind him.

Fecir roared, saliva flying from his jaws as he clawed the bars madly. But no matter how hard he tried, how loud he cried, he couldn't reach Chak, and he wouldn't wake up. He watched helplessly as the scarred man dragged him around the corner and disappeared from sight. Fecir continued to scream for Chak even after he heard the loud clang, and the lights flickered off overhead, returning the animals to darkness.

The screams began once again. And Fecir joined them. He howled with all his might, but it was no use. Chak had been chosen. Chak was gone.

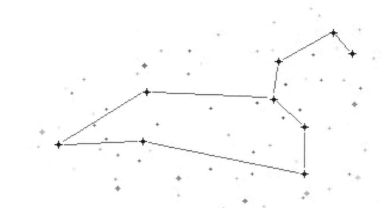

Chapter 22

Trust

"Fecir."

Fecir refused to hear him. He sat with his back to the other cats, his head hanging low in solemn silence.

"Fecir!"

Fecir finally turned around. Mahkuu stood facing him across the walkway, and his yellow eyes seemed to have grown old and dull with sympathy. He looked sadly at Fecir's face, trying to show him that he understood his pain.

"It's no use," he said sadly, shaking his head and ruffling his ragged mane. "There's nothing we can do now. He's gone."

"No," Fecir snarled curtly, turning away. "Be quiet."

"Just let him be, lion," Paggick sneered. "He'll get over it."

"You be quiet, too!" Fecir snapped. "Don't talk to me."

"Well, isn't someone getting all huffed up?" Paggick growled, showing her teeth.

"She-cat," Mahkuu snarled coldly. His legs became rigid and his mane bristled outwards in anger. "That's enough. I've had enough of your attitude. If I ever get out of here, I swear, the first thing I'll do is—"

"Shut up, both of you!" Fecir roared, but then his voice cracked, and he choked down a sob. "Please. Just … be quiet."

Mahkuu fell into a respectful silence, while Paggick turned away with a snort. "Crybaby," she insulted.

Mahkuu raised his lip in disgust of her, but then he turned to Fecir again. He seemed so sincere at that moment, so different from what he was normally like; so different from his usual vicious personality. So strange he seemed right then that Fecir could not help but listen when he spoke his solemn words.

"Nothing can be done for your friend," the lion said softly. "I'm so sorry, Fecir. But there's nothing we can do."

Fecir turned away and closed his eyes, refusing to look at anyone. How could this have happened? Just a few days ago, they had been living happily in the forest, spreading Panthera's message to all who would listen. How could things have changed so drastically, to the point where it cost his dear friend his life?

It all seemed so hopeless. The promise of all cats being free, the message that told of one day all cats becoming wild, all cages opening, all creatures running through the forest, now seemed like an impossible dream, a reality that could never be achieved. It was meaningless to ever believe in such a false hope. Fecir hung his head and growled.

A noise suddenly reached his ears, and Fecir opened his eyes. A sound hidden beneath the screams, yet it somehow broke through to him, called to him. The rattling of chains. A low, growling moan. A soothing purr. Fecir lifted his head. He knew that sound. He remembered.

The white giant was calling to him.

The giant stood near the door to the building, rocking back and forth on his sturdy legs, listening with his ears spread wide like wings. His brown eyes were closed as he groaned deep within his throat, letting the sound vibrate on the roof of his mouth until it came through his nose as a grumbling purr. And though the headdress had been removed, he reached up with his trunk and touched the middle of his forehead, as if searching for the tassels he once played with for hours. He tapped his white skin and growled, letting his voice vibrate through the dirt floors, the sound waves moving beneath the hooves and paws of the captives, until they came to Fecir, until he felt them in his toes. Until he heard the giant's words, for they were being sent to him.

He suddenly realized, as he felt those vibrations, what had been there all along. He knew, quite suddenly, the grand secret, and just that knowledge gave him power, gave him courage, banished his fear and sorrow. He knew who the white giant was. And he remembered what his destiny was. Fecir was the Pantheraseer. And this revelation, this sudden remembrance and realization, gave him, more than anything else, hope. He stood up and turned around.

"You are wrong, Mahkuu," he said suddenly, in a calm, clear voice. "There is something we can do."

The giant in his pen, though unable to see the cats from his location, flapped his ears as Fecir's voice came to him through the screams of pain and sorrow. He lifted his head up and listened.

Mahkuu looked up at Fecir and perked his ears. Fecir smiled before directing his voice to the whole building.

"Creatures!" he roared, and his voice was mighty and proud. "Cats! Hear my words! I am Fecir, and I am the Pantheraseer! I give you a message! Panthera is here! He has come, and we shall be freed! He will free us! Trust me!"

The animals quieted for a moment as they heard the jaguar's words. They murmured together, unsure of him, suspicious. Seeing this, Fecir spoke again, addressing them all.

"I am here!" he cried, "and I am true! I tell you that I am no lie, that I am the Pantehraseer. I have come to teach you! Panthera will come, but you must trust that he will. Have faith in him, cats! Have faith and trust him, and he shall come!"

"Would you shut up already?" Paggick snarled, whirling on him suddenly. "No one will believe you. They all think that Panthera has abandoned them. Stop telling lies and stop shouting. The Pantheraseer is a lie and Panthera is a lie. So stop claiming to be who you're not and stop promising a false future!"

Fecir fell silent for a few seconds. But then he smiled at her, and his smile was genuine and gentle. "Dear Paggick," he said. "You've changed a lot in four years; changed so much that you've lost your faith, lost that one part of you that made you who you were. So much has happened to you, but then, so much has happened to me as well. But I didn't lose faith, mind you. I found it. And you helped me find it, believe it, Paggick."

Paggick snarled, but her ears were forward to him. She was listening carefully.

"You were the one who told me about the Pantheraseer," Fecir said. "You were the first one to ever say that Panthera would come again. And I used to think you were lying. But I will tell you now that you were right all along."

"I was wrong," Paggick hissed, shaking her head. "I was a stupid cub back then. I didn't know any better than to believe in lies."

"Not lies, my friend. They were truths. For Panthera has come down to earth. He is here. I have seen him with my own eyes."

Paggick's ears perked, and a collective gasp swept through the cats in the cages, the cats who had been listening. There was a long silence as they all pondered, and then there was whispering among them, words of amazement and astonishment as they tried to decide if this cat was the real thing. If he really was the Pantheraseer, the one with the eyes to see his spirit.

A loud snarl broke the silence. All the cats looked to see Mahkuu standing tall with his teeth bared and fur bristled. But the lion wasn't snarling in anger. There was a new light in his eyes now, a light of recognition and renewal of hope, as he roared to Fecir in a loud, strong voice.

"I knew it!" he cried. "I knew it all along! I had suspected, when I first met you, that there was something special about you. And when you escaped, there was no doubt in my mind. You were the Pantheraseer. You would be the one to bring freedom to the cats. I knew it all along."

"Mahkuu," Fecir breathed in awe.

Mahkuu smiled, before directing his voice to the walls around him, and roaring as loud as he could, roaring in a mighty voice to the creatures living in darkness. "Trust!" he cried. "Trust! The Pantheraseer has come, you fools! Trust him! Trust him and be free, for Panthera is here! He's here and we will be saved! So trust him! Trust!"

As soon as his voice died down, the other cats instantly began to howl with joy, with faith and with a revived hope in their hearts. They lifted their voices to the ceiling, to the sky beyond it, to as far as the heavens above, for they were to be saved.

"Trust!" they cried together. "Trust!"

They fell into a chorus of excited snarls and roars. And amidst the words of faith repeated with new vigor and the voices of the cats yelping with joy, Fecir turned to Mahkuu.

"Thank you," he said, smiling gratefully.

"Don't mention it," he snarled, his demeanor changing back to his cold, angry self. "Just do your thing and get us out of here."

Fecir nodded. But next to him, he heard Paggick snort in disgust, as she sat in her cage with her head low and her fur bristling dangerously across her shoulders.

"Humph!" the she-cat huffed. "You cats are sick. You make me sick. You're praying for a miracle that will never happen!"

"And how would you know that, Paggy?" Fecir grinned. "Who's to say that miracles don't exist? Lend us your faith and maybe you will be proven wrong."

Paggick's ears perked at the mention of her old nickname, but then she snarled. "My faith is gone. It went with Tecka, or don't you remember?"

"Tecka isn't gone," Fecir said simply. "He is in the sky, with my mother and Tarunaq, and with Panthera. He hasn't left, and neither has your faith. You've just buried it. But now I'm asking you to exhume that faith, for the sake of everyone around you. For my sake, and your own. So please, Paggick. Trust me."

Paggick's eyes narrowed. "You left me all alone, without even saying goodbye," she growled darkly. "Why should I trust you, after you left me like that?"

"Because I came back. Because I'm here, now, with you."

"I suffered on my own. I was so lonely."

"You won't be anymore," Fecir promised firmly, stepping toward her. "Please, Paggick. Just trust me. Trust in Panthera. Please."

The she-cat was quiet for a moment, as she thought about his words. She sighed and hung her head, turning her head away from him. Fecir took a step toward her, about to plead again, when suddenly she lifted her head and smiled.

"Okay, Fecir," she said, and it seemed that her old playfulness and spunk had returned to her voice. "I trust you."

Fecir smiled gratefully and nodded. "Thank you."

At the front of the building, the white elephant flapped his ears and lifted his head, smiling to himself victoriously. Then, with a low groan, he snaked his trunk around the stake in the ground, the rod that anchored his legs to the dirt. He yanked it out of the earth and cast it aside before taking a section of the rope fence and lifting it, unhooking it from its post. Letting the rope drop, he stepped out onto the dirt path and walked heavily between the rows of stalls, moving toward the back of the building where the cats were kept.

The building grew silent as the animals watched in awe the magnificent beast walking freely through the stalls, dragging his chains behind him; the only sound heard was that of the clinking metal. When he came into view, the cats gasped, and some backed away in fright. The elephant did not stop walking – he moved quietly, gracefully, swaying his great head back and forth until he came to Fecir's cage.

The giant stopped and looked down at Fecir, and he almost seemed to smile at him. Fecir smiled back as the elephant lifted his trunk toward the top corner of the cage. With one quick movement, he flicked the bolt sideways and unlocked the door. The bars swung away with a loud, metallic creak.

The cats watched in astonishment as the elephant backed away, and Fecir stepped out onto the walkways. They were amazed as the jaguar stood between the rows – a free cat – beneath the giant head of the white elephant. Fecir looked up and nodded at him, and the beast nodded back. He lifted his trunk, reached over to his right, and slid the bolt on Mahkuu's cage. Mahkuu burst out of his kennel with a roar.

Now all the cats were yelping and shouting, calling for the elephant to open their cages next. The white giant went to each one and slid the bolts on all of them. One by one, every cat burst out of their restraints and ran toward the exit. Fecir followed them when the last one was freed.

When the elephant had finished with the cats, he turned his attention to the rest of the captives, quickly moving to all the stalls, all the kennels, all the cages, and sliding the bolts on each. Animals of every kind and size started to join the mix of cats in the hallways, adding their vociferous voices to the ever growing number and volume of excited yelps, roars, neighs, and howls. The white giant moved through every row, every column, every line of stalls, and he did not stop until the last animal had burst free of its confinement. They grouped together with the others in the darkness, waiting in front of the massive metal doors that blocked them from the outside, and stamping the ground impatiently as they waited for their breath of fresh air.

Now the miraculous elephant trudged his way through the mass of animals, and Fecir found him in the crowd. The giant touched the jaguar's fur, and Fecir felt his limbs go rigid as an image flashed across his mind: a constellation of nine stars, shining bright in the darkness. Panthera's stars.

The image released Fecir, and he looked at the giant. "Yes, I know," he said. "I figured it out."

The giant purred and touched his trunk to his forehead.

"Fecir!" call a voice. Fecir looked and saw Paggick weaving her way through the crowd. She pushed her way through and stood by Fecir's side.

"We don't have much time," she said breathlessly. "We have to hurry if we are to get your friend out of peril. He's probably in the corral by now. We need to open the doors now."

Fecir's eyes widened in alarm, and he turned to the white giant. Without making a sound, the giant nodded and raised his head up high, facing the metal door. Fecir knew immediately what he was planning to do, and he called out loudly to the crowd.

"Make way! Make way or get trampled! The elephant will bust us out!"

The crowd, hearing his words, quickly parted to form a runway between the elephant and the door. The great beast lowered his massive head, and with a mighty bellow, charged forward. His battering-ram skull hit the metal with such force that the whole building shook for a moment, and the door simply fell away from the blow. A blast of fresh air instantly blew in to grace the faces of the newly-freed prisoners, and they blinked as they looked upon their world, darkened by night. The stars were shining overhead, and Panthera's constellation was in the middle of the sky, blessing them all with his light.

The cats hesitated for a few moments, as if frightened by the feeling of being free. But then a shout rose up from one of the cats; a cry for victory. "We're free!"

Upon those words, the animals leaped out into the open air, flowing from the hated building like a river of ants. They were a writhing mass of moving bodies as they pushed their way out into the night, spreading out and galloping every which way. Fecir charged with the crowd, until suddenly he found himself out in the open, crouching low to the dust in the middle of a group of buildings. And that's when the humans began to scream.

The people milling about the ranch cried and started running, moving with the herd of frightened and angry animals. They ran to their trucks and jumped inside, as antelope leaped over and crashed into their vehicles in their desperate flights. With a snarl, a small leopard saw a man reach for his rifle in the bed of his truck, and, acting quickly, she lunged at the man, knocking him over and hissing in his face. The rifle clattered away and was trampled under the hooves of a frantic wildebeest.

Within the thick of the chaos, Fecir looked around desperately, trying to find Chak in the swarm. He spotted the corral in the distance and raced toward it. Beside him ran Paggick, snarling as creatures and people ran everywhere in their confusion. The Dark Place was suddenly ablaze with no longer the screams of the captives, but the cries of people as the animals exacted their revenge upon them.

In their desperation to get away, the humans fell to the ground and were trampled by the hooves and claws of creatures running for their lives. Those who reached for weapons became victims to the teeth and claws of the predator animals that had all their lives been mastered by the rifle. Now the scales were even. The animals could fight Man, fight back like they never could before, and fight they did. The smell of blood scorched the free air.

Fecir ran toward the corral, dodging the legs of animals and people, the horns of creatures and the bullets of Man, as he made his way toward the wooden ring. He heard a loud bang, and a bullet zipped past his ears. With a snarl, he turned his head to look back, and he saw, quite suddenly, that the white elephant was charging along behind him, as animals and Man dove to the side to make way for the angry beast.

They finally made it to the corral. With a snarl, Fecir bunched up his muscles and took a flying leap up and over the railings. He landed inside the ring, and there was Chak, lying motionless in the middle of the ring. Fecir froze, thinking that his worst fears had been realized. He rushed to the white cat's side.

"Chak!" he yelped, sniffing his and nudging his with his nose. Behind him, Paggick leaped into the corral. She ran to his side.

"Chak!" Fecir barked again. "Are you alright?"

Chak didn't answer. Paggick sniffed him once and lifted her head.

"He's alive," she reported. "He's just unconscious. He's not hurt, but the drug hasn't worn off yet. He's okay, thank Panthera."

Fecir sighed in relief, but then he growled. "How will we move him?"

At that moment, there was a loud crash. Startled, they looked up to see the white giant standing with his ears forward and his trunk touching his face, among the rubble of the wooden fence. The beast had broken the fence down, and now he stepped calmly forward, purring in his strange way. Fecir and Paggick backed away as the white giant approached the white cat.

The giant felt the cat with his trunk, as if checking for injuries, before lowering his head and wrapping his trunk around Chak's abdomen. He gingerly lifted the cat up and tossed him onto the back of his neck. There, Chak lay on the leathery back of the white giant, safe behind the shield of the creature's two wing-like ears, which hid him completely from view.

Now the white giant motioned to Fecir with his trunk, swinging it from the ground to the top of his head. Fecir immediately understood what he wanted him to do. Taking a running start, he leaped up and scrabbled onto the elephant's back. And there he sat, overlooking the world from his vantage, and the elephant started to lumber slowly toward the exit. Paggick followed at his side as they headed back into the fray.

As they walked, Chak began to stir. His whiskers began to twitch, and then his claws flexed. His ears flicked and he moved his leg. Fecir sniffed him curiously, gently prodding him with his paw. Finally, his green eyes cracked open and he looked around. His vision swirled and he frowned in confusion. He saw Fecir and their eyes locked.

"Fecir?" he asked slowly.

"Yeah, Chak," Fecir said in a relieved voice. He stood up to go to him. "I'm right here."

"Where are we?"

"You wouldn't even believe," Fecir growled, just as the elephant reentered the mass of panicked animals.

Rifles were firing in all directions, and both Man and animal were falling from their wounds. Blood spattered the dust and earth, and bodies lie in pools of red. Bullets flew through the air like birds, whizzing over Fecir's head and striking the ground beneath the giant's feet. A few men took their weapons and set the crosshairs upon the great skull of the white giant. They pulled the triggers and fired at him, but miraculously, the bullets bounced right off without so much as leaving a scratch. The giant just continued walking indifferently.

Chak now sat up and looked upon all the chaos around them. And he saw the bullets hitting the white giant, saw how no blood appeared on his skin, how he remained completely unharmed. His eyes widened in amazement.

"Fecir!" he cried. "It's him! It's Panthera! The white giant is Panthera!"

The elephant bellowed as he made his way through the bloodshed, following the other fleeing animals toward the road and the forest just beyond. Swaying his head and touching his nose to his forehead triumphantly, he picked up his pace a bit, eager to move away from the harassing bullets. Fecir could see the green of the jungle ahead, and he sat up eagerly, ready to be free.

A bullet grazed his shoulder, searing his skin just above the bone. Fecir snarled in fury as he was nearly knocked off the giant's back. Chak gasped in shock.

"Fecir!"

"I'm okay!" Fecir growled, clawing his way back on top of the elephant. "It's just a cut! I'll be okay!"

As he said that, he saw the culprit of the shooting, standing there with his rifle in hand, aimed for another shot at the jaguar. The scarred man snarled as he looked into the crosshairs, and Fecir closed his eyes when he squeezed the trigger. But no bullet erupted from the barrel.

Fecir opened his eyes when he didn't feel any pain, any indication of a bullet hitting him. He saw the scarred man blink in confusion and pull the trigger again. But still there was no fire. The rifle was jammed. With a roar of anger, the man threw the weapon on the ground and drew a knife from his pocket. Letting loose a wild, angry scream, he charged toward the lumbering elephant, his eyes set on Fecir.

The scarred man leaped up and tried to jump on top of the elephant as it was moving. But he didn't jump high enough, and so just barely managed to get his arms up over the top. He stabbed the knife into the giant's white skin and held onto it, hanging off the ground as the elephant continued to walk on, indifferent to the fact that he'd been puncture by a knife. And now, Fecir looked down into the eyes of the snarling scarred man, and he looked back with the intent to kill.

Fecir did not know what to think. What he did know was that now, at that moment, he could kill that man. And the scarred man realized it, too, realized the situation he'd put himself in, that the jaguar had the higher ground and that he'd stabbed his only weapon into the leathery skin of the white elephant. His eyes widened, but he was too frightened to let go.

Fecir stared deep into the man's eyes and snarled, raising his paw up to slash his neck open. His claws glinted in the moonlight, and he roared, wanting to bring that paw down on the man. But he didn't. He paw remained in the air above him, poised to strike, but Fecir couldn't bring himself to kill that man. Even after all the suffering the humans had caused him throughout, it just didn't seem right to take is life. And so, he sighed and lowered his paw. He looked away from the man, for he wasn't worth his claws.

The man snarled and saw his opportunity. Hoisting himself up, he swung his left arm, seeking to punch Fecir off of the elephant. But he never connected, for right at that moment, the man was suddenly tackled to the ground. With a sharp cry, he fell beneath the massive paws of an African lion. Mahkuu roared in his face before sinking his teeth into his throat.

Fecir saw the whole thing unfold, saw how Mahkuu saved him. When the man had died, the lion looked up at Fecir with blood dripping from his jaws. He nodded as the white elephant passed him by. Fecir nodded back, knowing that he was in debt to the lion, and forever thankful for him.

The elephant reached the road and crossed it, moving out of the fray of gunfire and into the trees. Pushing his way into the brush, the great beast felt the leaves and mud beneath his heavy feet. With a happy rumble, he flapped his ears and disappeared into the shadows of the forest, finally free.

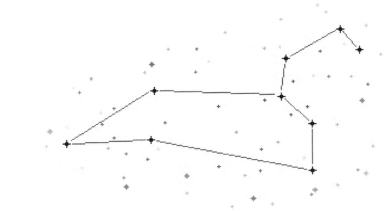

Chapter 23

Safe Haven

Dawn was just approaching when the elephant finally slowed to a halt.

The sky was beginning to turn gray in the east as the color heralded the coming of the sun. The stars above were barely starting to fade, and the trail of stardust, the arm of the Milky Way, still glowed with the brightness and potential of the waiting universe. At the edge of a meadow, in which the green grass swayed with the blowing of the soft breeze, the white giant snorted and stayed his stiff legs. He knelt down low to allow his two passengers to slide off.

Chak was the first to jump down. With a wild, happy whoop, he immediately ran to the nearest mud puddle and began to roll in the slop, coating his pure white fur with the brown of the earth. He was exhilarated to back in his home, among the trees and the grass and the earth. He rolled away the stinging scent of metal and Man, and replaced it with the natural scent of mud and forest.

Fecir stepped down next, though he did so cautiously and carefully. During their trek into the deep forest, he had licked away the blood from his abrasion, and the wound had begun to scab over and heal. But the scab was new and young, and so easily breakable. He slid carefully down to the earth so that the wound would not reopen and bleed again.

When Fecir was safely down, the elephant stood up and ambled away, out into the sea of grass, leaving the two cats on the dividing line between tree and open sky. Fecir smiled as he watched his best friend – his brother – frolic about in the dirt, speaking words of praise on his lips as he expressed his gratitude toward the fading stars. Fecir marveled at how much he'd come to care for the strange, annoying, amazing little cat, and he looked out onto the meadow, looked up at the stars shining down upon the dancing blades of grass, and sent his silent thanks to the shining lights of heaven.

He had come a long way, he realized. He thought back to a time when he had vowed to never trust a divine soul, and to never return to his true home in the forest. How much he had changed since then. In his heart, he now felt the complete trust that Chak had been born with; that trust in Panthera and the Star Lord's plan, that everything would turn out well and that the full spring would come. And it had.

The dark hatred, mistrust and the feeling of betrayal that had once blocked his faith and barricaded hope from ever entering his soul, had completely dissolved. Panthera had come for him, had come for all of them, and had stayed true to his word of legend. He had brought the spring to this land. He had brought the freedom, the liberty to live happily without the worry of iron bars or cages, of bullhooks and whips, of rifles and Man. Sovereignty had come.

The cats were now free to roam where their hearts desired, to be elusive as was their nature, to hunt their meat and drink from the rivers of the jungle, to live in solitude or in company if they so chose. And to tell their stories. To tell the legend of the Pantheraseer, the new and the old, to all who would lend their ears to hear, and to pass this tale down to the next generation of cats – the generation born free.

Fecir smiled up at the dark sky, and it was as if the stars were returning his gratitude, as they twinkled and winked at him from their lofty perches in darkness. They knew that Fecir would trust them now, trust the Star Lords to forever guide his path, as they would for all cats, all creatures, and that the spirit of Panthera would protect him, always.

Chak finally stood up and shook his pelt, splattering the foliage with mud. His eyes were bright green with the energy of the forest, the ecstasy of the wilderness flowing through his veins. He leaped into the air and kicked his back legs up, yelping with uncontrollable happiness.

"Fecir, we are free!" he roared breathlessly. "You've done it, Fecir! We are free! Finally free!"

Fecir chuckled at his antics, nodding in agreement. Chak finally settled down to simple prancing, for he was full of boundless energy. And Fecir looked about, seeing the forest around him, seeing the home of the wild jaguar, and he knew that Man would never follow them here, that he had been beaten. In this part of the world, at least, Man would never find them again. For the jaguar is elusive by nature, after all. What chance did the humans have now?

Chak's ears suddenly perked up, and he stopped, looking out toward the meadow. Fecir noticed and followed his gaze, and that's when he heard the voice in his head. The voice of a thousand whispers, breathing into his ears, into his mind, calling to him.

"Fecir."

He saw the white giant standing in the center of the meadow, facing them, his body glowing against the blackness of night. He lifted his nose to his forehead and flapped his ears, letting out his soothing purr that echoed over the silent grass.

Fecir felt the sound vibrate through the ground and into his paws, and he smiled, remembering the first time he'd heard that noise – the same call that had began his journey, that fateful day when he free the white giant from his ropes. Once again, he felt the tug of the elephant's call, so he stood up and waded into the sea of grass, toward the giant in the center. Chak watched at the edge of the meadow and smiled. Panthera wished to speak to his Panthera-seer alone.

Fecir approached the magnificent beast and stopped before him, and the elephant lowered his trunk and looked into the eyes of the jaguar. They stared into each other's souls for a long while, until the voice spoke again, and Fecir's ears perked to the sound.

"*Fecir.*"

Fecir blinked, realizing that this was the voice of the white giant, of Panthera, speaking to him through their minds.

"*Well done, Fecir,*" the voice hissed. "*The Second Panther-aseer, the one who brought freedom to the cats. They will always remember you, Fecir.*"

Fecir smiled. "But you were the one who opened the cages. All I did was speak to them."

"*The power of the spoken word is far stronger than bars of metal. Your voice inspired the faith long buried in the hearts of the cats, and even unlocked your own. As Seragah found hers at the very end of her journey.*"

Fecir closed his eyes. "I find it funny," he said softly, "how for many years, I thought of you as a bane. As a traitor and murderer. He who killed my mother and lied to all of us. I realize now that you were never the cause of all that has happened. It was Man who killed my mother. It was always Man."

"And it shall always be Man, for he is the greatest creature of them all. The greatest creation to ever exist, for he has the mind and image of a god."

"What will you do now, Panthera?" Fecir asked, calling the Lord by his name. "Now that the cats are free, what will your purpose be? Where will you go?"

"To the stars, dear Fecir," the voice breathed proudly. *"To the stars, where I can look down upon the world and watch over you. Where I can cast my light upon all the cats and inspire their hope in their own survival. Where I can rest until needed again."*

"Will you come again, ever?" Fecir asked hopefully.

"Pray that I don't," the voice said. *"Pray that I never need to. Pray that you all will find a safe haven away from Man, where you can live freely and roam beneath my stars."*

The voice was beginning to fade. Fecir opened his eyes.

"Don't go yet," he whispered.

"You shall guide them, Fecir. Guide them in their faith, and in their freedom. I leave the forest to you, my friend. And I shall protect you. I shall always watch over you."

He looked up to see that the elephant was no longer in front of him. He was walking away, moving towards the forest and the shadows, where the sky over the canopy was growing brighter with light.

"*Farewell. I have faith in you, Fecir. Always remember that, when you look up at the stars. For your journey is not over. Your story has not ended. Continue to inspire trust in me. And speak, my friend. Speak loudly and confidently, and remember the power of words.*"

Fecir wanted to shout, to run after the giant, for he didn't want the beast to leave. But he stayed silent beneath the stars, watching the elephant walk from him.

"*Have faith, my friend. I will always be with you. In the stars, in the trees, and in your heart, I will stay. So be strong, Fecir. And good luck.*"

"Goodbye," Fecir whispered sadly. "I'll never forget you, white giant. I'll tell your story to every creature that will listen, for I am your Pantheraseer. It shall be my story as much as it will be yours. Thank you, Panthera. I'll never forget."

But the white elephant had already disappeared into the trees. It left not a trail in its wake; no scent or sound remained of the giant creature. It was as if he had never been there at all.

Fecir closed his eyes, vowing silently to keep his word. As the First Pantheraseer had been a preacher, so he would become one as well. He would spread faith through the jungle as Seragah once did through the snows, and tell the story of the First True Spring, when all the cats became free.

"Fecir! Fecir, look!"

Fecir's ears perked, and he looked to see that Chak had bounded up beside him. He stood up and followed the cat's excited gaze to the forest around the meadow. And looking upon it, his eyes widened, for the forest was filled with lightning.

Thousands of tiny, glowing insects were flitting about the leaves, blinking their green, chemical lights in unison to create flashes of neon in the shadows. They were floating in the meadow, above their heads and within the grass, blinking to let the world see their lights, to speak their message of safety in their wild, magnificent display. The fireflies had returned to the forest, had returned to dance in the last hours of night.

"It's a sign," Chak said breathlessly. "It's a sign that this place is safe again, that spring has truly come in its fullness. Don't you see, Fecir? It's here! Spring is here! And the fireflies have come to celebrate!"

"Yes," Fecir murmured, looking up at the sky. He saw that most of the stars had faded now, but that one constellation still twinkled brightly, lighting up the last bits of darkness before the sun took over. Fecir smiled and nodded to Panthera, to the spirit cat that drank the darkness. And he almost thought he saw the white jaguar lift his head and nod back at him, before swirling away to the night.

Fecir chuckled quietly and lowered his head. He batted Chak playfully with his paw, as they both looked out upon the jungle and the sun just breaking the horizon. It was the dawn of a new day. The first day of spring.

"We are safe now," Fecir growled. "We are free."

The End

Some Big Cat Facts:

- The jaguar is the largest cat is South America, and the only cat of the Panthera genus found in both North and South America.
- The scientific name of the Amazonian jaguar is Panthera Onca.
- The name "jaguar" is said to come from the Native American word "yaguar" which means "he who kills in one leap".
- The difference between a leopard's coat pattern and a jaguar's coat pattern is that jaguars have spots inside their spots. These spots are called "rosettes".
- Black panthers are actually black jaguars or leopards. This black coat pattern is called "melanistic". If you look closely at a melanistic jaguar, you can still see its spots!
- Male jaguars can grow to be up to seven feet long (about 2.1 meters) and can weigh up to 200 pounds (about 90 kilograms).
- Jaguars are more commonly found in Central and South America, but some have been spotted at far north as Texas.
- Jaguars face many threats in the wild, which include hunting and deforestation by humans.
- Like all big cats, jaguars do *not* make good pets. Even though they may look cute and cuddly, these animals have the strongest bite force of all the big cats – enough pounds per square inch to crush their prey's skull.
- Circus cats, like lions and tigers, often do not live healthy, happy lives. In order to make them perform, animals are often beaten, starved, and confined to extremely cramped cages for long periods of times. Though it may be entertainment for people, it is not at all fun for the cats.

Some Big Cat Facts derived from:

"Jaguar." *National Geographic*. Web.

"Jaguar Facts." *Big Cat Rescue*. Web.

"Circus." *Big Cat Rescue*. Web.

"Circuses." *PETA.org*. Web.

About the Author

Morgan L. Booth is a high school student in California. At the time of her writing this book, she was sixteen years old, but had been writing since the age of six. She never knew she had a talent for writing until the fifth grade, however, when her teacher introduced the Masterpiece Project. This project was a semester-long writing assignment, in which students were made to write a story one sentence at a time. Only one sentence of this story was written per week, but that sentence had to be the best sentence they'd ever written in their entire lives.

It was this project that made Morgan want to become a writer. Aside from writing, she has many other hobbies, including dancing, drawing, and reading. She loves animals and enjoys writing about them. She wishes to someday study veterinary medicine and become a veterinarian, and be able to work with animals every day.

Morgan is now on Facebook! Check out her page at:
www.facebook.com/AuthorMorganLBooth

Look for the sequel to
The First Spring

The Endless Summer

Coming soon!

Turn the page for a sneak peek!

The land baked beneath the merciless heat of the sweltering sun. The trees, spread few and far between across this dry, flat landscape, offered scant relief from the burning warmth. The sparse grasses that attempted to grow from the dusty, cracked earth were yellow and withering, as they clawed their way up to a sky that produced no rain for them, no nourishment. On the horizon, with its image distorted by the boiling heat, was a small range of sweltering dunes and orange plateaus that rose high to face the raging sun, taking its wrath in full-body. The rocks were marred with scars.

The beasts of summer walked across this dry, endless land. Giant gray elephants trudged quietly beneath the blazing sky, led by their matriarch mother, the wisest of their herd. Small, agile antelope grazed quietly on the dying grass in the distance, looking up every so often to scan the prairie for predators. And the Cape buffalo, with their backs twitching and their deadly horns lowered in frustration, snorted and mooed as they moved in herds of thousands, trotting incessantly across the savannah as they searched for green grass. Joining them were hundreds of zebra, weaving their way into the marching bulls, as the elephants and antelope looked on curiously. And the hungry vultures sat in the trees nearby, waiting with quivering feathers for the time to take off and circle above the sweating animals – waiting for the inevitable, for the death of an animal, for the hunt to begin.

Made in the USA
Lexington, KY
01 April 2015